I0788115

First Printing: 2018

ISBN 978-1-9993471-3-0 (eBook)

ISBN 978-1-9993471-4-7 (Paperback)

ISBN 978-1-9993471-5-4 (Hardback)

Offworld Publishing

www.offworldpublishing.com

This novel's story and characters are fictitious. Certain long-standing institutions, agencies, and public offices are mentioned, but the characters involved are wholly imaginary.

CONTENTS

A race across time to save a child from never being born

MACHINE
SENSE

DOMINIC
SCHUNKER

1

tomatopaccio

History. Izzi didn't want anything to do with history, especially Nazis and concentration camps. Assholes.

Her dad was an asshole. He'd seriously pissed her off last night and here she sat in this airless, sweltering classroom that contained no-one else wanting anything to do with Nazis and concentration camps either, including Mr. Perkins.

Why not put everyone in a class of what they want to do? Sure, in third grade the fireman and astronaut classes would be full to bursting and it would be an underwhelming lawyer class but by the time you get to thirteen like Izzi, you know if you're going to want anything to do with Nazis and concentration camps. Even at Izzi's age, she already thought wouldn't it be nice if those class ratios persisted into later life.

Izzi kept her eyes open as a courtesy to Mr. Perkins. After her dad's weirdness yesterday, she couldn't focus on anything else. There was something different about last night, something she'd never felt before from him. Why was he being so secretive and annoying? Izzi's friend, Sarah reckoned it was another woman. Maybe it was time to do some detective work on him.

And then there was that horrific dream that woke her up soaked in sweat early this morning, sat bolt upright with a wide eyed panic, trying to breathe. When the air finally came, the nightmare remained vivid and the fear still clung to her sweat. She looked round her room to recognise items of reality, things that told her it was OK. Her massive Fozzy Bear in the corner was just grinning at her. A smile flicked the nose of fear and fear was gone. Then her dream showed itself.

She'd been drowning, so deep underwater she couldn't even see where the surface was. All her friends were there as well and lots of people she didn't know, all drowning, some already dead. They were all reaching out to her to help but she just couldn't. She tried to extend her arms to grab onto them but she was incapable of any movement, trapped as a useless witness to this death scene. When the dream finally oozed back into its terrifying realm without her, she centred herself and closed her eyes to put consciousness away but her eyelid darkness kept bringing it back. She couldn't close her eyes or get back to sleep for hours and only managed it as her room started warming to the small early light.

Izzi seemed at peace. She had her head on the desk and was taking in the picture of outside as presented by the two large windows.

Outside was sunny and bright, and she knew what it smelt like: jasmine and toffee apples and the sea. Perhaps, if her timing was spot on, she'd be able to avoid the performing dicks in the parking lot and get off to the boat quick smart. A tiny fragment of her dream resurfaced. The dream had made her feel scared of water. That was the most horrific thing about the dream. Sure, there were drowned floating classmates and a scene of horror but the open water was the only thing that made Izzi see the real beauty of life and escape her other life. How hideous would it be to be terrified by her only salvation?

The problem with today, apart from the residue of her nightmare and her legs once again feeling like they belonged to an old lady getting out of a chair after six hours of TV, was her silly dad. He never had secrets from her so what the fuck was this?

As of four days earlier, in the midst of an angst born of so much more than simply being a teenage girl, Izzi had cast aside the cute blond look. She'd put away the skip-thru-the-fields girlie dress for ripped jeans, a hoodie and navy-blue hair wrapped round her little ears like an elf.

In keeping with that theme, and still unbeknownst to her dad, bless him, a tattoo of a disturbing looking demon coming to get you, had materialized in the middle of her back. It being summer and all, she'd be forced to fess up before long on that one. On the face of it, the elements were aligning their ethers and creating a time to remember for Izzi.

It would all be swimming if it wasn't for the fact that Izzi was old enough and smart enough to recognise she might be starting to lose her grip on broader reality.

It's like the first time you get that little twinge of pain in a tooth, you just know eventually it's going to need something doing. And so it was with Izzi. The signs were clear to her. Something was seriously fucked up. It was now a matter for her to address it or hide from it. She expected changes at her age but didn't think this is what they meant.

The wind had got up a bit and was tinkering with the trees, teasing them into a casual sway. The boat would be bobbing up and down, little bells and rigging would be singing its tune and the sound of the waves would join to make it just what she wanted.

Izzi thought about heading to the harbor and getting out into the ocean just like she did pretty much every day. She had her phone countdown from the minute she arrived at school to the minute she thought she would get onto the boat. As soon as school threw them up onto the sidewalk, that's where she was headed. When her dad finally came to get her that's where she'd be, if he actually did come today. For all she knew it would be Sarah's mom picking her up.

She'd known how to sail since she was about eight years old. It seemed the first real deep breath of the day came at that time. Their little boat was a middle-aged Cole 43 with one or two teeth missing, enough downstairs to make for a cosy little party and comfy sleeping afterwards. It was all she could remember about the ocean. Her mom and dad had taken her on it when she was a baby and told her stories of almost dropping her over the side. Since then it had been her second home.

Izzi rubbed her left leg to try and ease out the pain and closed her eyes. She thought about that day not so long ago. It was the most awesome day of her life aboard that little boat with her mom and dad. It was tinged with some great oddness though. Mom and Dad had woken up far too late for little Izzi, she was up and packed and dressed before coffee was considered. She'd even put most of their stuff in the car ready. It was the Saturday she'd been hanging off for weeks.

Once they were all on the same page, after Izzi had thrown a few toys out of the pram, they started off with a bit of breakfast at the Harbor Cafe and she was a little more at ease. It was another glorious sunny morning in San Sebastian, the breeze would lift a sail or two and all was right and smiley with the world.

Izzi had lived here all her life and knew it like the back of her hand. It was a very Mexican style town, tiny side streets and white-wash and a feeling of complete peace, there were no feds scoping nasties here, there wasn't a Microsoft or some other country-sized thing camped out nearby, it was just a school and the sea and a few buildings that were of little interest to her, apart from Flat Eric's Burgers, of course.

The boys on the fishing boats had finished their day and were having a few sneaky ones at the harbor bar, putting off their return to duty at home.

Izzi's mom ordered tomato slices with a gentle oregano sprinkle. They called it tomatopaccio and she was hoping there may be a little lemon garlic dressing going on. Izzi and her dad needed fruit and lots of it, in this case, 'Izzi, number four, melon slices with a tickle of maple.'

The cooling breeze slipped between the boats and washed over them, tickling their legs under the table and fluttering the light drapes behind the double doors to inside. A little scratty dog was taking a pee against the side of the nearest boat, breeze flapping his little ears back, tongue hanging fully out to one side and generally having a good time. But a shout from its owner and the owner of the boat brought this little mutt down to earth and admonishment was expected. The day was set fair to be a good one.

Soon breakfast arrived and all three of them took possession of their melon slices and maple. Izzi's mom thanked the waitress and picked up a slice. Mom and Dad chinked slices like a glass of bubbly and were upon their melon quicker than the wasp that had arrived around her ears.

Izzi looked at the retreating waitress and then back at her mom and dad and then back to the waitress, who was wiggling away with apparently no drama to be had here.

But there was drama to be had here dammit, care of Izzi. Pretty far from happy with the available human response, she picked up the menu quite venomously, making sure her nails scratched on the distressed blue pine table top, and would prove her point quickly and to the embarrassment of everyone else.

It took her a few seconds to realise it. The menu was a completely different design and color scheme to the one she had literally just used to order her melon. And it took her a few seconds more to realise the bar was apparently called the Harbor Bistro not the Harbor Cafe.

On further examination of the menu, she confirmed the melon slices were still pretty much top of the bill for breakfast and now even had a little gold star, but after two or three ever more careful scopes, ever decreasing circles of desperation, she couldn't see tomatopaccio anywhere on the damn thing.

Preparing to admit defeat, Izzi turned her eyes to the boats in the harbor, jingling and swaying softly in the breeze. It usually brought her a clarity but today there was only another instant departure from her recollection.

A large yacht, tallest mast in the place, sat just four or five boats along the walkway and that bad boy had not been there when she got here a few minutes ago. They don't just rock up and park like a little car. On this beautiful vessel was an even more beautiful woman, tall, slim, bronzed in an orange bikini and looking straight at Izzi's confusion until Izzi spotted her. The woman calmly smiled, turned away and slid below deck. Izzi was sure she'd seen her before somewhere but couldn't place it. She wanted to be that woman one day but returned to her present turmoil.

She looked back over at two completely oblivious parents actually being quite annoying and friendly with each other. There was no sense to be had there or from the menu or from anything in the scene around her.

In the absence of any sense, Izzi summoned the waitress back over with a smile. In the several seconds the waitress took to gather herself, she managed to look deflated at being called to action, primed her notepad and finally plotted her swing over to Izzi's table.

In these very same seconds, Izzi wondered if the acid that was meant to be in the punch last night at Dana Jolly's party was suddenly kicking in. Did it really take that long?

'I'm really sorry but I've got two questions,' said Izzi. The waitress turned her flirty smile at Izzi's dad back to Izzi and offered the slightest tilt of the head to indicate, 'and they are …?'

'First, have you re-branded and put new menus down, like in the last five minutes?'

Without quite appreciating why a person would ask this, the waitress was confident she knew this one. 'Nope, it's been called Harbor Bistro for about ten years but you live here don't you? Aren't you Izzi?'

Izzi was and took a moment to look above her head at the sign just under the awning. 'Harbor Bistro.' A menu switch for a subtle rebranding might have been possible but a six foot sign being changed above her head as she sat there, not so much.

Disappointed by question one and deep down knowing the answer, she felt compelled to pursue question two.

'And my mom actually ordered the tomatoes, not melon.'

Her mom looked at her dad, slightly ahead of feeling the confusion, while her dad looked Izzi right in the eyes, offering little emotion. Izzi avoided that paternal gaze with all the strength she had as punishment for his indifference at all of this as it was happening. Poor skills, Dad.

'I didn't order tomato anything darling,' said her mom. 'Don't be silly. Eat your melon and let's get out on the water.' Her mom beamed a lovely, honest, warm mom smile at Izzi but Izzi could only eye her coldly back.

Both parents were clearly useless in this episode from The fucking Twilight Zone and there was only one thing you can do when you find yourself here in a land where logic sits starved and imprisoned: seek a release, find that logic in this world and, more importantly, find something you can blame.

It was Mom who ordered the damn tomatoes. Was this strong lovely woman she so admired frightened to make a scene or was something else afoot? Izzi had never witnessed her mom back down, yield or fail to kick off royally if something got under her skirt.

'Mom, seriously you didn't order that, for fucks sake.'

'Izzi!'

The thing was, Izzi kinda knew this wasn't her mom's fault. Her mom genuinely couldn't order something off a menu that didn't have it. Izzi rolled this through her head and she knew her game was up. Leave it, send away the waitress.

And don't think she didn't still see her dad's eyes searing into her from over there. No use, too late, that father, seriously if you've got something to say, say it.

At this point, the waitress added, 'Yes actually, she did order the melon,' and she said it with a certain tone.

Izzi knew this line of inquiry was going nowhere. It was now time to analyze her dad. He needed to step up. He'd know. She trusted him as the final arbiter, but he just looked back down at his melon and tucked in.

'Nothing? Dad, seriously, what the fuck?'

'Izzi!'

This was followed by something Izzi always seemed to do when she was annoyed or upset. What she was trying to say was something along the lines of 'are you seriously fucking telling me you didn't hear her order fucking tomatoes' but it emerged from her as 'Rugummum ul nisme izzakara suati?' Sounded more Klingon than human.

She'd been doing this pretty much as long as she could form speech and usually resulted in her mom and dad cracking up laughing, which in turn propagated the Klingon. Dad was sensible in holding back the chuckles today though.

Izzi had a naughty joint every so often but there were other drugs that produced exactly the nonsense of this harbor morning and she'd thought about them lots. If acid was in the punch at Dana's party and this is what all the fuss was about, they can all abandon themselves to the daft chaos of it and go fuck themselves.

The waitress edged ever closer to a place waitresses call retreat, slipping doorwards at a slow but intended rate. Izzi recovered decorum to thank her, which officially released the girl from this oddness, and Izzi was forced into a little contemplation.

The rest of the world was carrying on as normal, Mom and Dad behaving like this never happened and everything here at the cafe, or fucking bistro or wherever it's called, maybe Club du fucking Port in the next ten minutes, was, on the face of it, at ease with itself.

But Izzi wasn't at ease with shit. She knew what she saw, she knew what she heard, all this shit just happened, plain and simple.

No-one was going to listen to her and she thought it was perfectly reasonable to fester for a while, considering toys and prams.

Then Dad looked over when he knew her mom wasn't looking and just gave her the shush, we'll cover it later sign.

In this cocky gesture, Izzi saw a serious underplaying of what she needed but she also saw a chink of light and agreed to lock eyes with her dad purely to signal yes, motherfucker, we will cover it later or prepare to face your doom.

Perhaps her dad could solve this little riddle, maybe her mom wasn't well, or was she sad or was she finally certifiably mad? She didn't seem any of these really. Izzi would collar the old man soon enough for some proper input and give him a decent kicking for the lack of that input in the first place, leaving her in tomato-fuelled limbo.

This confused twenty-seven minutes neared its finale. Izzi had dispatched some but by no means all of the melon and left the rest in disorderly fashion on the table to lodge a subtle if squelchy protest at parental performance not to mention that tart of a waitress wanting to jump her dad for fucks sake. She smeared a bit of maple on the table top to give that slutty waitress something to do.

They were quickly on the boat and hitting open water, cruising slowly past the mystery yacht and its hidden beauty as they exited the harbor. Izzi was solo at the back, controlling the movement of this slinky cool vessel, she handled all of it. Her mom and dad continued their annoying closeness and cuddled on a bunch of cushions by the steps with a curiously early glass of something Izzi wasn't allowed yet.

She'd be heading to the little island about five miles off the coast and they could all pull up and wander about there. She'd get hold of the old man for a legendary kicking at that very opportunity.

So here was this nirvana right here just off the southern California coast. What more could she need than a face full of salty spray every so often, the peace and giant power of the ocean, the occasional cackling seagull saying hi? A few days ago there were no caveats but today this ocean carried with it questions unanswered.

Izzi's dad came up to her about a mile out from the island as she was starting to imagine her shower in the lagoon waterfall. 'Lagoon, right?' He knew it and she knew it. Right in the middle of this island, there was a beautiful clear lagoon with a waterfall at one end. After you leave the beach, there was about a half hour trek through some pretty thick forest to get to it. There was a decent-sized ledge behind the waterfall. You could take refuge between moments of experiencing the full power of the drop and you could just let the day tell you it loves you.

Behind this waterfall was the spot Dad chose to tell her the news. Mom smiled and wiggled up next to him and he asked her if she'd ever thought of having a little brother or sister. She had, lots. Her face lit up and she ran in for a massive hug.

They sat down behind the waterfall, watching its power hammer into the lagoon and Izzi put the tomato shenanigans to one side. Izzi had been snuffling about looking for something like she knew it was there and she finally found it. She said she'd seen this last time she was here but couldn't find it again but now she had. It was a smooth, perfectly symmetrical 3D eclipse, an ellipsoid. It had an equally perfectly round hole in one end which emerged as a smaller hole at the thin end. It was beautiful.

Izzi had figured it out quickly. She was so happy to have captured this cool thing. Her Mom and Dad tried to play it but all they got was breath from one end exiting the other as breath. Izzi snaffled it back quick smart. It was her stone pipe thing.

Izzi stood just behind the waterfall so she caught the cool spray of it, blew into the thin end and produced a pure perfect tone. It was so hypnotic. They were so chilled out behind that waterfall, they all found themselves waking up. It was the most beautiful day. Izzi got up and dived through the waterfall back into the lagoon and they all made their way home.

The bell went and history was over, another hyperspace lesson, and that was it for the day. All her thoughts and smells were now real and she was third out of the door only because the large and slow Maccio brothers hovered and chatted in Flat Eric's Burgers format through the door.

The thing she had to discuss with the waves this time was her dad. He'd been super weird for the past few days and certainly last night. She reckoned this was all to do with why she thought Mom ordered tomato that day and all the fucked up things she'd seen since then.

He'd taken her by the shoulders and looked into her eyes, she had to go stay at Sarah's house. He had stuff to do and he couldn't take her to school in the morning. Fine, that happened all the time but the forever hug and secret obvious tears laid into her shoulder seriously scared her and for some reason what the fuck are you talking about didn't have time.

So, yes, today Izzi had stuff on her mind. The tedium of school was past and she could now head to the ocean. It was a quick five minute walk to the marina for someone on a mission and she was out of the school gates and left down Ocean Walk as the sun ducked behind the palms on the other side of the street, strobing her as she walked.

There was a little cafe called Frio on the left, halfway to the harbor. The newer bit of San Sebastian was pretty basic, several straight roads heading to the harbor and none straighter and more direct than from the school past Frio.

Most times she'd meet Dad there after school and she used to meet Mom and Dad there before the mom thing happened, but today its outside tables were deserted apart from this old guy having coffee smiling at her as she wandered past. Him again. When Sarah's folks drove them to school this morning he was outside the gates just standing there looking at them get out of the car and head inside.

He had the same grin and he was looking right at her again. There was no-one else around, just her. She'd never seen him before today. It meant nothing to her when he first appeared, apart from a brief Stephen King thought, but here he was again. Maybe he'd just moved here and he was really friendly. Did he stare and smile at everyone like some lunatic or was he a preacher from another world looking to offset his alienation in this one?

A chill wind created for this moment invented itself and whistled up ocean walk, wrapping round Izzi, inspecting her as it left on its way up the street to someone else. It bound her eyes to his and everything was still and quiet.

2

the preacher and the cardinal

The sun wasn't even the hottest it would be today but he could feel it burning through his black trilby hat, bringing his already sweating head to a level of dripping discomfort he would only tolerate for this. He had the hat down over his face and all you could see of him was the stubbled jaw of an old man perhaps in his eighties. Every car that pulled up outside this little wooden church kicked up more dust. He looked down at his brown leather shoes and wondered what the point was of anyone polishing fucking shoes in this godforsaken armpit of a place, desert one way and desert the other and so fucking hot.

There must have been thirty cars, giant lumps of post-war metal and maybe sixty people all suited and booted now inside this church. From across the road on this low wall, as he sparked up another smoke, he had to wonder where they'd all come from. He'd driven for miles of just cows and horses to get here. He concluded wherever they came from, they sure did need to see their God on a Sunday.

The smoke from his cigarette lingered around his head for the briefest of seconds before the breeze took it away, like it was trying to tell him something but didn't have time. He always preferred the forties. It was where he was from, he fit in better but he'd never seen this side of it. He heard someone spark up the little organ inside and their curious ritual began. Guide me O thou great redeemer. The doors were left open as a courtesy to all inside, fans were swishing, jackets covertly removed and everyone was fidgeting in the sweat of it.

The open doors and the hymn asking for peace were drawing

him in. He wasn't here for this but what harm would it do to go inside and take a seat? After all he did need to be sure this guy was his guy. He pulled out a folded piece of paper from his inside jacket pocket and opened it out to get a picture in his mind. The cigarette suddenly made hot fire on his index finger and was cursed into the road. He timed his stroll across the deserted road to drop a punishing shoe on the offending smoke and continued towards the steps.

He hit the bottom step, looked up into the open doors and wondered why the doors that really mattered had never been open to him. He'd busted his guts all his life, done good things, about to do even better things, but even then that one door to the elite world he knew existed always stayed shut, looking down at him like he was inferior, unworthy even of an interview. On merit that door should be opened to him first over all others but this wasn't merit, this was bloodline. He knew what went on behind that door and he'd never be a part of it.

'Fucking inbred pricks,' he muttered as he hit the top step and stood still to absorb the scene. His shadow drew the attention of a sweating bald guy on the back row, who turned round briefly to see who'd arrived.

The silhouette of him and his hat slid into an empty row back left. He could see his guy was his guy because there was his guy standing up there telling these sixty people that there's only one side to be on when the end of days comes upon us.

These sixty people were doing well. They were paying attention to the sermon amid the horrific fidgeting that accompanies hot sweaty clothing invading parts of the body it doesn't belong. Considering where they were, only a cheeky tug as they stood for the next hymn could ease it. Ladies' fans were fluttering. The ceiling fan was attractive but futile and this hot moment in the universe was only going to get hotter after another couple of hymns.

He then focused back on this preacher, his voice, his movements, was he a genuine man? Did he believe? Then he realized he didn't give a shit. He was annoyed he didn't get here when it was just him and the preacher. It was too hot for this singing and standing stuff, words needed to be had.

Those couple of hymns came and went and finally the preacher started mentioning 'next week' and other things that signalled the closing of this service. It was time to get back to his wall and wait for everyone to leave.

Before too long the chatter and life of the day hit the steps and oozed slowly away into their cars, preparing to re-enter a desert with even less than this in it. It would be many decades before even the notion of getting something cold and fizzy on a Sunday would appear so it was home to some of Grandma's lemonade and a cheeky swig of something in a drawer, probably the same stuff Grandma puts in her lemonade.

One by one, they all hit the road and eventually created a thirty car trail of dust and sand all the way back to wherever they were going. He pulled his hat over his face and cursed the fact he'd be finding a fair bit of sand in his pockets later.

Once more he sat on the low wall opposite the church. He lit another smoke as the dust slowly settled. He'd give it a few minutes, make sure there was no-one else but him and the preacher.

When the dust was near enough where it started, just a single car remained so, unless this preacher was giving someone a ride, it was time for that chat.

He was back up the steps and inside quickly, this time listening out for anything going on in the place. The main church was empty. All that remained was the smell of sweat and Sunday best perfume. And then there was a sound from a little room off to the right of the altar. He skirted round the wall until he was outside that room and the sounds became a single person moving stuff about.

The preacher looked up smartish. 'Can I help you?' he said,

offering a warm smile, putting a book down on his desk and clapping its dust off his hands.

'William Simons?'

'Yes.'

'Born February ninth 1910. Your father is Claude Simons?'

'Yes, but I'm sorry, can I ask what this is all...'

Enough said, one in the head, one in the chest. This innocent preacher had done nothing wrong. He was probably a nice guy. He looked like a nice guy. But he had to die for a reason he couldn't possibly imagine.

He crossed the deserted road and wondered who was next due to drop by here? Who would find this preacher? Maybe it wouldn't be till next Sunday's cars started the whole thing again.

At the same moment William Simons breathed his last breath, some eighty years later, some of the cardinals moved inside from the balcony as yet another flight went over St. Peter's square. It was another hot one in Rome and cassocks were starting to ride up a bit. It was time to get on with the business of the day.

As they all filed in and took their seats, Cardinal Simons started to feel strange, like he had heat stroke, but it wasn't heat stroke. His stomach was twisting and he was losing the feeling in his legs. He felt his leg but there was nothing. Then his arms went limp and suddenly he had no control of his body. He sat in his chair looking at everyone unable to speak or signal to them. Is this what a stroke feels like?

A vibration started behind eyes fast losing focus. He heard the names of the eight of them here called out in latin to log attendance. One by one he recognized those on the list until there was one name he didn't recognise and where was his name? He was sitting right here, one of the eight and that was the last he knew of it.

3

the fight

A deep growling snore and chaotic bundle of bedcovers hid most of Izzi's dad, Zak, with only a lone foot dangling over the bottom corner to signal its freedom.

He managed to occupy every square inch of the very big bed he was in, some of it was drool, one sock, most of it body parts.

It was about seven in the morning. He had a slice of slim sun sizzling through a slit in the curtain right onto his emerging face and was showing signs of leaving sleep behind and joining the world.

He rolled over and kicked a blanket onto the floor, disgusted with its impertinent trapping of his balls to his leg. He was starting to fidget and fuss and was passionately involved with something in his dream head.

It was cold, black water, he was out of breath, barely enough energy to keep afloat. He could see the shore but it was just as far away as when he started. It felt like there was something in the water with him. He tried to look but he couldn't see more than a yard into it. His arms and legs got slower and heavier as they floundered further under the water and soon his head slipped under too.

Zak felt the cool crackle of a fresh sheet on him and rolled to bring it in and kick out that dream. He felt like he'd been shat awake onto this pillow. His eyes opened to scan the room, taking in details, making sure he was joining it as he left it. A sigh of relief suggested he might be. The next thing to introduce itself to his mind was Izzi.

He swung himself round to get up and hundred-year-old man syndrome struck again, like every day. This was really starting to piss him off. Modern medicine was consistent in 'we haven't got a clue.'

He was never too stiff to feel fully out of order and it was usually only first thing. It just made a lot of things tedious, especially the stairs down to the kitchen.

A few lurches and the odd grunt got him halfway down them and then he heard movement from the kitchen. There was news on the TV and a chink of coffee mug on coffee mug and he felt that little bit better. His joints lubed themselves up to something approaching free movement and landed him safely at the bottom of the stairs and there she was, his little munchkin, just that little baby they nearly dropped in the ocean, magical sea fairies and pink, toys and prams, dramas and joy, now taller, bothered by something and making him coffee.

A covert sneak up behind hug was perpetrated by father on squeaking daughter along with a big strong kiss on her head and tug on her left ear. Izzi fended this off later than she would have liked due to coffee paraphernalia and smiled do that again at her old dad. She handed him a coffee, punched his shoulder and pointed. The idea was 'off you fuck, go watch TV.' Izzi was doing stuff. Parent handled. Next? Parent was flat out on the couch. He'd already spilled some coffee on himself and was watching some news.

Until recently, Zak had been fine-tuning his plan for the first boyfriend he met. He was pretty sure he could be cool but that had taken a back seat for other things. In any case, this blue-haired strip of attitude standing here was in control of her own world and she was good at it.

She had Zak's green eyes and dark blonde hair, almost a clipping apart from those eyes of hers weren't always green. They changed color from velvety fighting Irish green to the bluest of crystal lagoons for no apparent reason. He could be looking right at her and it would happen in front of him. She wouldn't know it was happening.

It was most likely mood, which made the approaching teen years an interesting prospect, a strobe show of data. It was some kind of mix they couldn't get, completely random, obeying a rhythm from another dimension.

It was the most beautiful thing they'd ever seen. The perfect mix of Megan's piercing blue and Zak's embattled green eyes and here was their little Izzi.

Zak's attention was drawn back to the TV. The news reporter was reeling off the questionable actions of this cardinal in Rome, who'd been accused of doing all sorts of things, not least lining corporate pockets. It was a super scandal and 'no comment' was the reply but you could just see it on his face, he was guilty as fuck. He didn't even care how obvious it was. Zak shook his head. This sort of asshole got right in his shorts. There's always been a time when people have lied. Then there was the time when people lied and tried to cover it up. But now people lie and they don't give one solitary fuck who knows it. Zak wondered what the next logical step would be but didn't find any peace in his answer.

The days always felt lighter and his pain even eased a bit when he saw his little Izzi first thing. But the thing about Zak was, he never knew if his timeline was going to be the same timeline from one moment to the next and definitely each time he woke up things could be very different. He'd still ache like a trenches veteran but the world could be a very different one to the one that sent him to sleep. It could be a very small change, like he could have sworn that ad campaign had a different strap line, or a 9/11 of a change like a few countries vanishing in favor of one big new country.

This made him nothing like everyone else. He saw things around him change and nobody else saw any of it. To them, it was always like that but Zak knew it wasn't. To everybody else, the way it was right now had always been the way it was.

Things would be in slightly different places, signs would change, people would no longer be where they were meant to be and sometimes they wouldn't know him anymore, he could never be sure today was going to be based on yesterday.

A few weeks ago he'd dropped into the Harbor Bar for a swift cold one after his shift and headed on over to chat with his buddy, Ryan who was on a stool at the end of the bar. He'd known Ryan since school. They were at the police academy together but Ryan preferred not being in the police. Zak did but the things him and Ryan did would put either of them in jail.

That day Ryan looked furtive as Zak made his way over. He sat on the next stool to Ryan and held his fist out for a pump, but a pump wasn't returned. He looked at Ryan and Ryan looked at him like *who the fuck are you* and took a little ale.

Zak had learnt not to challenge it now, something had happened in the timeline that meant him and Ryan never became buddies. Yes, he was used to this happening all the time but this was a big one. Here was a guy he knew better than any other male human, a guy he could unload on about Megan and all his shit. It was still there for him but not for Ryan any more.

What shitty thing would bother to direct such a mean and pointless alteration to a person's timeline but there it was. To this day, he wasn't buddies with Ryan. And if that can happen, what if one day he'd never met Megan and they'd never had Izzi? He could handle the ones that didn't get too close to home but not anything that put her existence in doubt. Do anything you want to him but touch his little girl and you've got a war.

And then there was the tomato thing. Until that, he thought maybe she was safe from it but he hadn't seen any more signs of it from her since then, until yesterday.

They were watching TV and Izzi just said, 'Brave color dad, what sort of green is that, it's like a dark vomit?' and threw some popcorn at him.

'Olive green, baby,' said Zak and the feeling he had at the bistro that day came back to haunt him again. Before yesterday the wall had been yellow but Zak woke up to it olive green. She saw it too.

She's seeing the changes. If she wasn't that wall would have always been green to her. But the day before it had been yellow to her as well. Zak had to be ready with the answers she would need and he would give what he never had, someone else like her.

Zak'watched his little girl as she continued with 'something' over there on the worktops. He checked to see if her hair was the same pretty cool color, any sign of tattoos. What else might have changed? This was the daily checklist for any teenager's parent. He was pretty sure she was exactly the same Izzi as yesterday so he sat back and tried to imagine what the day would bring.

'Hey, Izzimena, what's for breakfast?' said Zak.

'You're holding it or most likely pissing it all over yourself.'

'You just watch it, you little blue muppet. I might have to turn you upside down. You are way short of too old for that.'

'Standing right here, ancient retard.' Izzi had a spare little tiny tomato to hand and it missed Zak by a fraction, ending up spinning like a top in front of that stupid corner table that no-one ever uses for anything.

'Remember when I taught you to fight?' said Zak.

'Which tedious time would that be, Dad?'

'Natalie Anster'

'Natalie Anster, awesome, but I knew how to fight, Dad, you just said I should, Mega-tard.'

A couple of years ago, Izzi was a pretty little eleven-year-old with the little button nose and all the coochee-coo trimmings but she was also no stranger to swerving bullshit.

Her presence allowed her to stand calmly, looking up at people much older, who were usually pretending to be much wiser, and fix a glare on them that would raise a little sweat. Some of them had to sit down for a bit, just a little freaked out at how an eleven-year-old can totally uncover them and then govern them so quickly.

These qualities set her at odds with a few girls a couple of years older than her as they saw boys their own age finding little Izzi far more interesting than them. These girls were fabulously mean and they designed their response. The delicious irony was this tended to endear the victim even more to the people that mattered.

There was a large boy at school in Izzi's year, Diego Santos. He was a sweet kid but, school being school, this decent nature played second fiddle to his tragic waistline and wasn't helped by his tendency to emit a certain boyish odor.

One text was all it took. One text explaining to the ever keen audience of these mean girls that 'Izzi Kramer got to second base with Diego Santos.' Izzi liked Diego and was one of the few who did bless him but not like that and Diego respected that. She was greeted that morning by the glances and chuckles associated with being the object of something, she was suddenly in focus and she soon discovered why. She knew Diego wouldn't have said anything and her first order of business was to let him know she knew that.

Finally, one of the recipients was forced to yield the name of the text sender and Izzi knew, because it was the mean but popular girls, her fate was sealed and it was to be that sort of day. To further compound their felony, they cobbled together a crude picture of Izzi and Diego's yearbook pictures with some love hearts and such like and smashed it out all over instabook and beyond.

Izzi was locked in her room all weekend damning her smallness and the temerity of the parents who brought her into this shitty world. She came out only to act on her dad's advice. Zak's advice was simple.

'Remember what I told you?' he said.

'No.'

'Find a place you won't get in trouble, get in there before they even start to think about it, smack them right in the sweet spot with a…'

'Solid left cross. Yes, Dad, I remember.'

'Make em dizzy, they'll change their thinking.'

Izzi had left the house, claiming a head-clearing cycle ride, but she cycled straight round to Natalie Anster's place and summoned her out front for this exact purpose, returning seven minutes later with a massive hug for her old dad. This was followed, as such a hug always was, by pushing him away and offering a cursory 'silly parent' before slipping back upstairs.

Until the phone started ringing, Zak was unaware of the terrorist emerging in this fabulous daughter and was proudly at one with his parenting skills. He rewarded himself with a beer. She was right on the button with all of it apart from the getting in trouble bit.

People would from this point start to understand there was so much more underneath her than her 'not sure if they're green or blue' eyes and that little nose.

Over the coming week or so, Izzi proceeded to wallop each and every one of the four mean girls involved all over town and left them changed and far more wary of things around them. They compared their big red blotches, they took two weeks to disappear, and by that time, Izzi had rendered them subservient.

So standing here right now was someone who could now throw him over her shoulder and fix a knife in his throat before he landed. There was no finer feeling.

It was about this point in the day he remembered Megan. She would be standing over there where his blue muppet was now, doing 'something.'

Zak knew Izzi wasn't far away from detecting it and she'd be in to make it better. It was happening less and less but it still happened.

Megan, died last year. Zak disintegrated into useless dust and flickered off with the wind with no-one to hear him go. He'd proven he was useless, unable to ride to the rescue of the thing he loved, he'd failed. The universe became evil for a long time. It was Izzi who pulled him back from the edge, like constantly waking from a dream with her smile and outstretched hand looking down on him. All she ever needed to do was look at him.

Zak and Izzi took turns in fully melting down and losing it and took turns in helping each other out the other side. There were nights sat in the rain in a field together, trips to the island and the mountains and several with the wine and music at home.

Izzi filled his coffee and pulled his ear.

'Stop it, Dad, do something, change channel or something.'

If there can be one cancer nastier than another, the cancer Megan got was a full-on dug-in demon asshole of a cancer. She was about three months pregnant with Izzi's little brother. It attacked her brain and that proceeded to shut everything else down quick smart. It was about three weeks from diagnosis till the end. They were dropped into a new hell as someone pulled the sheet over her face.

Zak camped outside Izzi's room when it happened and still does now from time to time. Neither of them know whether its for him or her but they both feel safer.

The first time they really cracked up laughing, some story about this guy and a chicken, they both stood back and wondered if they should be cracking up. That was also the first time they realized they probably should. They knew they'd never get Megan's smile back. In its place were dismantlement and recon-struction.

'Anything odd happened today,' he said.

'You didn't shit the bed?'

'Seriously, nothing else?'

'Dad drive me to fucking school already. Go get the keys. Vamos. Off you fuck.'

Izzi was ready to move the day on. She was always ahead of the game, planned, prepared, ready for everything before anyone else.

Zak took the hint. He got his gun and his badge and they headed out to the car for the trip to school and then onto the precinct. Leaving the driveway, Zak noticed the real estate sign outside the Fernandez's place opposite was no longer orange but a nice sky blue.

He checked out of the corner of his eye if Izzi had noticed it but her little nose was glued into her phone and wouldn't have noticed it if the sign came through the windshield and asked her for a date. It could just be a re-branding but probably not.

San Sebastian came into full view as they turned the corner from their place higher up on Benissa Street and from there it was a short drop past the precinct to Izzi's school.

All Izzi said before she shut the door was, 'You're such a dick, Dad, hey, Dick Dad, sounds like a football commentator.' And with a little 'tada' she was off towards the front door.

Time to get to work. The precinct was just round the corner. Most of the time when he thought of work it started with him getting arrested after that bar fight and talking to the cops on the way to the precinct. The confusion had taken him to breaking point, a point where removal of consciousness was the only option. A bottle of rum and a humdinger of a wild west bar fight was his shout out to the world. It was the first time he wondered how soon before he really did belong in a padded cell. Zak had sat there in the squad car with a mouth that looked like it was stung by a football-sized wasp and mouthed off to the cops. He repeated the scene in this morning car with a smile.

'If you'd seen what I'd seen, copper, you would shit,' he said, playing himself.

'And if you'd seen what I'd seen buddy you wouldn't be able to shit, now pipe down,' he said playing Martinez, accent and all.

He'd seen a brave new world, taking an element of control back. He became a cop and he was now Detective Kramer.

He'd always had one of two options: pray he stops seeing things when they do change, drop him back in normal ignorance, or do something about it. Zak had strayed both sides of that fence. After so many years of this shit, why not just settle into option one, Right? No. He still had plenty enough of option two in him. If he was going to be confused, be confused with a gun and a badge.

Today in this car alone with the freshly risen sun Zak felt that same spirit. The game had changed. It really was now all about Izzi so option one was binned and option two was about to step up. He had no idea where to start looking but he did know there had to be such a place. There had to be clues. Nothing happens without a reason, nothing is truly random. Even the universe has a pattern. Everyone has a tell and everything gives itself up somehow.

First, precinct then off to Bayside Sanitarium. This was going to be a tricky one.

4

veto

Just when it was all going to open up for him and his cause, the only fucking cause he ever believed in, a free pass to being excellent for ever, everyone else said *no way, fuck off*, and that was that. Then it was a skin of the teeth escape by accident. His own people didn't want him alive but the enemy certainly did and his own people were no more. He had skills and he had information but all these skills and all this information still did nothing to gain him entry to the one place he knew he belonged.

There was so much work to do, so much future to conquer and then the neanderthals got freaked out and stopped it. He cursed the stupid and the inbred with equal venom and spat that venom onto this leafy street, taking a little time to use an elm to hide from the warm afternoon sun.

The thing was fuck them, the tables had turned. He could conquer the past to conquer the future. This wasn't just the idle boast of the disenfranchized. He was in control of something they couldn't get their shitty six-fingered little hands on the fucking assholes. It was time to forget knocking on the door, time to kick it down and expunge the unworthy pricks inside. But even as he imagined looking over the burnt embers of his conquest he'd always know he didn't belong. If he had one wish it would be not to care.

Today was a tricky one even for him. It was a six-year-old boy. This was a boy who would father a president and that president needed changing. It just so happened the perfect window occurred here and now.

There was the house. He'd grown up somewhere like this. The

little boy in the backyard of this house was him in another country in another era but that thinking will get him killed. He tuned his mind to an inanimate target, not someone with a name, a favorite toy and a pair of eyes. Then he heard a high squeak of play from behind the house and that was the sign.

There was a six foot gate open to the right side of the house. This was a time of day when both parents were out, leaving Garfield junior sitting in the back yard with a ton of toys while the babysitter-maid-cook-confident-and-surrogate-mother did something inside. It would take a minute or two of that curious silence for her to look up and wonder.

5

bayside

Zak had to be at the Bayside Sanitarium at ten o'clock. There was this guy, Terry la Croix. Zak needed to interview him about a missing kid, Celine. The kid just didn't come home from school one day. Over the next twenty-four hours, the whole world shat all over her parents. Celine was the same age as Izzi so Zak was double keen to figure it out, get her back safe.

Given where Terry la Croix was currently residing, who knew if a prosecutor could get his testimony to stand up to the chuckles and orange M&Ms from the opposite bench, even if he did know something. But you never know till you know. What he did know is, if it led to catching the sicko red handed, Terry's testimony wouldn't be important.

'So wassup, compadre?' said Bob, Zaks lieutenant. 'Bayside today, right?'

'Yep, one Terry la Croix, or one of his personalities,' said Zak, zoning out a bit. He was thinking of the place, the institution, the buildings of Bayside, not Terry.

'You ok?' said Bob.

'Sure, just that fucking place.'

'I know, bud, it freaks me out too. Do you want Martinez to take it?'

'Nah, Bob, it's cool, I got it.'

'Sure? Or he can come with you?'

'Nah, it's stupid. I'm fine. It's just I know the joint. My folks almost sent me there when I was a kid. Some fucking shrink.'

'Everyone's got a story about Bayside, bud. Back when I was a kid and the school was being sorted out after the flood, we had classes up there. About a week. We hated it. You'd be surprised how many people have been there for some reason or another.'

'Yeah right, well, it totally freaked me out.'

'What happened?'

'Nothing. My old man just said it was teenage shit, leave him alone, but my mom wanted me to get some help. It was just when they brought me there to meet this guy, Jesus, I'll never forget driving up to it. It just looked like a building would look if it was insane, gives me the chills just thinking about it.'

Bob wasn't about to get the full details but teenage Zak had made the mistake of mentioning a few of the things he was seeing to his folks. He had the feeling his dad was seriously onside though. His dad normally looked at him like he was an idiot when he was in trouble but, with this, he looked at him like he needed protecting, not punishing. Eventually though, his mom had her way and proved Zak's initial theory was just fine: tell no-one, on no account, ever. It was the last time he spoke to anyone about any of it.

Zak didn't know Bayside. Sure, the changes were confusing but he got some sort of super-driven power from the whole thing. He didn't understand them but they made him feel more than anyone else, better than a secret, a superpower, although a superpower of dubious benefit. So he didn't care what they were thinking of doing, he wasn't going to do it.

'So did you go back there for tests or whatever they wanted to do?'

'Evaluation. Nah fuck that. I got the four AM bus to San Francisco, furthest I could get with sixty bucks. Fuck Bayside.'

'Shit, you ran away?'

'Sure, I did. No-one asked me if I wanted to be fucking evaluated. There was nothing wrong with me.'

'So, what happened in Frisco then?'

'The only thing I saw of Frisco was the bus depot. Twelve hours on that fucking bus and my folks and local PD were there to meet me.'

'Fuck.'

'Yeah, fuck. Must have left some pretty big clues for them.'

'Being the highly effective detective you've always been. So you never saw Frisco, shame, what then?'

'A twelve hour drive back to San Sebastian in the car of frozen parents. I knew my Mom sneezed at one point and Dad definitely farted, deliberately hit static between radio stations to try and mask it. But that was the only noise to come from the front seats all the way home.'

'Kinda got the point across to your folks though, right?'

'Right. That was the last I heard of going to fucking Bayside for a fucking evaluation.'

'Solid tactic, bud. The less anyone sees of that place the better they'll be. So anyway, you got a deal for this Terry la Croix guy today?'

'Review board meeting and ice cream. He wanted Pistachio flavor.'

'Ice cream. Jesus, you gotta love these nut jobs.'

If you drive a few minutes past the original church of San Sebastian up over the south side of the bay and head out to the point as far as the track goes before you hit the cliffs, you will find Bayside, looking down on the whole of San Sebastian bay, on the face of it, quiet and at peace with itself, a hub for the disturbed since 1927.

Folklore invents more than can possibly be true about places like this so no-one knew what was true and what wasn't. One thing was true though, once the whitewashed expanse of Bayside came into view from the track, it filled Zak with that same sense of imprisonment he got when he saw it from the back of his dad's car, a danger that something was at risk if he went in, something would be irretrievably lost.

Some of the inmates were outside in the gardens, enjoying a dance of a different design. Zak was up the few stone steps to the front doors and into the shiny floors, the slipper shuffling silence and that smell, ingrained in all surfaces, like it was projecting a slow airborne venom to entrap all comers.

You can walk into places like this just to deliver a chair and end up lost and hidden in its bowels, going slowly mad in its corridors, guided by someone into a room pending a fucking evaluation you really didn't ask for. You become a de facto inmate and you have no guarantee you can ever leave. Someone may tell you that you weren't here to deliver a chair. You're not a deliverer of chairs and you don't even have a van with chairs in it outside.

Bayside lures you in, demands you're analyzed and then finds you wanting. It wants you to stay forever within its walls, looking out at freedom.

'Not fucking today,' said Zak. 'In and out.' Zak was already feeling the coolness of a very large glass of something afterwards.

The main doors opened again and a young woman strolled in, leather jacket and jeans, dark shoulder length hair pretty much anywhere but where it was meant to be, in no fit state for a cocktail party. Allie's aim was true for the front desk. She glanced down the corridor at Zak looking for his designated door and was happy to reach a friendly face on reception.

'Hey Becky,' she said, peeling her shades away from crystal blue eyes and reestablishing hair control with a solitary left handed sweep. She signed the register. *Who's that?* she thought, someone called Hendricks had visited her mom a few days ago. Allie didn't recognize the name and there was always someone dropping in for a secret snoop. Maybe it was another doctor.

'Jesus, can it ever be too early to be fucked off with the day?' she said to Beccy, firing a warm smile over the desk. Beccy's own smile did know that it certainly could not. Allie fumbled for something in her back pocket and eventually revealed her dog-eared visitors permit. They didn't really need to see her pass, they all knew Allie, they'd known her as long as any of them had worked here. Allie had been coming for years to see her poor old mom.

'Hoskins asked if you can drop by before you see her. You know where you're going by now, girl' said Becky.

Allie did indeed know where she was going. She could do it blindfolded and backwards on a Segway and was on around the corner towards her mom's room at pace. She would have been able to see Zak at the end of the corridor, pissing about, looking for another corridor, but she wouldn't have paid him any attention. There was stuff on her mind and it seemed like just about everything today was already conspiring to prevent her from doing it. She wondered if Hoskins had anything more interesting to say than he normally did. His door was open, like it always was, and Allie offered a little tap on the door to raise his head from what he was doing.

'Allie, nice to see you again,' he said. 'Please take a seat.' Dr. Hoskins had a calming voice. He put people at ease quickly and they tended to stay there whatever he had to tell them.

'Everything OK, doc?' said Allie.

'Yes, fine, same as normal, sorry didn't mean to scare you. It's just your mom's still saying these strange things.'

'What, unlike any other day?'

'I know, but there seems to be some consistency to this.'

'The animals?'

'The animals. It's a new one for us, are you sure you never heard her say it before. She gets quite upset when she says it sometimes.'

'And she can still say it when she's lucid or… otherwise?'

'Yes it's the only thing she says in either state, like it's coming from a deeper place.'

This was why Allie was particularly keen to find her mom in a state of lucidity, something she could converse with, something she can work with. When Hoskins had first told her this a couple of weeks ago, it struck a chord with Allie but she knew well enough by now to deny all knowledge of such things with the powers that be. Revealing stuff like this got her mom stuck in here in the first place.

'Don't think so, doc,' she said. 'When you ask her about it, when she's lucid...'

'She doesn't remember saying it even after she's just said it.'

Allie's mom, Katherina, was brought in one night twenty years ago when Allie was about thirteen. Katherina had been found by her and her dad on more than one occasion, standing in the rain, talking to someone not there. Sometimes she was just crying. This time, though, they were all watching TV when Katherina just got up a walked outside and kept walking until she was halfway across the field in front of the house and heading for the river. Allie's dad just about got to her before the current took her. All Katherina could keep repeating was 'the animals, oh my God, the animals' but she could never remember why. And here it is cropping up all these years later. What about the animals?

Katherina had told Allie and her dad many years ago she'd been seeing things most of her life. Her dad seemed resigned to the woman he loved being a little different and Allie just thought it was funny. Her mom was still functional in every other way. To her these things were real. It was everyone else missing things, not her. Her doctors said if illusions go on long enough and people can't reconcile them with the real world, eventually people just leave the real world behind.

Allie used to come once a week with her dad to visit but just sat there dealing with whatever pink toy they'd given her, unable to recognise this woman that had always been there to cuddle into. She saw the occasional glance that indicated it was still her mom but not enough to make it feel anywhere near alright.

She spent her time here trying to figure out what was wrong with her mom. Even when she was in her mom's room, there would be plenty of time for this contemplation as her mom zoned off somewhere and offered a few surreal statements from another dimension.

Allie knew there was something in there that needed to get out. From the rare lucid moments they'd shared, she knew what that thing was. It was the same as her but she couldn't prove it to anyone and pushing it might see here right in here with her mom.

The problem was the lucid moments came as a real shock when they did appear. They sprayed out from a background haze of nonsense, like radio waves with a coded message.

Her mom would start talking about things Allie recognized from her own life. They were both in the same dimension for blissful seconds and then her mom would call her Mary or ask her to fetch her binoculars to track the man who's been watching her or some similar nonsense.

It was near impossible to figure out if lucid moments spoke the truth or not. Were they real or just madness dressed up in finery? Whatever they were, Allie had to be ready to seize them. Allie might walk in and her mom would be her mom again. 'Hello darling, would you like some tea?' like it had always been, or bat shit somewhere else entirely, recognized nothing or nobody from this world.

'So, if this animal thing is a new development,' said Allie. 'A consistency between mental states, it's some kind of clue right? Does that change anything? Is it still the same diagnosis?'

'As far as I can see, nothing's changed, Allie. I'm still sure it's schizoaffective disorder and I still know there are things she's not telling me. I can't move it on until she does.'

'I know doc. I'm trying as well and I'll ask her about it as well as soon as I see my real mom.'

'I know you are, Allie. I guess all we can do is try.'

With that, friendly smiles were exchanged and Allie found herself back in the corridor heading for room twenty three.

This schizoaffective disorder did go a fair way to describe Katherina's actions and some of her approach to life as seen by this world. You hallucinate, see things others can't, you're paranoid, depressed and you have serious mood swings. To Allie, this ticked a hell of a lot of boxes with her mom but didn't get anywhere close to the plane of existence her mom actually inhabited.

When Hoskins first described her mom's 'disorder' he also mentioned it was a hereditary condition. This eventually ticked Allie's last box as she went through her own life and started seeing the same things as her mom did but at that moment it also occurred to her: If she had this same condition as her mom, how could they both be seeing the same things? How could their hallucinations be the same hallucinations?

What they were both seeing was real. Modern psychology had not understood what was going on here. Modern psychology would shit itself and throw away the key for both of them if this was revealed to them.

Her mom never had anybody there to tell her 'it's OK, I see it too,' and that persistent loneliness created the disconnect and brought her here. Allie didn't have that loneliness because of her mom but she also knew, the less lucid her mom became over the years and her own isolation grew, well, she didn't want to imagine, neighboring rooms, attempting a connection with her mom when neither of them could guarantee lucidity?

Today, her question for a mother hopefully compos mentis remained the same: The animals, but this question was joined by a theory and another question. If this animals business demonstrated the first crossover between mental states for years, it had to mean something. It had to be a clue, something her mind really needed to get out. This was her first real sign since she could remember coming here and it was Allie who needed to wrestle it out. The doctors would get nowhere. The other question: Who was this Hendricks character who came to see her a few days ago?

If her mom was lucid, she would most definitely cast a classy and considered shadow on it. This shadow, when cast by a Katherina in formidable and fabulous mood, was gold dust and a splash of unashamed sense.

The light pouring into Katherina's room through the large double sash windows was interrupted only by the silhouetted chair and partially hidden form of Katherina herself, still and composed, facing out to the lake.

Allie knew this was to be one of those days not yielding much at all. A fully lucid mom would have turned and smiled and got up and said a huggy hi. This mom was in her own place entirely. Allie needed to cover something with Katherina but it seemed again she was going to have to put that on hold.

Allie sat on the bench seat in front of the big windows and looked at her mom.

'Hey Mom, so what's up?' but this extracted nothing but a recognition that some of her light had been taken up by something. Allie sat back against the window's side panel and shared Katherina's view of the lake.

'Sold a painting this week,' said Allie. 'That nice big one I told you about, the blue one.'

Allie's attention swayed to the gardens. She absorbed the serenity and panorama of the big blue sky and its lake flooding over the window sill into the room. A flock of birds glided quietly past and a black dog was having some fun chasing a few sticks.

'I saw Hoskins again,' she continued. 'He says you still know when people are here. Come on, Mom, talk to me. I need you to talk to me.' Allie moved closer, see if she could detect anything from her mom's face, but no. 'Which world are you in now, Mom?'

She moved over to her mom and kissed her on the forehead. It was warm, like there was a hot battle in there trying to release something.

'Tell me about the animals, Mom,' she said. 'And who was this Hendricks that came to see you?'

Zak had reached the deepest bowels of this place and there was room forty three. He would be face to face with Terry la Croix in the smallest seconds. He'd prepared about as best he could. Terry on a good day was just a sweet confused guy, completely unaware of his Mr Hyde operating in the background, waiting to show himself. Terry on a bad day, Mr Hyde front and centre, was the Terry who took young girls then tortured and killed them. Interviewing Mr Hyde was the only way to get into his head because the normal Terry was unaware of there even being a Mr Hyde.

Zak pushed open the door of the interview room. He was surprised it was open in the first place and even more surprised to see a hospital security guard and an orderly standing in the room and no Terry. There was a fair amount of liquid on the table and floor, it looked like blood mixed with something else and the orderly was looking a little queasy as he made his way round the cleanup process.

'Where's Terry?' said Zak.

'He was here, Detective,' said the security guard. 'But he wasn't Terry, he was the other one.'

'What happened, is that blood?'

'The time it took to uncuff him and cuff him back to the table he turned. He got hold of Bill and bit half his lip off. I've never seen him like it. He was laughing and frothing at the mouth like some diseased dog.'

'Where's Bill?'

'He's getting stitched up but he won't get that lip back. Terry chewed it up and swallowed it like it was prime steak and no-one was going near that mouth, even licked his lips afterwards and said 'yummy.''

'Jesus.'

'Jesus wasn't around, Detective, I guarantee you that.'

'So no chat with Terry'

'Nope, probably not for a while,' said the security guard lending a hand moving the table while the orderly located more oomska. 'Oh hang on,' he said, turning Zak from the door. 'Just before we all got him on the floor he left a piece of paper on the desk. He said it was for you.'

The security guard pulled a piece of messy paper from his pocket. Zak put on his gloves and unfolded it.

I am a leader of men
I am a killer of men
I care for my flock
And I feast on them at night
I killed them all
I drowned them all
The real evil is in the water
The water that's not meant to be there
Be careful how deep you go, Detective
Look in Sacramento

'Sacramento?' Zak asked himself. 'What the fuck about Sacramento?'

'He didn't say anything else, just the note,' said the security guard.

Zak had something he needed to ask Dr. Hoskins and he was quickly at his door.

'Hey doc, you got a minute?'

'Hello Detective, please take a seat.'

'Well, I came to see Terry.'

'Yes I've just heard. Doesn't appear to be in receiving mood.'

'He doesn't. Is Bill OK?'

'Not really. I mean, yes he's OK but the ear thing...'

'I'm so sorry about that.'

'So what can I help you with?'

'I need a list of anyone that Terry talks to please.'

The positive thing about Bayside is Hoskins and others knew what San Sebastian PD were dealing with. They saw their troubled souls and called them patients after PD had dealt with them as sickos. It had long been a policy at Bayside not to put PD through the ringer with warrants and the like when it wasn't really necessary. Hoskins called up the 'known associations' bit of Terrys record.

Zak checked the screen had things like addresses and more known associations of these other people when they were free men.

'That's great doc, thanks. Can you ping it over to my email?'

Zak shook Hoskins hand and he was back in the corridor calling Cassie at the precinct.

'Cass, Za... Hey. I'm gonna send you a list of names. I need you to check out anything you can on them, there might be something that relates to Celine... cool, thanks Cass. Oh, and by the way, if anything you find even hints at anything about water or Sacramento, give me a call... Yep, Sacramento... Thanks.'

Zak made his way into the main corridor from Hoskins's room. It was a long corridor back to the front desk but it could be seen small and bright from all the way down here. Zak made his way towards the light. There was only one other interruption to the dark shiny corridor and that was a door on the right slightly ajar, allowing light and sound to seep out towards him.

In the otherwise sedate environment it was hard not to focus on that door as he slowed to walk past. The closer he got to the door, the stranger he felt, like there was something he knew behind the door, something he had to see.

The sounds gained volume and started to reverberate in the corridor, bouncing off shiny wall and shiny floor. He couldn't make out the words but it felt like a conversation he'd had with himself many times. He couldn't take his eyes off that small gap in the door, watching for changes in light, moving shadows, a sign of the room's contents and something he was convinced he badly needed.

He was pretty much stopped in the middle of the corridor soaking in this scene when he was suddenly brought round with a bump, like waking up, and realized he'd had his eyes shut.

'Get all that did you?' said a young woman, suddenly up close and personal as the door clicked gently shut behind her. For a few moments they shared a few inches of headspace and felt each other's breath on their faces.

The music from the front desk, a gorgeous deep lingering cello tone with a clarinet melody was joining the scene and the movement of a few people down that end of the corridor changed the light enough to jog them out of it.

The spell was broken. Allie backed off away from Zak. The absence of any immediate response from him urged her to move off down the corridor towards the light.

Zak managed to halt her escape by a touch of the arm and, 'Hey, hang on.'

Allie stopped and looked at that spot on her arm and then back into his eyes like she'd never left them. Her heart was racing. She didn't understand why but she knew there was a reason for the two of them to be in this corridor at this time.

One or two of the ceiling lights, accustomed to offering an inert low deep yellow hum of light, started to flicker a little and strobed the corridor around them. It all seemed set up for these humans, the fanfare had been played, the audience had quietened and now for the show.

Zak moved a little closer to Allie. Had they just shared a telepathy, exchanging data in a few moments? The way she looked into him, he was convinced this woman knew all about him and his fucked up existence.

Until this moment, the idea of saying what he was about to say would have filled him with shivers, an abandonment of a lifelong promise to himself, a risk of ending up right back in Bayside. But right now, all this fear was gone. Now was a different time, a time to seek and find the truth and if that landed him in the shit, then so be it.

'You're seeing the changes aren't you?'

Allie remained physically still but inside she was twisting. At the same time, his words stabbed her with the fear of being uncovered but also offered her complete peace, an ally, finally? Her and her mom called them time shifts but she knew exactly what he meant by 'changes.'

'Things suddenly not what they were before?' he added.

Allie thought 'yes and fuck yes.' It was loud in her head but may as well have been echoed far louder in this corridor. Yes she was seeing the time shifts, all the time she was seeing the fucking time shifts, every day another mystery.

It was the same for her mom in the room behind her. Allie's deepest desire to talk with this person for fucking ever was balanced by the prospect of being given her own room here. Her approach had to be denial.

'What changes? What the fuck are you talking about?'

Zak saw it. The detective in him had analyzed 'what the fuck are you talking about' from day one. Allie was good but he saw it. He knew. Maybe he should review his approach, how quickly this woman could run for assistance, like a kid in a playground from some asshole beckoning from the fence. But Zak knew she wanted it too so he didn't care.

'Kalenjin,' he said.

And suddenly here was that moment for Allie, the moment she'd been waiting for all her life, the moment that stopped her brain in freeze frame on this one word. Doors bursting open and men in white coats taking her away were gone, she was drawn to the flickering lights for a microsecond but then back to Zak.

'Ethiopia, Somalia, Kenya,' said Allie.

'When did that happen, about four years ago?'

'Fifteenth of June 2013. Ethiopia, Somalia and Kenya suddenly never existed.'

'And Kalenjin always had.'

'The PC you were using wasn't Apple,' said Allie.

'Never had been apparently.'

'It was Hershel Electronics.'

'About ten years ago?'

'Seventh of December 2009.'

Allie wanted to wrap herself up in him and cry out the years. Waves were running over her shoulders as she swam deeper into a calm midnight sea, but as she thought of it, she thought of just being close to him in that sea, holding him, touching him.

She pulled back away from Zak and rested her back against her mom's door. Her head was now tilted slightly to the left, like the left side of her brain was getting heavier and heavier and a hypnosis was creeping up on her.

She delivered a 'doors have ears' signal, touching her ear and the door at the same time, and started walking slowly along the corridor, maintaining the migration to sign language by gesturing him to follow.

She knew where they could go and talk, a quiet part of the garden down the steps and a bench in the avenue of trees leading to the lake. Not a word was spoken as they escaped the building and walked into the bright sunlight. Every step felt safer, partners against a bizarre world.

They descended the twenty or so stone steps and a little pathway led them to the avenue of trees. They took their seats on the stone bench in the shade.

'First time I saw you back there, I thought you here to throw me in with my mom. I'm Allie.'

'Zak. I'd be right in here with you. Your mom's here?'

Still, Allie's default position was caution. It was taking her time to adjust to the fact that this guy really exists, sitting here next to her.

'She's been seeing what I see, what you see, for fifty years,' said Allie. 'She doesn't belong here the same as we don't belong here.'

'When I was fifteen, I started seeing them,' said Zak. 'Just subtle ones like someone's car would be a different color or something, you could just about convince yourself they were possible. Then there was the one that threw all that down the drain. There was this show called *The Next Place*, awesome sci-fi show, aliens, ghosts, weird things going on across the universe. It was like I felt safe looking at supernatural stuff, kinda made my stuff more real, more...'

'Acceptable. It was *X-Files* for me.'

'Then, one spring morning, everything changed. I'd been looking forward to the next episode. Picard from *Star Trek* was presenting it.'

'Make it so, number one.'

'It was late. I checked the schedule a million times to make sure I didn't miss it but no episode of *The Next Place* began. Instead, there was something about how washing machines came into being, bold as you like, silly music blaring out at me, not giving a shit it was replacing The Next Place. I dug out the TV schedule again. This time there was no mention of The Next Place. I looked at last week in case that had been the season finale but no, the show that I had actually seen last week wasn't there either, nor the week before. It had never been on the TV.'

'So there was never a show called *The Next Place*.'

'Never. I thought I was in an episode of *The Next fucking Place* but there had never been such a show. I even called the TV station. I told em about last week's show, electrons vanishing and reappearing again somewhere else, do they go to another dimension? The guy had no idea what I was talking about but said it would be an awesome show. I said it had already been an awesome show and at that point I gave up. There was nothing else to talk about. I'm guessing you've never heard of it either.'

'No. Sorry,' said Allie.

'I'd tried to wrap myself up in *The Next Place* but *The Next Place* was now a cheating girlfriend. Was it just the show that vanished or did electrons not do that anymore? How deep did it go? Not long before that, this shrink thought it was a good idea to come here and now I wondered how close I was to that padded cell. For a few hours I didn't care anymore.'

'The one that told me there was no going back was when I was a kid, my best friend, Nancy didn't know me anymore. Never met me. Didn't even go to my school anymore.'

'Same, few years back. Ryan, my best buddy.'

Allie sat back and looked in the eyes of a person she knew wasn't running anywhere.

'Where the fuck have you been?' she said.

'And where the fuck have you been?'

'You can't be proactive, that's the real fucker.' said Allie. 'You just have to check before you say anything, try stay away from things like history.'

'It's like I'm saying it myself,' said Zak. 'I tried to figure out why it was happening to me but but the only thing I could do was give in to it, manage it as best I could.'

'Same here,' said Allie. 'It's OK most of the time.'

'Most of the time,' said Zak with a smile.

'So what the fuck is it, the universe's little joke, a mixing of dimensions?' said Zak. 'I mean, most of the changes are so meaningless, there can't be a rational reason for them. It has to be random.'

'It's not random,' said Allie.

'How can it not be random? If an infinite number of dimensions had always existed in sync with each other, maybe we're seeing one of those other dimensions invading this one, lost in this place and lost in meaning here.'

'But why only to you and me and my mom?' said Allie.

'Is it just us though?'

'Have you ever met anyone else in, what, fifteen years?'

'No.'

'It's not random, Zak.' said Allie again. 'Mom said the time shifts used to be much more obvious when she was younger. Countries would be called something else and wars raged in places that hadn't been at war. It eased off over the years, settled into more subtle changes, sure they seemed like meaningless changes but what if these were a fine tuning of whatever they needed to achieve.'

'They?' said Zak.

'Yeah, they. There's no way it's random. Mom always said it was all by design, not some universal tomfoolery or any design from the gods, design from right here on Earth. This was being done deliberately by something sentient.'

Just as Zak was about to ask *how does she know that and who?* his phone rang. He left it in his pocket. He couldn't tear himself away from Allie. She glanced pocketwards and thought *for fuck's sake, get the phone*. It wasn't that she wanted him to lose focus, it's just a phone not being answered bugged the shit out of her, the monotonous, pleading little shit.

Zak picked up. The tone of the voice the other end was sombre. It was Mrs. Adams, the head teacher at Izzi's school. Normally he'd be up and into the trees for privacy but he had no secrets from this woman.

'Hello Mr Kramer,' she said. 'First of all, Izzi's fine.'

'OK,' said Zak.

'It's just something's happened and I think you should come down.'

'Happened? What's happened?'

'It's OK, she's fine, she's just quite upset about something. It really is better if we see each other. Can you make it into the school any time soon?'

'I'll be there in ten minutes,' said Zak and he turned to Allie. 'Allie, I gotta go. Izzi.'

'Izzi?'

'My daughter. It's her school.'

Zak gave Allie a hug goodbye that said the next time they meet that hug will be back for more.

'To be continued,' she said.

'Harbor Bistro, Friday? One o'clock?'

Allie nodded and pushed him away to his daughter. Zak turned with a smile but as soon as the car door was closed he was focused on Izzi. Allie regained posture on the bench and watched every second of his departure as his car miniaturized down the drive. For her this was a rebirth, something to grab hold of after all these years. She felt an attraction of mind and spirit not to mention body and she was pretty sure he did too. Friday.

6

mr. sanchez

Mrs. Adams came out of her office to greet Zak. When they went back inside, there was another teacher there, standing by the window.

'Detective Kramer, this is Mr. Rolon, Izzi's Spanish teacher.' Formals were concluded and everyone sat down. Rolon occupied a position slightly back and left of Mrs. Adams. It looked like he'd be chipping in when she said he could.

Zaks head tilt said *Speak, woman, speak.*

'Izzi's not in trouble particularly,' said Mrs Adams. 'But she was very distressed today.'

'Distressed? How so distressed?'

'Confused, angry. We can't figure out why. She won't say.'

Zak pictured his little Izzi sitting somewhere in this building, probably on her own. He just wanted to go get her and wrap her up and take her home.

'I'll let Mr. Rolon take you through it.'

Rolon was up, sooner than anticipated, but he looked calm and prepared.

'We were talking about Alhambra, you know Alhambra?' Zak shook his head. Mrs. Adams shuffled a few papers and Rolon considered himself jogged along.

'The class was quiet. I was writing some dates on the chalk board and then Izzi shouted a swear word at Rachel pretty loud.'

'Rachel?'

'The girl sitting next to her, her friend.'

'What did she say?' Rolon checked any movement from Mrs. Adams. 'She said 'fuck off, Rachel.''

'Right.'

'Well, the class thought it was funny of course and I asked Izzi if she'd like to add anything.'

'Right.'

'She asked what happened to Mister Sanchez.'

'Who's Mister Sanchez?'

'Precisely. Who is Mister Sanchez? You don't know any Mister Sanchez?'

'Nope.'

'She said she didn't know Mister Sanchez was away. I asked her who is Mister Sanchez.'

'Right. So what did she say?'

Rolon looked at Mrs. Adams again and Mrs. Adams raised her head to focus more intently on Zak. Zak got the feeling this was the rub of it coming right up.

'She asked where is our usual Spanish teacher? I thought she was joking with me. She does sometimes. I said 'Come on Izzi, I've been here longer than you,' and then her face just went white, like she'd seen a ghost. She just looked me right in the eyes.'

Zak was sitting down but a cold flash still managed to travel from his butthole to his brain, culminating in a sudden itch behind his ear. He knew this moment Izzi had just gone through, the moment you know never to speak of things like this again, the moment of acceptance, all is not well with the world.

'Izzi stood up and shouted something at me.'

'Something?'

'It wasn't English, it wasn't Spanish. It didn't make any sense. Does Izzi know any other languages?'

'Nope,' but Zak knew she did and he knew when she did it. It was time to get his Izzi.

'Where is she now?' he said.

'Mr. Rolon called me and said Izzi's got a problem and I came down and took her into the room next to this.'

Zak looked at the wall her head pointed to and stood up.

'I need to get her home,' he said.

'Detective?' said Mrs. Adams. He knew what was coming.

'Is everything OK at home?'

'She misses her mom very much. Sometimes she shows it. It's OK. I'll take her home and we'll have a chat. Thank you for letting me know, Mr. Rolon. I'm so sorry about this.'

Rolon quickly held his hands up to suggest *Please, it's OK* and then Mrs. Adams released into the room some of the bile from this morning.

'Detective. There is one option you might like to look at.'

'What's that?'

'Maybe it's an idea to ask someone to talk to Izzi.'

Mrs. Adams was a nice woman and he knew she was good for the kids but she can publicly fuck right off thinking he's taking her anywhere near any shrinks or fucking Bayside.

'I appreciate that but I will talk to my daughter,' he said. Formals were concluded again and Zak was quickly inside the room next door and there she was. She looked calm, more bored than anything. She strayed a glance at him and was up and moving.

'Home, Father,' she said aiming to bypass him for the door.

'Excuse me missy moo. Home, daughter is the instruction here and get in here for a hug.' Izzi did get in there for a hug and a tight one, pulling back from it with 'silly parent.'

The car journey home was quiet for under a minute.

'Baby, tell me what happened.'

'Nothing, Dad.'

'Definitely not nothing, Iz, come on.'

Izzi shuffled in her seat, flipping her phone over and over in her hands and staring at San Sebastian going past the window.

'Rachel Delaney is a dick,' she started.

'Fair enough.'

'She just pissed me off that's all.'

'Why?'

'I got confused with the name of this teacher and she was just a giant dick about it.'

'Mr. Rolon.'

'Whatever.'

'He said you shouted at him, Iz.'

'Little bit.'

'He said he didn't understand what you said. From what he said it sounded like that funny language you speak sometimes.'

Izzi dropped her head into her hands.

'Oh God no, I didn't do that again did I?'

'I think so, baby. What were you trying to say?'

'You don't want to know, Dad.'

'Oh, trust me, squirt, I really do.'

'OK father of mine, buckle up,' she said. 'I said *fuck you and fuck everyone else in this shit hole of a fucking classroom, what the fuck is wrong with everyone?*'

A few moments of silence persisted until it was broken by Zak, who couldn't mask the snort he needed to. Izzi quickly matched it with a smile.

'Well, I guess at least if he didn't understand it,' said Zak. 'You didn't really tell them all to go fuck themselves.'

Father and daughter shared eye contact and that was it, they lost it all ends up. Zak had to slow the car to compensate but felt the pressure release from both of them.

'Talk to me when you feel like it, baby. Love you.'

'Love you too, Dino-tard.'

The front door clicked shut behind them and Izzi spared no time to turn and grab her dad by the jacket and bring him back in for a supermassive black hole hug. She made the only point she needed to make. The prospect of tears were making her eyes fat. Soon she would cry but not here, upstairs in her room. Within seconds she was there doing that and Zak was here.

She would have her space and he would have his space, a space he didn't want, he wanted to camp outside her room for the first time since Megan died, but he couldn't.

<h1 style="text-align:center">7</h1>

sacramento

Zak woke up outside Izzi's door after all but Izzi had already gone. A quick call to Sarah's mom. 'Dad's asleep in the hallway again,' and she was safely off to school. Zak was late and he was greeted by a smiling Cassie as soon as he got to the precinct.

'Kramer. Sacramento. Water. Solid intel man.'

'What's the story, Cass?'

'There's this inmate at Bayside, Osiris Alasar, his brother, one Simon Alasar, well he's got this place just outside Sacramento right on Folsom Lake.'

'It could only be him, Cass, awesome job.'

'Sacramento PD are hitting the place now.'

'Fuck yeah,' said Zak.

'Fuck yeah,' said Cassie. 'Oh yeah, Bob said he wants a word.'

Zak tapped on Bob's door.

'Hey Zak, what's up compadre?' said Bob. 'Take a seat, awesome job on Terry. PD up there are going in now. Just wanted to tell you.'

'Yeah, Cass told me, thanks Bob, see if it pans out. There's something I wanted to ask you anyways.'

'Shoot.'

'It's about Izzi.'

'She OK?'

'Yeah but she's not handling things right now. If I don't get her sorted, the school's going to start getting antsy. I know it's been a while since Megan but something's not right. I need to spend some time with her.'

'What can we do here?' said Bob.

'Just give me some leeway, Bob, that's all. I just need time.'

'You're taking a vacation. take her to Rome, take her to the beach, take her fishing. Four weeks full pay.'

Only a bear hug would do for Bob and in it came.

'You're tired. You look tired, buddy. I've seen the changes in you these last few weeks.'

Zak couldn't help an internal smile at Bob's choice of words.

There was a bang on the door for show but Cassie didn't need an invite.

'They got the prick. He had Celine in his basement.'

'She OK?'

'Fine, just dirty. Fucking guy, his wife's upstairs doing the dishes and he's got a teenage girl tied up down there.'

'The wife didn't know?'

'Said she didn't. Kinda believe her too.'

'Great work, Cass, I guess Terry can have his ice cream now.'

'Yeah, hope it goes down easier than that guy's lip.'

Cassie left and Bob turned back to Zak.

'Take off, bud, we got one today. Go be happy about it. Go see Izzi and make it all better. Anything you want.'

Zak made his way home slowly. Izzi won't like it but he'd be around a lot more, four weeks at least, try and get a handle on things, make sure she's OK.

He'd also not be risking the mistakes that were starting to creep into his work. When it came down to it and it was him and his crew doing what Sacramento PD did today, could he be confident he'd be master of his own world at the time and do what was needed of him? He got the feeling Bob wanted to say something else when he called him in. Maybe this was it, he was going to suggest a bit of time off anyway.

8

sentience

Friday came round quickly. Zak shuffled in his seat, see if he could shake out the twinges in his back but they weren't shifting. The news on his car radio served to warn him of any changes to the status quo of this new day but immediately that status quo was upside down.

The newsreader was talking about President Valdez addressing the senate and doing all sorts of other things a US president would do but Zak lived in a world with President Garfield not President Valdez.

He'd always liked Garfield. He was believable, like your grandad's shed. He also had the same eye thing going on as Izzi, sometimes green, sometimes blue. Garfield was the only other person Zak had ever heard of with it but suddenly there was no President Garfield.

Zak parked up and rounded the corner from the car park and through the archway towards the boats and there she was, kicking back in the afternoon sun at one of the tables closest to the water outside the cafe, legs crossed, tight black knee length dress, knee high boots and the darkest silky hair flicking up in the breeze.

She was composed and gorgeous and unknown, in the middle of a healthy slug of Americano, replacing the cup only to pull out a cigarette. Her large, bold and very gold Sophia Loren sunglasses reflected the metronomic disarray of the masts in the windy harbor, like they had windshield wipers attached to them.

Zak was pretty sure she'd seen him. She pretended she hadn't, changing position just a shade to show him what she wanted to show him, annoyed with herself for not having this already set.

Detectives and many others know, just because you're not being watched with eyes, it doesn't mean you're not being watched. As the yards between them dwindled, Zak and Allie were now on stage, lights coming on, makeup girls gone, cameras buzzing, everything ready to roll. Like he'd just hopped off his Lambretta in that Sophia Loren flick in some Roman piazza, Zak was quickly standing in front of her and pulled up a chair.

'Hey.'

Allie looked over at him and he sensed this wasn't as promising as he'd hoped. Her look wasn't 'hey' or anything remotely friendly.

'Excuse me?' she said. 'Do I know you?'

Here we go, thought Zak. Of course, why would life just happily trundle along as it should? Here was a wasp in the ear of a change. It showed him this fabulous woman on Tuesday and removed her on Friday. Fucker.

He held her gaze for at least three deep breaths. She looked at him all lopsided, like she was looking for a way out of this bistro quick smart. The only thing for him to do was go.

'Naaaah. Zak, kidding, jeez man, come on, a bit of time travel humor?'

'Fucker.'

She was a fabulous sixties Russian spy, missing only the black mink and long thin cigarette holder. Right on cue she flicked her cigarette into the harbor like she'd hit that spot a thousand times, and gestured him closer.

'You're a dick. Waiter, yes please, espresso.'

Their heads lowered, almost joined above the table with a glorious amateur sleuth panache and quickly parted again as the waiter scratched the vinyl and delivered espresso.

'I still would have asked you, just like I did on Tuesday,' he said.

'No, you wouldn't. You were about to run for hills, you massive chicken,' and Allie's chicken noise had Zak sat back in his seat and some of the ladies in the bistro looking on.

'Less covert than expected,' said Zak.

'Did you see about fucking Garfield?'

'Who the fuck is Valdez?' said Zak. 'Sorry about the other day by the way. Izzi was in trouble at school. I'm pretty sure she's seeing these fucking changes as well.'

'Probably.'

'What do you mean, probably?'

'What is she, twelve, thirteen?'

'Thirteen.'

'That's when it hits you, puberty, remember?'

'Yeah, I remember, been trying to pretend it won't happen to her.'

'Well, it will, looks like it has. You need to have the chat.'

'So. Tuesday. Continue,' said Zak.

'It will change the way you see all of this,' she said. 'I'm pretty sure about how it's happening but I've got no idea who's making it happen.'

'What, who?' said Zak. 'It's random, universally random, people can't fuck with you like this. What, some Blofeld, sitting there in a massive office under the sea with a cat, being shitty to everyone?'

He got a wicked smile back from Allie. Her dark fringe hovered above her eyebrows and one of them lifted ever so gently.

'It's not random,' she said in her best late night weather voice. She leant in and placed her hand on top of his on the table. 'Not one little bit. Even God isn't that cruel.'

'You want to know how cruel God is?' he said.

'What I'm going to tell you will stop your jibber jabber. It might even make you nauseous. Just bear with it.'

Zak did his 'bear with me' claws and instantly drew a blank from Allie. Too soon? He didn't want her to start thinking he wasn't taking this seriously.

'There are people going back in time,' she said. 'Making changes to things in the past, changes that mean we suddenly see something different today. This is what me and my mom and you and

Izzi are seeing, the results of these changes in the past. Until the other day it was only me and mom seeing it.'

'Time travel,' he said.

'Look, just shut up and listen. If you still don't get it once I've finished, fine, disappointing, but I'll buy the drinks and you can get up and walk away.'

Zak was back in his box, trying to keep an open mind.

'It's some bunch of assholes making this happen, not some shitty god or some shitty random universe.'

'Let's take the boat out.' He leant in closer and this pulled her face to him. 'Peace, no people.'

She had this look on her face, it was a half smile, delivered a little sideways with a dressing of 'not quite sure you're with me yet but let's do that.'

She got herself in shape to move. Zak threw down his espresso, put a ten under her ashtray, led her down the pontoon and they boarded the boat. Conversation only restarted when they were out of the harbor and heading out to sea. The sun bounced off the water and the breeze was warm.

'It always benefits someone,' she said. 'There's always a winner. Think about it, think of all the changes you've seen.'

'OK, say the changes benefit people. Who does it benefit and why would they bother turning a real estate sign from one color to another. What's the point?'

'I don't know but I know there are people and they're getting something out of it. It's all by design.' Allie took a deep briny gulp of air and felt the freedom she could shout it all across the open sea.

'When Mom was younger, she was closer to ground zero.'

'Ground zero?'

'The time it all started. That's what she called it, ground zero. She was thirteen like Izzi. The time shifts back then sounded crazy. Suddenly the world had a billion more people in it and people were writing messages using the phone lines. There wasn't a month that went past that a different country didn't appear with some different fuckwit in charge of it.'

'Well, the Garfield thing is pretty fucking serious.'

'Yeah, but imagine that every day. Look, 1962. Mom was eighteen. Serious cold war shit. You know Khrushchev?'

'I do.'

'Cuban missile crisis?'

'Yep'

'You want a ground zero time shift, here it is. Khrushchev wasn't Soviet leader in 1962, someone called Beria was.'

'Nah, it was Khrushchev.'

'Nah, it wasn't. It was Beria. Stay with me. Everyone knew Beria wanted a Soviet first strike, just get it over with, go back to whatever's left. There was no backing out of it. Fingers were quivering on buttons. This was it, the big one.'

'What?'

'And one day he wasn't leader of the Soviet Union, Khrushchev was.'

'Holy shit.'

'Yes, holy shit. Khrushchev was a little more... sane. The rest you know. Things were worked out.'

'My dad told me about all that,' said Zak. 'The end of the world. He said the TV and the papers were just telling everyone to run for the hills.'

'So, did your dad tell you who we were running from, Beria or Khrushchev?'

'No.'

'If your dad saw the same shit as us, and you know either him or your mom had to, he'd have seen that time shift as well. My mom was eighteen years old and she saw it. This one saved the world.'

'I've never heard of Beria. What happened to him?'

'Long before any Cuban missile crisis, he'd been arrested for treason and executed in 1953.'

'Fuck, and your mom saw all this?'

'She did. When she's with me, she has her moments.'

'Motherfucker of a change but it doesn't tell me anyone's doing it, just the universe doing its thing. Maybe it's looking out for us.'

'Really?'

'OK, so it's the Russians doing this or something?'

'No. Not the Russians.'

Zak shifted slightly to get the boat in line with the right spot on the island. She had him at 'ground zero.' He stayed quiet so she could let it all out.

'In sixty-seven, my mom was at university at Berkeley. There was this guy, Friedrich. His father was some war refugee. Friedrich and his mom were brought over two years earlier to be with him.'

'Right.'

'She said back in sixty-five, Friedrich was twenty years old and he got a call from the police in Munich asking him to come into the station. When he got there, he was shown into a room deep inside the building. He was seen by some pretty serious striped-up US military. They said his dad was still alive. He was in the US working for the military and Friedrich and his mom needed to join him.'

Allie stopped and looked at Zak. Zak was concentrating on the ocean. Can a man can do that and listen to her at the same time?

'You still with me?'

Zak nodded.

'It's just this is where it starts to go a bit sideways.'

'Why?'

'Twenty years later?' she said. 'So, why the delay? Why bring over a war refugee after the war but only bring his family over twenty years later, twenty years after the war ended?'

Zak had nothing.

'This was the first time he'd ever met his father. He'd only just been born when his father was supposed to have died. Once the hugs and tears were done with, Friedrich couldn't believe how young his father looked, exactly like the photos from when he was born, exactly like the photo he had in his pocket.'

'I don't get it.

'You're not supposed to yet.'

'OK.'

'There was this top secret Nazi project in the war, an experiment in anti-gravity propulsion or some kind of free energy machine, anyway, it looked like a big bell. The Nazis called it Die Glocke and Friedrich's father worked on it. There was no sign of any bell by the time the Soviets reached where it was meant to be in Poland, just empty buildings, scrubland and a strange concrete structure, like a little Stonehenge.'

'Izzi learnt about that in school. She told me.'

'In 1965, just a few months before Friedrich and his mom were brought to the States, something crash landed in Kecksburg, this little town in Pennsylvania. Half the town saw it smashing through the sky in flames, heading for the outskirts of town, out there in the deep woods. When the various people that had to be there got there, reports and conspiracies aligned in a single truth, it looked like a big bell and no-one knew what the hell it was. The military said they'd got hold of the thing in the war. The thing was, that didn't explain the twenty year gap between getting hold of it and Friedrich's family coming over. Someone had left Nazi Germany and turned up here in the US of A in 1965.'

'Jesus, what?'

'Travel in time, Zak. So, what if that bell shaped thing in Kecksburg in sixty-five was the exact same bell shaped thing the Nazis were working on in forty-five? Why else would they only bring the pilot's family over in sixty-five?'

'And someone is using that bell, that time machine, to go and do all this stuff, make these changes.' Zak shifted forward. Allie had to let him get there on his own.

'Someone from 1945...'

'Friedrich's father, the Nazi...'

'Friedrich's father, the Nazi, time-travelled using this bell machine thing, ended up in the woods somewhere in Pennsylvania twenty years later in 1965 looking exactly the same age as he did in 1945.'

He got the nod, he got his gold star, good boy, a glimpse of full color.

Allie maintained her fierce eye drill and saw the moment of his turning, his revelation. At that moment he looked right back into her and offered a small smile, not a eureka high five quite yet, but slowly slowly, catchy monkey, he was closing on where she was.

Zak wondered briefly if it was the frequency of her voice, just resonating with him all up and down that could be swaying his opinion but he had to accept her hypnosis.

'Offer this power to any single human being and they'd take it,' she concluded. 'Tell me you wouldn't.'

'I would,' Zak said. 'But I don't care. Izzi and everything I know is at risk, always has been. I just get the feeling it's happening more, getting closer.'

'So we find it and kill it,' she said.

'We kill the fuck out of it.'

The boat was approaching the island and Zak had to take steps to get it close to the beach. He was going for Steve McQueen but turned into Spongebob as the nose end grounded out a little and then backed off the beach. He let her drift and settled for a spot about thirty yards out.

'Sailing skills, Zak.' It was finally time to flick her nose so he did, and got a cheeky smile back.

'So if you stay seeing changes at puberty, do they fuck off again at menopause?' he said. 'Has your mom… you know?'

'Mmm hmm,' she hummed. 'It didn't fuck off.'

She got up, stripped off to her underwear like a wiggling pro, planted a surprise kiss on Zak's cheek and dived over the side into the water. Zak tracked her round the boat as she swam.

Her teeny white underwear held fast around her smooth slim body but only just. Backstroke was her choice and for all the right reasons. That smile she had, she knew something he didn't, an aphrodisiac, and she was fucking beautiful in the water.

'So which one of them?' she said, creating an echo in this little bay.

'Which one of what?'

'Your folks. I reckon it was your dad who passed it down to you. I just get the feeling males pass to males and females pass to females, kinda makes sense.'

Zak added up all the little snapshot memories of his dad and it did indeed make sense. That look he got when Zak's own first change happened, his dad fighting against bayside, he knew. But he just said 'these things happen' and left Zak to figure it out by himself.

'It was my dad. He just couldn't share it.'

'Couples hiding it from each other, parents hiding it from their kids, kids hiding it from parents.'

'And all of us hiding it from everyone else.'

Allie spat a little stream of water towards Zak.

'If it wasn't for my mom, if my mom hadn't made the decision you have with Izzi, I wouldn't know any of this, they're would be no clues, we'd all go round in this nightmare forever.'

'Or until the pricks doing it finally blow the planet in half.'

'I've brought the clues. Time to solve them, detective.'

She smiled as she turned over, put her little bottom above water and started off for the beach. That smile meant competition and Zak was overboard and smashed and crawled to join her and they raced to the beach. They were too close, too little time to kick and pull each other back, although Zak got the smallest touch of her toe at one stage. Allie finally won by a short nose, got to her feet quickly and celebrated it loudly with a chicken strut.

They crashed back on the warm sand and Allie resumed.

'The thing is, because we can see the changes, we can see the evil happening right in front of us.'

'Why are they evil though? They made sure Beria wasn't in

power and stopped a really bad version of the Cuban missile thing. Why is that evil? Good thing, right?'

'That had to happen. They had to ensure a world that's not a barren, crispy nuclear wasteland or what do they gain? Then it got ugly. Just talk to my mom if you ever manage it. People have been disappearing and getting replaced since mom was aware of it in sixty-two and who knows before that, probably all the way back to forty-five. They're killing people, Zak, erasing them from history, making changes that no-one can see. But we can.'

'I remember stuff about time travel from The Next Place.'

'That show?'

'You can't travel back in time before the time machine was invented.'

'Right'

'I'm just saying whoever's doing it can't go back before their time machine was invented so if it was this Nazi bell, that's 1945.'

Allie wasn't convinced of the link.

'It means there's a limit that's all. Maybe it doesn't matter but they can't go back to the stone ages, kill Ig of the swamp and that's a few billion people less today.'

'So was that show telling it like it is or did Klingons suddenly appear and get all frowny?'

'Straight up, it was Carl Sagan.'

'So they've got a limit.'

'Feel any safer?'

'No.'

Zak and Allie faced each other laughing on this beach and it just happened. Maybe it was being opposite a beautiful, dripping, half-naked person. Maybe it was the gravity of being two of only four like them in the world. Maybe the sea gave them shelter and it had just been a really long time.

Zak moved his hands either side of Allies's face and stroked her hair back, pulling her towards him. He held her there for the briefest of seconds as her smile persisted and he kissed her. Her tongue folded into his and it was only a few more seconds before she rolled over on top of him, dropping water and sand on him. She smiled and launched into her own long soft kiss, grabbing his wet hair and merging it with the wet sand.

She was breathing so deeply, like she'd just come up for air after a dive. Her kiss melted him to the sand. Before he knew it, he'd peeled her little panties off with his feet and he was inside her. The sand and the sea rubbed and cooled them to orgasm and they freeze framed the moment until the last of the feeling subsided. They wrapped each other up here on this beach. Zak stroked any wet hair off the side of her face that wasn't embedded in his chest.

'So...' said Allie.

'So...' said Zak. 'We know how they're doing it. How do we find out who's doing it?'

She looked up at him and kissed him on the end of his nose. 'That, my friend is our mission if we choose to accept it.'

'And we fucking do. Truth or Bayside.'

'Truth or Bayside.'

'There's something else,' she said, comfortable and confident in her sandy repository. 'Something else my mom said from when she knew Friedrich.'

'What's that?'

'Well, Friedrich was always saying to my mom how pissed off his dad was all the time about the people who sit at the top of the tree, the club, he used to call it, a club that wouldn't let him in. Friedrich said sometimes he was pretty scary, shouting at someone who wasn't there.'

'Club?'

'All she could remember beyond that was something Friedrich said about the Sumerians but she never managed to tell me what. Sometimes she doesn't even remember what I've just told you.'

'Sumerians?'

'Sumerians. I took a bit of time and learnt about the Sumerians. You believe in aliens, right?'

'I do,' said Zak by virtue of The Next Place et al and the mathematical improbability there weren't aliens. His face was quickly rid of smiles to greet Allie's sudden look. If she felt he was humoring her there would be a tweak of some of Zak's thinner skin.

'Aliens came to Earth thousands of years ago. They wandered around pretty much like gods, playing their part for the monkeys trolling about on this planet, can you imagine the fun? One day they came back and there was a new kind of monkey. This one wore clothes, made fires, had a language. This species might start to understand them. This species could be genetically modified. They created a super race, part human, part alien. The muppets running the place were forced to let them handle things or get squished.'

Allie appreciated someone with nothing to say not saying it.

'Their alien ancestors did literally come from the skies with all sorts of great chariots and holistic diets and stuff. They first cropped up in our written history in ancient Sumeria. They were superior in every way. The senior locals lapped it up, gave them as many houses and fruit as they needed. They called them the Annunaki.'

'Annunaki?'

'It means godlike offspring in Sumerian. Zak, the descendants of these hybrid alien offspring are the people at the top of that tree.'

'And that's the club this Nazi couldn't get into? Where's the proof?'

Allie had now risen up from the sand, water slipping slowly off her breasts, tickling over her nipples as it planned its descent over Zak to the sand.

'One in a thousand of our genes isn't shared with any other terrestrial life form. Even us monkey bloods are made of at least some watered-down alien.'

'Seriously?'

'Seriously. Who else could it be? If anyone on this planet would end up with a time machine, it has to be the people who control everything. They've been pulling the strings so long.'

'So who are these people? How do we find them?'

'There are symbols everywhere. They're pretty easy to spot once you get your eye in.'

'Like what?'

'One of the recurring symbols on Sumerian sculptures is the double coiled snake.' Allie showed Zak the image on her phone.

'The symbol for medicine?'

'Yep and the British royal family. The Queen's royal carriage has an ancient Sumerian symbol on the back. It means humans born of aliens, beings of this place made of alien blood, Zak.'

Ok so the British royal family, we'll never get close to them or their club, and medicine as a whole is a little broad.'

'Like I say, this is our mission, should we choose to accept it.'

Zak laid his head back down on the sand and closed his eyes.

'Blue bloods,' she said.

'Blue bloods?'

'These aliens had copper based blood. Copper turns blue when it oxidizes. Their offspring from back then to now have copper-based blood, rhesus negative, and you only get into that club if you have the purest blood. They mix with each other, not the rest of us iron bloods, bloody red blooded peasants we are.'

'So that's why the Nazi never got into their club. It's all about the bloodline.'

'All about the blood. You know what blood does?'

'What?'

'Creates those that qualify and those that never will.'

'And the Nazi didn't. He didn't have the blood.'

'It didn't matter if he had a time machine or a pill for everlasting life, he'd never get in.'

'So these people at the top of tree ended up with this power as well,' said Zak.

'That's why they'll always be top of the tree.'

'How the hell do we find them? I mean, if you've got a time machine, would you ever be found if you don't want to be?'

'We've only got one clue. Start where it all started. Let's find that Nazi fucker. We need to ask your mom.'

'She's not seen Friedrich for fifty years. Even if he dropped in for tea twice a week and brought cakes, I still don't think she'd remember.'

'Paperclip,' said Zak.

'Paperclip?'

'Operation Paperclip. Bringing Germans to the US after the war, Nazis or not.'

'Paperclip was done by 1959. There's nada, nothing to say he was even here.'

'Apart from your mom. Who else? Military?'

'It's a Roswell job,' said Allie. 'Initially they said they found the bell in forty-five. Then they said what the fuck are you talking about, what fucking bell? Good luck with them. And we do not want to get on radar with these people.'

'That reminds me. Don't call or text till I get you an app to use.'

'What app?'

'Just a friend. He'll give us something no-one can track.'

Zak looked up. Allie was pretty sure he was still trying the 'who else' angle.

'No. It's still not the Russians,' she said. 'We can only look at what we know, the top of the tree.'

'The Queen of England?'

'No. There are more of them. Follow the symbols. Follow the clues, Detective. Something will show itself.'

'We've got what we've got. Plan.'

'Plan.'

'We'll find our enemy or we'll find another clue.'

'Either way, we're in the right place.'

9
flag

How come so little time was gained by not working? Two weeks of being as close to his Izzi as he could get away with. She was fine, never been brighter, like she knew something. She knew what he was doing and she didn't give him shit for it, just hung around, time with his Izzi. There were water fights, food fights, breakages and spillages. It was just normal. They talked about everything but this.

It was also time to get that day with Allie through his head. The day it all went more upside down than he could have imagined, but upside down with a plan and a view to a target.

Yesterday he'd had a chat with Manuel 'Manny' Zamora. This kid was next level genius, a little hacker now living with his third or fourth foster parents. Manny was special. He was in trouble more than he wasn't but Zak knew his story. Hacking the California Cannabis vote was Manny's own personal favorite. Some channel even did a show on it. When they're special, and it's not their fault, they get help. They also get help because they can get you places you couldn't get on cases.

Zak knew Izzi would fall in love with Manny immediately, which is why Izzi would never meet Manny.

Manny had some tech. All Zak knew was he could search anything and stay invisible, something about bouncing searches around the world and ending up originating from Saturn or something. If they're diving into a world where people change presidents because they can, they want to be invisible. They now were.

Allie got a text from Zak to say *only use this app*. He got a smiley face and a flowerpot back with a message. *2213 Alliss Street, Tomorrow. Midday x.*

This was that morning. There was the smell of coffee and the scuttling about of his little Izzi in the kitchen.

She turned and smiled and then a surprise Yoda said 'eggs, Father, made for you I have.' She showed him a nicely dressed table and physically sat him in a chair.

Coffee was one thing but breakfast meant she had something on her mind. This was the chat. Step up and don't fuck up.

The eggs looked good. Bless her little socks, she'd sprinkled a little oregano on top and stuck a little red flag in as well, causing a breach in the left egg, a slow yellow bleeding out.

When things were busy and 'Dad, can we talk' didn't quite hit the mark, this was Izzi's way of telling him 'look seriously Dad, sit down, shut up, we need to talk.' This was a flag.

It was agreed, when there was a flag on the play, it could not be ignored, time had to surrender to it no matter what. Zak was usually out of his quota of flags quickly in the average month. Izzi had only flagged him a handful of times. She never did it without a good reason, apart from the times she just wanted a big cuddle hug.

Zak would buy a little cake or something and plant it in that or stick it in the headphone socket of her iPod. Either way, Zak and Izzi knew the meaning and substance of the flag.

A flag always started with a smile, exactly what a chat between dad and daughter needed. The accepted format of the flag system was for its target to take the flag and hand it back to its planter, thus officially accepting it.

Izzi took a seat and happily received the flag back, sucked a little egg off its stem and laid it down next to her plate. She looked up and had to smile as her silly dad was doing what he always did when he was a little nervous, he twisted his hair into two little horns at the front of his head and stared straight ahead, this time at an unsuspecting coffee pot. She tapped one of his hands to remind him 'Dad, stop it, what are you, six?'

'I was just thinking back to one of the first times we took you on the boat. You were so tiny.'

'I know, Dad, I've heard this.'

'Mom was on the way from front to back down the side with you in her arms and tripped on a rope. You were heading over the side.'

'Dad, hello, I know.'

'The whole thing lasted a couple of seconds. Mom said you were like a bar of soap, a slippery Houdini baby. She got the faintest grip on the string of your little baby hoodie.'

'Dad.'

'It stretched and you dangled by the skin of it but this string wouldn't hold.'

'But then came Dad-o-tard to the rescue,' and Izzi made the trumpet noise game shows use to announce the winner.

'Yes, he did, what, Dad-o-tard, Iz, seriously? I've never held onto anything tighter. I got hold of some of your flabby baby middle and you started laughing. You kept laughing for so long, we thought...'

'Dad. Flag. Shut the fuck up.'

Zak was back on dry land and focused on that baby as she is now.

'We kinda got off topic a while ago.'

'I know, baby, that day in the Cafe?'

'Bistro,' said Izzi.

'I'm sorry, baby, it's just with your mom and stuff and I wanted you to be ready to talk to me about it.'

'I know, Dad, chill, I get it. And here I am.'

Izzi topped up Zak's coffee.

'OK, so father of mine.'

'Daughter of mine.'

They both made Zak's crazy ugly face because they both needed to keep tension off the table. Crazy ugly face always achieved this, it was an extreme gurn, cross eyes and a drooly lopsided grin. They both reeled at how ugly each other's crazy ugly faces were and a quick fist pump got things started.

'So, I know you knew something about that day,' she said. 'It was written all over your silly face, and then there was Mom's news.' Zak saw Izzi's eyes start to shine with the an early tear and he put his hand on hers. 'Did Mom already know she was sick?' Izzi was deflecting. If today was only about that day, this might have been a valid question but today was no longer just about that day and she knew it.

'No, baby, she didn't.'

'So you saw the same thing right?'

'I did, baby. When we got there, we sat down at the Harbor Cafe and Mom ordered tomatoes. By the time our waitress brought us breakfast, the place was called the Harbor Bistro with a shiny new menu, no tomatoes in sight, and Mom had ordered melon. Good melon through right?'

'Yes, Dad, awesome melon and thank you, finally, and you didn't paint the wall green.'

'No. Baby, I'm so sorry it's taken so long to get to this. I didn't want it to mess with you. My folks let it mess with me. I don't think you or me had our heads on straight, maybe we do now.'

'We need to, Dad and what do you mean like your folks let it mess with you? Let what mess with you?'

Little Izzi had tried but it was time to accompany the protocol with tears. Zak had been ready for it since he mentioned her Mom. Izzi leaked one from her left eye and Zak pulled chair and daughter in for a hug.

Zak's own tears were on the way up from that place that stores them and can't wait to tell everyone, but he had to be strong for his little girl.

The only way into this was straight in. Zak separated from a calmed Izzi and wiped her eyes with his napkin. A little kiss on the nose accompanied him pushing chair and daughter back to where they were with a smile and 'silly daughter.'

'The first time I saw it with you was at the bistro but I hadn't seen it since, till a couple of weeks back.'

'Oh there's been plenty.'

'As soon as I heard about Mister Rolon I was sure.' He cupped both of her little hands underneath his big right hand on the table. 'When I was about your age, I started seeing things.'

'Things?'

'Changes, Iz. Suddenly I'd find out that there was something very different with the world from what I knew it was.'

'That's exactly it. What the fuck?'

'That's what I thought. The problem was no-one else saw it change. One day there'd be some new country or the Governor of fucking Nebraska would be someone else but to everyone else, that country had always been that country and that governor had always been the same governor.'

'And Mister Sanchez had always been Mister Rolon.'

'Yes. When I told my folks, my dad looked at me and I was sure he knew something, just like you did but my mom didn't. It freaked her out totally and then it freaked me out totally. I had to see a shrink and was nearly sent to Bayside. Dad made sure I wasn't but I never found out if he really knew what was going on. We never talked about it. I had to figure it out on my own. That's why you and me are dealing with it now. You're not alone, you'll never be alone. I'm right here with you going through the same shit.'

Izzi became more animated. She wiped away the last of the tears no longer required and ran into her old dad for the biggest tightest squeeze hug he could remember. He returned it with interest and planted a long kiss on the top of her head.

'So what is it?' she asked, adrenaline trembling her voice.

'Somehow, time is being screwed up. No idea how, no idea why it's just us that sees it. What else have you seen apart from Mom's tomatoes and the Mister Rolon thing?'

'The real estate sign over the road. It used to be orange now it's blue. And this one was really bugging me,' she continued pointing over at the wall. 'That wall was yellow then it was this weird olive green? I know you, Dad. You don't decorate.'

Zak knew she was a smart little cookie this daughter of his. She was spotting these changes and that would help her.

'So it's like some fucked up sci-fi movie,' she went on. 'You and me are out of the normal time loop.'

'And the rest of the world just carries on like nothing's changed, totally oblivious lemmings. Kinda makes you feel special if it wasn't so fucked up.'

'And, Dad, it is fucked up.'

'Seriously, baby, when the tomato thing happened, it was all I could do to keep my shit together. I prayed it wasn't happening to you but it was. I'm so sorry.'

'Dad, chill, it's fine. We're on the same page. We can help each other out, right?'

'Right.' The threat of tears was averted by another fist pump and Zak continued.

'So we have to do things a little different now.'

'Like what?'

'Well, there are changes that happen all around us all the time. Most of the time we don't know they've happened. The ones we see straight away are the tip of the iceberg. Then we start blabbing on about something a friend did last week and find out they weren't even at that thing last week or maybe they don't even exist anymore.'

'Embarrassing.'

'More than embarrassing, baby, people start to wonder.'

'They sure did when I handed it to Mister Rolon.'

Another tension relieving chuckle followed and another solidarity fist pump.

'Poor Mister Rolon. Seriously though, baby, we need to be more reactive now. Assume something you know isn't true any more.

Zak took a moment and let Izzi zone into outer space a bit and absorb all of this. He was confident she was capable but everyone needs a little metabolic leeway.

'And some of the changes are really small and stupid. You just can't figure out what the point is,' continued Zak.

'Like what?'

'The ones that make no sense? Countries appearing and disappearing and assassinations of presidents you can kinda get your head round if it's people who are doing it.'

'People? So it's people, Dad?'

Shit. Idiot. He wanted to give her a friend not give her the same fight. Give her a sniff of it and she will. Idiot. Divert.

'I don't know, baby. Probably just random, might just be a shithead of a universe.'

'Dad, you said people.'

'I know, baby, but I don't know. It could be anything. Just thinking out loud.'

'I've told you about that, Dad.'

'Right.'

'So what was the point of the day of the tomatoes?'

'That's just it. I don't think there was a point. What possible big picture could mean a person suddenly ordered something else for breakfast?'

Zak remembered probably the only conversation he had with his dad that could have been about all this. Maybe the only way his dad could deal with telling him was being cryptic.

'My dad said some things just don't make sense in life. If you see something that doesn't make sense, it's just a consequence of something bigger that did make sense. It's like a big river splitting out into tributaries and then smaller streams and each tiny branch eventually comes to rest where it does. A milk carton ends up caught in the brushwood in a stream somewhere. There's no reason for it to be there.'

'Or is there?'

'Very Zen, daughter. Wise beyond your years you are.'

'Dad.'

'It's just one of the millions of tiny results of something bigger upstream, something that did mean something. So I guess what he meant was if time is the river and something is changed at its core for whatever reason, there are repercussions all the way down the line, some trickling onto you for no apparent reason, like the tomato nonsense. On their own, there's no reason for them but as a consequence of that bigger change they're inevitable.'

'So the tomato thing was like a milk carton that washed up at the end of the tiniest stream. It had no business being where it was but it still was.'

'Not everything means something.'

Zak smiled at his little girl's immense ability to process stuff like this. Izzi had an ally and that ally was her dad, the only human being on God's green earth she truly trusted.

'So how come it's just us?' she said.

'That's something else I need to talk about. I just found out it's not just us. There is someone else, but first I need to ask a couple of questions.'

'Intriguing, my father, shoot.'

'Do you ever dream of water, like you're drowning?'

'Shit yeah, only all the time, started a few weeks ago.'

'Me too, a few weeks. And do you ever feel stiff in the morning like you ran up a mountain yesterday?'

'That started the morning you, me and mom went out on the boat, the day of the tomato.'

Then Izzi's eyes started to change, one at a time, gradually changing color from the pupil outwards from her current emerald green to her mom 's crystal blue and Zak could only smile at the sheer beauty of it. It was mesmerized, stopped time in its tracks and reminded him of the truest beauty there was in the world.

'They just changed again didn't they?' she said.

'Yep.'

'That's so fucked up. Has that got anything to do with it?'

'No idea, baby, I just love seeing it.'

'You're so weird.'

'Look, I've been aching every day since I was your age. Don't worry, it never gets too bad, you just know it's there, right?'

'Right.'

'I saw the doctors and they had not one fucking clue but we'll go see them anyway.'

'Don't let them do tests on me, Dad.'

'No way, baby. If they don't know, they don't know. I'm pretty sure it's all part of these changes somehow. I just don't know why now.'

Zak reached across and needed both her hands wrapped up in his for this.

'There's one more thing, baby'

'Me too, you first.'

'I met someone,' he said. 'Allie. She sees the changes too and so does her mom.'

'So basically everyone sees the fucking changes?'

'No, just us four and they've never heard of anyone else seeing them either. We're linked to them somehow. These changes seem to run in families. It starts when you go through the hormone change, you know, when a girl starts getting her... you know...' That's it he was in, no going back. 'You know, boys start being even more stupid but with different haircuts?'

Zak looked literally everywhere around this room apart from into her eyes.

'So how's that all going for you, baby? Have you... er... you know... gone through that other kind of change?' he said, seriously cracking her up with a new and fully nervous crazy ugly face.

'Dad, gross, please.' Izzi put her head in her hands. Zak just about heard a muffled 'yes' through her fingers followed by something that sounded like 'barra abum.'

A teenage daughter, however close she may be to her dad, is still less likely to chat about such stuff with dad than mom. She knew there wasn't the option here but still, gross.

'Great flag, Dad, thanks.' Their third massive hug took place, no less intense than the others, and Zak sat back as little Izzi removed the plates of untouched eggs.

'What was that other thing you wanted to say, baby?' reminded Zak.

Izzi wondered if she should tell her dad about the other thing. She knew it would worry him but there was still a flag on the play and she had to.

'There's this guy.'

'What, Brandon from school?'

'No, this other guy. He's older. Even older than you. It's just really weird. I keep seeing him looking at me.'

Zak perked up and was right over into seriously fuck someone up mode. 'What guy?'

'A few weeks ago, he was outside school when Sarah's mom dropped us. Then he was at Frio later on my way to the boat. I've seen him walking past and driving past. I don't know, never seen him before he's just started showing up. He's always smiling and looking right at me but never comes close and never talks to me.'

The detective in Zak went into overdrive. Not only did he have some sick fuck stalking his little girl, but he had to wonder if the 'who' in Allie's analysis, the seriously high end individuals they were about to seek out, were onto them already somehow and tracking Izzi.

'How long has this been happening? What did he look like? What was he wearing?'

'A few weeks, Dad. I never feel threatened. He looks smart and civilized, not like some sicko.'

'Sickos don't have a dress code, baby. At no point go near him or talk to him, right?'

'Right, Dad.'

'And call me as soon as he shows up again. And if anyone else you don't know starts looking at you, call me as well, especially if they're fucking smiling.'

'Right, Dad.'

Zak was now cold all the way up from his ankles to his neck. His next task this very morning was ask the boys at the precinct for one or two drive-bys the school and Frio.

Had these hypothetical fuckers just shown themselves? He and Izzi were way deep in this now. He knew Allie was right. They had to find out why this was happening and kill it and there was less time to waste than he thought.

Zak took a quick shower and was ready so head over to Allie's.

'Iz, baby, just going out for a bit.'

He listened for an answer but there was probably music or some other contemplation up there in Izzi central. He jotted a note, *baby, just going out for a bit.*

10

billings montana

Allie was coming up fast, toying with the mountain edge, emerging from her dream, pushing through it to the surface. It wasn't like the recurring dreams she'd been having recently about being stranded in the sea, in this dream there was a little boy. She knew his name was Aaron and she was pretty sure this was her little boy.

There he was in the front yard, about three years old, riding around on a little toy pedal boat and then he looked back at her through the kitchen window and smiled.

She opened her eyes and looked round the room, slowly releasing the dream and rediscovering her reality. She softened into her pillow again. 'Not yet.'

The next thing she thought of was a memory from a few years ago. She'd dreamt she was pregnant. It was so real, big lump, hard to move and the whole shebang, she got a test and, for fuck's sake, she was pregnant.

She didn't remotely love the father. She didn't remotely love any male kind. Men were assholes every last one. The only man she ever loved had fucked off with someone ten years younger and, not only that, he'd taken her old VW bug in the bargain. Men were a messy means to an end and nothing more and never did one get invited to stay the night. With that pregnancy test, she made a decision only women have the affliction to ponder, to keep her life her own for now.

Today, though, sleep was no longer possible for Allie. She was feeling nauseous. She thought of Zak on that beach, that kiss, him inside her on the sand, and she was hurled into the bathroom, head planted deep in the toilet ready to let it all go but it held, false alarm but had her dream recall of pregnancy become a fucking pregnancy again?

Today, she now had two things to do where once there was one. At time of going to bed last night, her schedule was meet Zak. But now inserted into that schedule, topping it quite easily, was a pregnancy test.

She was quickly in and out of the pharmacy and home without any other thought crossing her mind other than 'negative.' She slipped the test out of her bag and headed to the bathroom. 'Don't you fucking dare.'

A fucking ridiculous amount of time later, time occupied only by the little readout in the middle, all the molecules in her body downed tools and stopped. Her throat seized. The color drained out of her and started to appear in the readout, the sign of her new reality. Green.

Like when you get food poisoning you know it was that prawn. She knew who the father was and that prawn was Zak. This felt different to the first time it happened. She'd promised herself never again and, OK, fine, if again, you're having a baby.

A smile saw an opportunity and pushed aside a frown. Check again in a week but, Holy Jesus, a baby.

Before her revelation spread to notifying fathers, names and diapers and mom's groups and other things, she was saved by a knock at the door.

By the time Zak realized the flowerpot emoji didn't mean buy a flowerpot, he'd already bought the damn pot and here it stood with him outside Allie's apartment.

A few weeks had passed since their boat trip and he was a little nervous about seeing her again. Would she be embarrassed after their wickedness the other week or was he seconds away from more of the same?

Allie's apartment building was Spanish-Californian, whitewash and red terracotta tiles in a calm leafy street. Her front door on the second floor opened out onto a nice big communal terrace overlooking some secluded palm gardens, the distant bay and a kidney-shaped pool.

The door opened and he was greeted by an Allie in faded Levis and white cropped T-shirt, definitely no bra, a casual departure from the Russian spy the other day.

Allie took a quick look at his pot and smiled a beautiful smile and Zak was tugged inside. The place smelt wonderful, fresh laundry, flowers and most of all, Allie and whatever her scent was.

'Nice apartment.'

It was big, gorgeous splashes of abstract color delivered by the large paintings on all the walls, fat red leather couches, things Moroccan, stone floors. Zak didn't know what Allie did for a living but it looked like she was good at it.

Zak noticed a big computer screen over on an antique desk in the corner.

'Awesome place, Allie, what do you do?'

'I'm an artist. The pictures are mine.'

She was, in that case, a really fucking awesome artist. Zak wasn't a connoisseur and wouldn't know if the things were upside down or not, but he knew what he liked and he liked hers very much. They were almost 3D, deep burnt colors, looked like the globs of paint were still moving. They were about the size of him and they just vibrated, like they were deciding whether to govern the space or let it be. They were completely fluid.

'You shine lights through crystals onto the canvas and pour acrylic over it,' she said.

'So you do it on the floor.'

'Yeah.'

'Hang the lights and crystals above it.'

'Yeah.'

'Awesome, you should shoot some video of you doing that.'

'What, naked I assume?'

'If you prefer.'

Right. This can go one of two ways. Surrender to this delicious lust monkey standing in front of him, just run his hands right up the front of that little shirt and kiss her... or fucking be cool.

'Do you ever dream of water?' he said.

This turned her head.

'All the time.'

'Always feels like drowning or about to drown.'

'Yeah.'

'So does Izzi. If your mom does too, there's got to be something to it.'

Meanwhile, in the street outside Allie's apartment, the trunk popped open on Zak's car and Izzi climbed out. She knew he was off somewhere. Her and Sarah had plotted this a few weeks ago when he first started acting weird and Izzi stayed over. He was up to something and Sarah's brother, Kyle, was enlisted to provide the car. They'd followed Zak all over town last couple of weeks. They followed him up to this house on the point. He was there for fifteen minutes and went back to the precinct. Someone watched him from a top window as he drove away. Then she followed him to this weird Moroccan looking shop and saw him shake hands with someone outside and now here he is at this apartment.

She took a receiver unit out of her pocket and switched it on. There was some chatter about paintings and there was a woman there with him. The last of those hugs after her flag this morning had successfully planted the bug in her dad's pocket and she was receiving loud and clear. She'd got it from some guy at school, said he got it from this other guy up on the point, the guy can literally get anything, some kind of computer nerd.

Izzi headed over to a little green space and sat under a big oak tree. She knew her dad was keeping something back. He'd tried to divert from his glaring error about people being involved in these changes but she wasn't having any of it. Poor effort, Dad.

'Who's this woman? Oh God, please don't do anything gross,' Izzi said as a small fuzzy dog thought about lifting a leg on the tree next to hers.

'Thanks for the app,' said Allie.

'Manny said they can never trace it.'

'Coffee?'

'It's officially afternoon though. I'll join you with one of those if that's OK,' said Zak noticing an empty wine glass on the table.

Glasses were chinked and they took their seats on opposite couches. Eye contact became prolonged eye contact and a mutual smile reminded Allie of the beach and Zak of her pouring paint naked.

'Izzi said there's this old guy that's been turning up outside her school.'

'Old guy?'

'Yeah she'd never seen him till a few weeks ago.'

'Who is he?'

'No idea, might be nothing. She reckons he just smiles at her. I'm checking it out, just worried they're fucking with us'

'How could they know?'

'How deep do they go? Maybe they're the ones who monitor what anyone says anywhere in the world. Maybe they watch out for random chicken noises outside bistros.'

'Funny boy. So who's this Manny anyway?'

'Manny. Manuel Zamora. This orphan kid. One of these genius kids who can do anything. Helps us out on cases every so often. If he says this makes us invisible, it does. He was left as a tiny baby outside the police precinct in a cardboard box. The box once contained Manuel Zamora's Super Bueno Tortilla Chips. There were plenty of blankets but no note.'

'The day I saw you at Bayside,' said Allie. 'Mom came out of it for a few minutes. It was the weirdest thing. I'd given up hope till the next visit.'

'It came out of nowhere,' she continued. 'She was sitting facing out of the window looking at the sea like she always did. Some seagulls were laughing it up and circling something down below. She suddenly recognized me and smiled. I reached out and took her hand. I knew she was with me in the room again and I knew the first thing she'd say, the first thing she always says, are you pregnant yet, dear?'

Zak had to chuckle and Allie calmly picked out a little glass ball from the little glass ball bowl on her side table and aimed for Zak's glass. It fell just short.

'What did you say?' said Zak, this time drawing a salvo of little glass balls. Allie juggled for the faintest moment, what did she say or what would she say now? Do not go there.

'I said Mom, literally every time and she just said, one day the answer will be yes, my darling. Then she changed right in front of me. She looked up like I'd said something but I hadn't, looked straight into my eyes. She had these hollow eyes, the mom who's in another place. She said A man owns a tree but who gathers the fruit? Find the man with an apple and find the tree it came from. Then she suddenly turned and got up out of her chair and looked at the door, the door you were standing outside. It's like she knew you were there and that was the end of her brief shift in the real world.'

Zak remembered what Izzi said in the flag. That milk carton ending up at the end of the tiniest stream. It had no business being there, it just was.

'If we want to find who's behind it we have to find who benefits from it. We have to find that milk carton, that change that doesn't seem to have a reason. Who benefits from it? Find him and go up the channels, swim upstream, find who creates it.'

'Milk carton?'

'We know the changes that have been happening. We can find who's involved further down the chain.'

'People. I fucking knew it,' said Izzi shifting position under her tree. The little fuzzy dog had returned and was now sitting between her and another tree, staring at her. She saw it and willed it not to come over, she's busy and she would have to give it a good fluffing if it did.

'So where do we start?' said Allie.

'Changes. Think of all the changes you've seen, think of the ones that didn't seem to have a point. The ones that definitely had me convinced it was all random.'

'Why would a car or a wall change color,' said Zak.

'Why would a friend never have been a friend? Rum?'

'Splash of coke, hand squeezed lime? Said Zak and another three little glass balls missed his head by inches and signaled Allie's departure to the kitchen.

'Why would a TV show never have existed?' Zak said to himself and then he remembered one late night slob out in front of the TV not long after Megan died. Izzi was long since asleep and he was halfway through a bottle of rum, drifting in and out of sleep on the couch.

'The Mayor of Billings, Montana,' said Zak, sitting up on the couch and dislodging one or two glass balls onto the rug.

'What?' said Allie in the distance.

Zak joined her in the kitchen.

'The Mayor of Billings. It's a town in Montana. You didn't see that one?'

'Nope'

'Slow news day. They bring in regional small stuff, the stuff you would just never know about.'

'Out of there if literally anything else happens.'

'This guy was the Mayor of Billings, Montana

'Billings?'

'Yep right up there in... Montana.'

Allie turned with retribution in mind but couldn't quite find a safe place to throw him, too messy, breakages. She settled for a pinch on the arm.

'Where are your balls now,' said Zak as he dropped a glass ball in each rum glass.'

'And where are yours, Detective? Nice touch by the way.'

'This guy was re-elected by a mile. No-one really bothered running against him. Some schmuck was hoisted in there so they could claim democracy. Anyway, you know what got him home big time?'

'Nope.'

'There was this hydro dam and reservoir project they wanted to build there, snake river I think. He said no fucking way and he was Mayor for another four years.'

'And the point is?'

'The point is, two years later, big news. Not some shoe-in on a slow day. This was prime network gold.'

'What was it?'

'They had built a hydro dam and reservoir in Billings, Montana.'

'Surprise. Fucking lying scum politicians, and what?'

'And here's what. There were hundreds of people protesting at the loss of wildlife and all sorts but the company building the dam opened the thing anyway, they flooded the whole area.'

'Shit with all the protestors still there?'

'Yep. The news was having a real Cronkite moment. The humanity, one hundred and eighty people and all the livestock and wild animals drowned, floating in the water. It was like a scene out of the bible.'

'Shit, fucking assholes. Why would they do that?

'You know what they said?'

'Nope.'

'They said really sorry, it was an accident but maybe its for the best. They couldn't wait for vagrants and communists to get out the way forever.'

'Assholes. That was it?'

'Pretty much. And then they interviewed the Mayor asking how could this happen.'

'What did that prick say?'

'This is the kicker. It's not what he said, which was politician shit like it's a terrible tragedy, unfortunate accident and bullshit. It's who he was.'

'Who he was?'

'He wasn't the guy I'd seen on the news two years earlier, it was a totally different Mayor of Billings, Montana.'

'What happened to the last guy?'

'There was never any last guy. This new guy had been Mayor of Billings, fucking Montana forever. When I looked into it, there was no mention anywhere about the Mayor I saw on TV two years earlier.'

Allie handed Zak his drink and then something became clear to her.

'Dreams.'

'Dreams?'

'Water. We've all had dreams about water. It always felt like drowning.'

'Water. Jesus. I got a note from this guy I was meant to be seeing in Bayside the day I met you. It said *I am a leader of men, I am a killer of men, I drowned them all, The real evil is in the water that's not meant to be there.* That note led us to this guy, he'd taken a little girl. He had her in this cabin on a lake near Sacramento. We saved her. This Billings thing. The water that's not meant to be there.'

'My mom. The night me and my dad brought her to Bayside, she was shouting the animals, oh my God, the animals. She's been saying it again last few weeks right out of the blue. Did she mean this?'

'It's all pointing to this moment in history in Billings, Montana. What the fuck?'

'Our target that's what the fuck,' said Allie. 'From this Mayor, we get further up the stream and find the people who made things happen for him.'

'And the best thing is,' said Zak. 'With politicians it's easy.' He moved over to the computer with a massive light bulb hovering over his head and started typing.

'How?'

'This is why politicians make it so easy. All politicians have to publish who their backers are. Those backers have to meet certain criteria, no porn empires or Japanese whaling corporations, but good, clean, solid all-American money.'

'Find that list and we've found our suspects.'

Allie budged him off the driver's seat and quickly had a list of backers.

'You've got your usual suspects, local lumber mill, car dealership, all pretty sensible donors,' said Allie.

'Andersen Logistics? They're not in Montana.'

'Right, so why would they be bothered who the Mayor of Billings was? Andersen Logistics. They're owned by a company called... Island State Electronics.'

'And it's all owned by this one group... Rabbu Tahumu. Jesus, they're into everything, banking, oil, pharmaceuticals, aviation, chemicals.'

'The top of the tree.'

'The river.' said Zak.

'LA,' said Zak. 'Rabbu Tahumu has its HQ in LA, Malibu.'

'So what earthly business does Rabbu Tahumu have in Montana?'

'Who's the main guy there?' said Zak.

'The main guy is... Peter Hendricks. Where do I know that name from?'

'Then this Peter Hendricks fucker is our target,' said Zak.

They chinked glasses again and sat back like they'd just finished an exam early.

'Address?' said Zak.

'Fucking stupid thing,' said Izzi, shaking the squeaking idiot receiver in her hand. It was resonating between squeaking and static and biting it wasn't making it better. Izzi rebooted it but still the same. 'Fucking useless shit,' she said, eyeing up a neighboring tree to throw it at.

Zak and Allie soon found that naming company officers doesn't mean giving the addresses of company officers. An hour and two more rums followed without an address. Even Manny's dark search couldn't uncover one.

'We need to go to LA,' said Allie.

'We need to go to LA,' said Zak.

Zak stood over her as she shut down the computer and suddenly realized there was nothing to look at on the screen yet here they were still looking at it. His arm had been warming against hers since Billings, Montana and he could hear her breathing.

This moment of silence and success allowed him to smell her again. That peck on the cheek before her little bottom wiggled overboard, the water dripping off her breasts as she kissed him on the beach, being inside her.

Allie turned her head and looked up at him, her crystal blue eyes driving into his skull, down his spine and then everywhere. Zak fell to his knees and wrapped Allie and her chair into him and kissed her. She wrapped her arms and legs round him. The Russian spy was very much under that crop T-shirt. She slid her hands under his shirt and lifted it off him, burying her face in his neck. Zak ran his hands all over her naked back and round to her naked front, massaging her sit up, beautiful, handful sized breasts. The kiss persisted and breathing demanded fucking in seconds.

Zak picked her up and moved her over to the couch. Allie made it clear he sits, she wiggles. She pushed him backwards and rose up on him, looking him right in the eye as she peeled her shirt off and cast it away without a thought, causing something metallic to rattle on the little table next to the couch.

He rubbed her further up his body. Her breasts were mouth level and he invaded them, capturing her strawberry tip nipples and running his hands into her jeans. She rose up from him, attacked his belt and studs and he was free to be massaged and placed in her mouth.

Zak swiveled on the couch and peeled her jeans off. He licked every inch of available skin from belly button to her knees and finally embedded his tongue in her. Her hot breath on his cock got hotter.

Zak moved her up and down and Allie righted herself on top of him, coming in for another deep tongue kiss and he was inside her everywhere. She was flat on him, engulfing his neck as he moved her up and down.

Allie slowed to almost a stop, just one long slow thrust every couple of seconds. She became a very pretty statue and stayed where she was for just a second or two, eyes closed, trembling. They climaxed together on that big leather couch, looking each other right in the eyes. Allie licked Zaks face from chin to nose, she immersed her tongue in him one last time and collapsed next to him, wrapping her tingling body around him.

There was the occasional brush, flick and chuckle as they moved round the room to find their clothes.

'Coffee?' said Allie.

Izzi made one final attempt to get the stupid receiver to cough up some sensible juice. If it didn't work this time, she already had its fate planned. She would stand calmly, wind her arm up and pitch the fucker at the tree and good fucking riddance. She switched it on. No static. it was working. All she heard was a woman say 'Tuesday' and a door shut. Then just footsteps. Shit, he's leaving. She got up and hauled ass over to the car and she was back inside the trunk before Zak hit the bottom step.

They weren't far from home when Izzi's receiver offered an unwanted final splutter from its dormant state to punish Izzi for almost sending it into a tree. A loud whining screech lingered for about three seconds and then vanished along with its power.

Before long, she felt the car slip up the slope into the driveway and her dad's door slammed shut. 'He didn't hear it, he did not hear it.' Her dad's footsteps sounded like they were heading to the door but then they stopped. Izzi froze and suddenly the trunk was open, exposing her to the world of her dad and a look on his face that couldn't help make her smile. The only logical response to this was to give a muted 'tada' and a big fat cheesy grin.

'What the fuck are you doing there?'

'Dad that was halfway to crazy ugly face. Here's one back at you.' Izzi's crazy ugly face penetrated the hard shell of trying not to laugh and Zak crumbled.

'Come on Iz, out the trunk, seriously what are you doing in there?'

'Never mind about all that, father of mine. What are you doing there, randomly looking in car trunks and anyway, you stand accused, yes you do.'

Izzi composed herself after exiting the trunk and stood up to her full height some way below her dad's chin and poked him in the chest.

'You stand accused of the most horrible crime.'

'Iz what's going on?'

'The crime of breaching the flag.'

'Breaching the flag? When?'

'This very day. June 2nd 2017. How plead you?'

'Not guilty, now stop it. Come inside and tell me why you were in the trunk.'

'Not people you said this morning and within hours here you were discussing the very people that it apparently isn't with some woman.'

'That's Allie, baby. Remember I told you. She sees changes too, calls them time shifts, kinda like that.'

'Fabulous news, Tardimus. However, you are guilty of fabrication and not only that, fabrication on a flag day. The penalty is truth or death.'

'Baby, I'm not having this conversation in the driveway. Inside now please.'

The door was shut behind them but Izzi wasn't about to release him.

'People, Dad. Tell me about the people.'

'Baby, this morning I didn't know it was. It was just an option.'

'Option, right Dad, and your attempted diversion in the flag, bear in mind another felony, less than poor, as transparent as the hollow air escaping from you now.'

'Iz, what did you do when I was at Allie's? Did you hear us today?'

'Every snake-like word, almost.'

'OK tell me.'

'I heard about floods and I heard about some company, Rubber Poopoo or some nonsense. Need I go on? Oh, hang on, what's that you say, yes please, I must go on. Well OK, cunning and devious parent, and I heard about Peter Hendricks.'

Zak was numb. How dare she not fold under interrogation when he's just caught her scalping a ride in his trunk and spying on him. Fuck. What else did she hear?

'Hear anything after that, oh my little in-more-trouble-than-its-possible-to-be-in daughter?'

'No, technical problems.'

'Technical problems, what technical problems?'

'Never mind.'

'Thank fuck for that,' thought Zak.

'Pardon, Dad, what?'

Jesus did he say that out loud?

'I didn't say anything.'

'So start.'

She didn't hear about LA. He was worried about this exact thing happening. He knew she wouldn't let it go and she'd be in his fucking truck all the way up I-5 to LA.

'Dad. Dad! This Peter Hendricks. Is he the guy that's doing all this, making these changes happen? You're going to try and see him aren't you?'

'No, baby, we're not.'

'Only because you don't know where he lives.'

'That's right, we don't.'

'I can help you know.'

'Baby, the best way for you to help is to stay out of it and not get involved.'

'Not get involved? I'm involved, Dad. I'm seeing what you're seeing and now I know what you know. I can never unknow that but I can help.'

'No'

'What?'

'I said no. The same as if I was going to war, I wouldn't want you as my fucking driver. Drop it please.'

'War dad?'

'Figure of speech. Iz.'

'When you get his address, I'm coming with you.'

'No fucking way.'

'Way.'

'Look, sorry Iz but father here speaking to thirteen-year-old daughter. Even if we do go see this guy you ain't coming.'

'I am and you know why?'

'Do tell.'

'Because you need me. I know stuff you don't.'

'What stuff?'

'Lots of stuff dad.'

'Not good enough, daughter, reckon it's time for bed don't you?'

'Naturally I do not.'

'Bed now please and we'll talk in the morning about this horrible disregard for the rules.'

'Ha, says the flag-breaching parent.'

'Bed.'

'Fine, Dad, OK just before I go, how's your tech these days?'

'What?'

'What do you really understand about technology, alarm systems, where the street cameras are, covert stuff, in fact anything about technology since they brought out singing birthday cards. You're gonna need that sort of knowledge if you go to war,

Dad, and I'm not talking about standard cop issue. I'm here to assist.'

'Baby, please, the answer is no and that's that. Foot down, enough said, bed.'

Izzi smashed her way up the stairs accompanied by 'foot down, my ass. I'll break my foot off in you ass, stupid dad' and within seconds her bedroom door was almost slammed through its frame to the other side. She released what she thought were various expletives about how unfair it all is but actually it was just more Klingon.

Although the Klingon could only make Zak smile, she hadn't heard about LA and hadn't heard what followed. These were blessings in troubled times. She did make solid sense though. What did he know about technology? It wasn't quite as basic as birthday cards but they weren't going to get far without some serious advantage in the tech department. And for that there was only one man, actually one boy for the job. Manny.

OK so she did help but Zak knew on no account ever, while he still drew breath would he put his baby in front of the evil they might see along the way.

'And that's fucking final,' he said up the stairs, fairly sure it wasn't loud enough for her to hear.

Izzi did hear it but was no longer concerned. She will wage her own war on Peter Hendricks or whoever. She will find that little stream and follow it up to the river as well. She lay back on her bed and smiled. And she would do it without her silly dad and this Allie person. Hypertards. It was just tedious she only had a few changes under her belt. I mean, how far was she going to get with tomatoes and vanishing Spanish teachers.

Then she sat up. She knows a guy who knows a guy, the guy that got her the bug, that guy who lives up at the point somewhere. She would enlist that Geek-o-tard in her war and might have words with him about that piece of shit receiver in the bargain.

When she finds this Peter Hendricks character, they'll have to take her along. If they don't, she'll just go anyway.

Another smile brightened her face.

'Tuesday,' she said. 'Ha.' He didn't know she'd heard Tuesday. On Tuesday, she would be on him like skin from midnight to midnight.

11

i-5

It was Wednesday morning and Izzi was about to head off track and take the shortcut through the woods and up to the point. She had water. She had clothes. She had biscuits. She was all in order. Her guy at school had told her where this guy lived even though he'd asked him not to ever do that, but Izzi was persuasive like that. There were six houses right up near the end of the point, look for the one with the yellow door.

Izzi had woken up this morning deflated from yesterday. Tuesday my ass. She'd held off any further stalking till Tuesday. Don't risk getting caught, save her skills for Tuesday. She was only interested in what she knew and Tuesday was it. She was awake and ready to foil some sneaky creeping out Dad but Dad just slept late and when he did get up he spent the rest of the day annoying her throughout the house. Nada. Maybe it was next Tuesday.

For now then, back to Izzi's autonomous plan, it's Geek-o-tard day, secure the info and means to out-tech the bad guys and find this Hendricks. Jesus, she couldn't wait for her dad to say how completely invaluable she is and plead with her to help them. Maybe she would and maybe she wouldn't.

Pretty soon she was through the woods and up the hill and the six wooden houses came into view. She could see the yellow door from here. That was her target. When she got there, the first thought was you wouldn't want a serious wind to get under it. It didn't looked like it was nailed down somehow. It had space, lots of space. She stepped over a flat stone with symbols on it and headed for the front steps.

From behind this little house Izzi heard a cow, plain and

simple, clear as day, a cow. OK, well, why not? And she continued. Then she noticed something moving under the house behind the long grass and it was soon followed by a loud hissing noise. Izzi stopped in her tracks and back up a couple of paces. After a couple of chickens, a donkey and a UFO taking off she realized this guy was probably a dick. She hopped up the steps as the wildlife medley carried on around her. The curtains were drawn. What time was it? She wondered if some change could actually suddenly make it a different time for everyone and it was way too early to ring a bell.

'Nope, eleven-thirty.'

Izzi rang the bell and waited. After a few seconds there was the noise of something very big and heavy coming down the stairs inside, creaking and splintering the steps, and then a deep growl close to the door. It was already amusing but when the tiny voice of a tiny little mouse said 'sorry, no-one home, leave a note or come back,' she had to chuckle, this guy was a dick but he was a funny dick.

'Something's been bugging me since the Garfield thing,' said Zak as they headed down the ramp to I-5.

It was 11am and a two hour drive from San Sebastian to LA and another half hour to the Rabbu Tahumu offices on Latigo Shore Drive in Malibu. There was plenty of time for Zak to throw in a new curveball.

'Eyes,' he said.

'Eyes?' repeated Allie starting to feel the peace of the pacific but sensing 'possibly not yet.'

'It started with Garfield.'

'Garfield.'

'He had eyes like Izzi. They changed color from green to blue sometimes. That's what got me thinking about it.'

'Izzi's eyes do that? Thinking about what?'

'Was Garfield wiped out because they needed someone else in power...?'

'You know it. Just wait for this Valdez to do something really fucked up, outsource all military to some company or something.'

'Or was he wiped out because of his eyes?'

Allie wasn't close to being on the same page as Zak right now and she stared off to the ocean passing quietly by.

'I've looked into the ones I can remember,' he said. 'Garfield, obviously, and Brett Marr Junior.'

'Brett Marr Junior?'

'Famous philanthropist, or he was. Texas oil. More money than the rest of Texas. Gave away billions, half of everything he made every year. Allie, I just think there's more to it than money and power.'

'Like what, eyes?'

'I get it about the changes that benefit people, the President of Kalenjin, that Mayor of Billings, Montana, the reason we're on this road.'

'Yeah.'

'But there are so many that don't have any reason. I know the little ones have a reason somewhere up the line.'

'Milk cartons.'

'Right, but now there's a different pattern.'

Allie turned her head away from the ocean and into Zak's right eye. Zak's focus stayed on the lines in the road.

'A lot of these changes,' he said. 'The people who vanish to make them happen, they have one thing in common.'

'Eyes?'

'Their eyes change color.'

'That's crazy. Why?' said Allie.

'Any crazier than infiltrating the richest company in the world to find a guy with a time machine?'

'Fair point.'

'I had to look at it, Allie. If there's any link to Izzi...'

'I know. Did you find more people like Izzi around?'

'Just Garfield and Brett Marr Junior so far. I looked into them and tried to find if anything weird happened to any of their family from their past. What happened to them? Were they killed or had odd accidents and stuff? Maybe their descendants today were the real target.'

'And?'

'I knew what I knew about Garfield, born in Indiana, parents, brothers, all the family stuff, where he went to school, who his first girlfriend was. It turns out Garfield's father, the last in the Garfield line, was murdered when he was a kid, playing with his toys in his own backyard.'

'Jesus!'

'The case was never solved. No motive, no suspects, nothing.'

'So what about this Brett something guy?'

'Brett Marr Junior. I didn't know as much about him but I remembered him looking about sixty. So he was probably born in the late fifties, something like that?'

'Sure.'

'I found quite a few Marr families going back but only one stuck out. Someone called Brett Marr Junior would have a father called Brett Marr, right? And he did. His father was born in 1933.'

'So they couldn't kill his father before the time machine was invented in forty-five,' said Allie.

'They had to kill him after his twelfth birthday in forty-five. Like with Garfield's father, when he was a kid they just found him at the bottom of their garden, one in the head, one in the chest.'

'Holy shit. OK so this guy and Garfield, that's only two?' said Allie.

'So far. Two eye changers, two unsolved child murders.'

'Why would they get rid of people because their eyes change?'

'I don't know, maybe they're special or something.' said Zak. 'I've always thought Izzi's special but I guess I would. I just can't see the reason for them. There doesn't seem to be any consequence other than getting rid of people who had changing eyes.'

'There is though, Zak, come on. You can see a reason for Garfield and Brett Marr and two samples doesn't make a theory. Even if it wasn't as obvious as those two, maybe there's no consequence yet. Maybe they haven't become that president or songwriter or that Mayor who hates reservoirs.'

'I accept all of that but something's not right. I can feel it. It's not just about money and power. Money's not the object.'

'Money's always the object.'

'No. There's more. There's another mission.'

'What mission?'

'I think it's an extermination.'

'Extermination?'

'An extermination of people whose eyes change color. It's a pretty rare target. Have you ever heard of people's eyes changing color?'

'No, but I haven't heard of people born with massive orange toes either,' said Allie. 'But I bet if you searched for them there would be a few nasty endings.'

'Sure, but I think you know what I mean, Allie. Suddenly Garfield and Brett Marr Junior and whoever else we don't know about, they've never been here and my daughter's one of them. If it wasn't getting close enough anyway, here's Izzi in another fucking firing line. Maybe they're a threat to the assholes doing all this. Allie, if these people are the top of the tree, the descendants of the hybrids you were talking about, something's going on with them. Maybe some of them in that club have turned on the others, the eye changers. Someone's scared of them and someone's removing them. If you had a time machine wouldn't you go back in time and wipe out your enemies before they even were your enemies?'

'Right now Garfield and Brett Marr seem like nailed on targets for so many reasons, forget eyes changing color. Let's keep looking, see if it happens again.'

'If it happens again, it could be Izzi. There are the changes that maintain the power and money and security, the unassailable all-seeing eye, and there are the changes that exterminate the only threat they have in this world.'

'People whose eyes change color.'

'Alien credentials and all. And it's not just people at the top of that tree. Rich or poor, young or old. They're just another target. It's genocide. If we could find one more eye changer. An enemy of our enemy. They're an ally.'

'Provided they don't have us locked up, sure, but, again, two people does not a genocide make. We'll take any allies we can get though so let's keep looking. If these eye changers are the purest blood descendants of the hybrids, they'll be special. They'll be leaders, presidents, philanthropists. They'll be thirteen-year-old girls.'

'She's definitely not getting involved in this. I just want it to stop for her, have a normal life.'

'They'll be people who can balance it all, stop the shit, wake us up to what it's really all about. The next step in human evolution.'

'And someone at the top of that tree doesn't want that.'

The ocean was in danger of becoming hypnotic. A break was needed and Allie opened her window.

'Jesus, if you could go back before forty-five,' said Zak. 'Can you imagine the fucking Nazis? A few short trips to kill a few Jews thousands of years ago.'

'Or just the one trip, kill Adam and Eve.'

'Kill the whole idea of God.'

'To be continued. We need to think about the countless felonies we're about to shit on.'

Zak had done the honorable thing and suggested two rooms but Allie had overruled him. Their nice little double room facing the sea was secured, and a balcony and breakfast in the bargain.

As they set off on this mission, Allie started thinking. A mission, for fuck's sake, who has a mission? What were they, special forces? Were they lobbing themselves into something they could never handle? She knew somewhere along the line there would be a point of no return, where their heads pop over the lip of the trench and they'd become visible, put themselves in the line of fire, the whistle blowing its call to slaughter in some mud suffocated hell. That point of no return would be Rabbu Tahumu tomorrow. If she wasn't careful, logic could start to present solid reasons to turn round and stop being so silly. But fuck that. They were Butch and Sundance, loading their final rounds, joking and smiling ready for their final charge into a hundred guns, but in this version they escape, get drunk and make love on some beach later.

There was only the single option as Zak and Allie mulled their plan of attack. They knew they couldn't just stroll into Rabbu Tahumu and ask for Peter Hendricks. Secret and silent alarms would fester around them and forces would start gathering. They'd be very seriously on radar. It had to be covert and highly sneaky. As Izzi reminded Zak the other night, with any plan like this, there was only one person capable of making it work and that person was Manny Zamora.

They met Manny by the cliffs yesterday on the point near his place. Zak had this feeling Izzi was being way too nice to him, considering the unresolved trunk issue. She'd been bright and fluffy and in no way the ninja daughter he was expecting. Something was afoot. She was planning something. Anything was possible with his little squirt so he enlisted Manny once again, this time to simulate a sleeping, snoring dad without there being a dad there.

This was Zak's Ferris Bueller moment. He was pretty sure Izzi hadn't seen the movie either but it's all he had, the mannequin in the bed, timed to turn over as the door opened, snoring intensified, effortless. He even put a single sock on it, keep it real. It didn't just let him sneak out for the half hour he needed, it proved he was still the dad around here. She was thirteen for fuck's sake. He'd been uncovered before but not on Tuesday. He hovered quietly outside her bedroom door, seeing if she was awake and he had to smile. On Tuesday it was pretty clear her alarm clock was whining at a daughter who wasn't listening.

Zak and Allie walked up the narrow path towards Manny. He was sitting as near to the edge as he could and Zak wondered if he'd sat there before and considered something else.

He had his backpack with him and wrapped his arm through one of the straps in case the wind got hold of it. Manny had the same green eyes as Izzi and looked more like a surfer kid than a genius kid. He was living with these bohemian folks up at the point. His last foster parents had handed him back for a reason he didn't feel like revealing.

If the plan was to succeed, if Manny was to design their incursion into Rabbu Tahumu, he needed info but he didn't need to know about all of it. If he did, his blood would race and he would commit everything to take down the evil empire. This wasn't about taking down an evil empire. This was about finding one guy.

It didn't take him long, couple of bags of tortilla chips and a half ounce bag of weed and he had his master plan.

'They could stash their most secret files deep in the bowels of their servers, trust their defenses,' said Manny. 'Or not.'

Fucking cryptic kids.

'Or not?' said Zak.

'Or their really really cheeky monkey secret stuff might not be anywhere near anything digital.'

'Why?' said Allie.

'They know we can get into pretty much anything. They can build in nuclear level security but they still know we can.'

'So...' said Zak.

'So, the best way to keep that cheeky monkey secret stuff safe is real world.'

'Real world? Manny, I didn't realize you were such a master of suspense. I have a daughter at home.'

'Nice idea, Detective, maybe later. Look, real world. Have your

PA keep a piece of paper under her foundation at home, cut the lawn in a certain pattern. No-one can hack into a few pieces of paper stashed under floorboards.'

'Unless, of course, they're here to fix the floorboards,' said Allie.

'Ping. Top prize. Oh, that's fabulous, well done. It's all happened for this lovely couple from Mobile, Alabama here tonight, ladies and gentlemen. Let's see what they've won. Zak and Allie, you're going on a fun-filled trip to... the Faranga Water Treatment works in Papua New Guinea, yay!'

'Are you alright?' said Allie. Zak could only shake his head and smile.

'Reasonably. Not sure yet. Anyway, I hacked into their systems, didn't find any Peter Hendricks.'

'Shit,' said Zak.

'Fear not, brave warrior. Hacking is so much more than what people think. It's not just smashing through firewalls and whatever levels of cyber security. It's real world. The medium that holds the required information, boys and girls, demands a solution of the same age.'

'Which is...'

'Well we can't go look at the floorboards. They don't have floorboards, whole place is concrete. Although I have to applaud your grasp on the whole idea, Madam.'

'Manny.'

The plan was beautiful. Manny had hacked into the major tech suppliers in the area and had discovered that Ionic Solutions Incorporated, ISI, were responsible for the supply and maintenance of all Rabbu Tahumu technology and a fellow called Enrico Fermi was the ISI POC for this client. He then accessed their maintenance schedule for Rabbu Tahumu. ISI were next due to roll up and upgrade stuff there in a couple of months.

He'd looked into Enrico Fermi including photos, a bit of family background and listened in on a few calls he made. He now knew about a healthy chunk of his life and what he sounded like.

Manny knew a big prick capitalist shitbag corporation like Rabbu Tahumu would double check anything that entered its space so the email that Enrico unknowingly wrote to the bod in the company suggested they were bringing forward their regular maintenance to enhance security, oh the irony, and keep them on track to defeat the latest hacks and tricks.

That same day, as anticipated, the relevant bod at Rabbu Tahumu called Enrico to double check this schedule and was deliciously routed through to a fake ISI switchboard and then to Manny, who did a pretty decent impression of Enrico Fermi and confirmed the whole thing.

'I said we at ISI are super proud of our ongoing victories over nasty hackers and we can't wait.'

'Nice.'

'Maintenance and updates to Rabbu Tahumu systems are scheduled for Thursday at eleven AM.'

'So what if it's not digital?' said Allie.

'We're in the building and if we're in the building, we can be invisible in the building.'

'OK so we just stroll in and say show us to your servers?'

'Pretty much but this is the best bit, disguises. I fucking love this shit.'

'What disguises?' said Zak.

'You've got uniforms, ID badges, tools and the ISI employees you're impersonating have never been to Rabbu Tahumu before so no-one can recognise you're not them. The very fabulous and very clever ISI engineers turning up and carrying out this exciting maintenance and upgrade session are Ash Garling and Vikki Kay.'

It was a lovely sunny southern California day as this car trickled uneventfully along I-5 and the sun cast a short shadow off to the drivers side. The road was less busy than usual and nothing of any significance interrupted their gradual approach to their destination, that was until they both heard a defined and deliberate banging from the back of the car.

Zak looked at Allie and Allie looked at Zak. Zak was pretty sure his car didn't have the engine in the back so he needed to pull over and investigate. Maybe he'd run over something and it was caught in a wheel.

They walked round the rear of the car looking for bits that didn't belong to it and they were now very much more conspicuous than required. Then the knocking happened again, three precise knocks and they were coming from the trunk. Zak closed is eyes. She's done it again. Izzi. This would be a grounding of indefinite proportions.

They moved round to the back and looked at the trunk, perhaps waiting for one final knock to convince them to open it but Allie didn't wait. She popped it and there inside curled up and smiling was Manny.

'Manny, what the fuck?' said Zak. 'Jesus, what is it with you kids and my trunk?'

'Sorry man,' said Manny. 'I just couldn't stay in this tiny fucking trunk any more. What's wrong with American cars, dude?'

Zak and Allie had nothing. Before they could find something, with them still glaring frozen to where he once was, Manny had escaped and run round to take his uninvited position in the back seat.

Zak and Allie were back in and the doors were shut. Zak eyed the still smiling teenager in the back of his car and there were no words for a short time while he gradually digested their new situation. Manny broke the ice.

'So Zak, dude, you can hear quite a lot from that trunk,' he said, raising a few tingles in the front of the car.

'Like what?' said Zak.

'Like, it sounds like you guys are totally fucked up, and don't try to scan your brains for ways to bullshit what I just heard. Tell me.'

'Manny you can't come with us. I'm going to turn round and take you back.'

'Nah ah, buddy no way,' said Manny wagging a finger in the rear view mirror and maintaining his all-knowing smile. 'Three things. First of all I ain't missing this buzz for anything. Second... I can't remember the second one, but third, you need me.'

'Manny, look I appreciate you setting this up and you know I trust you but this could get ugly,' said Zak.

'Nice. I love ugly. I marry ugly and give ugly my ugly babies, even better. Thing is it'll get real ugly if you don't have someone with you who understands the tech. What if someone there asks questions about it. What you gonna say?'

Zak knew Manny was talking sense. It pissed him off he'd got him involved but he had to be involved. Allie's little shrug and her own head-tilted all-knowing smile told him to start the car and resume north. Manny fixed his stare on the passing ocean and there was quiet for several minutes before he posed a question neither of them had managed to tackle yet.

'So anyway, I figured something out in that mouse's shoe box of a trunk.'

'What,' said Zak.

'Why's it just you guys who see these, what do you call them, changes?'

'Yeah, do you ever wonder why it's just us?' said Allie.

The four other eyes in the car were on Zak.

'Yeah, for about twenty years,' said Zak. 'Maybe it's just natural selection. Nature knows it's wrong for people to be doing what they're doing. Maybe nature's lending us hand and somehow, we're the only people who can stop them.'

'Uh uuuuh,' said Manny like he'd hit a blank on *Family Feud*. Zak had failed so a disappointed presenter tried another contestant.

'Allie? You're up,' said Manny.

Allie felt the audience on her. The clock was ticking away. The whirr and grind of broadcast technology was probing all over her, waiting for her answer to draw the 'ping' of success. Manny preferred brains that simply functioned instantly and so he gave her a clue.

'Allie, it's you and before that it was your mom. Zak it's you and now it's your daughter, what's her name?'

'Izzi.'

'Izzi. Is that her picture?' he asked, seeing the photo on the dash of blue hair and leather wrapped round eyes he could probably get on with.

'Yep.'

'Smoking hot, dude.'

'Manny, she's thirteen!'

'Sorry man. Look, it's only y'all that's seeing this and it's running down your hereditary line. Take that line back to where it started. Did anything happen to any of them way back?'

'Well, all I know is my grandad died at Auschwitz.' said Allie. 'We know it's something to do with the Nazis and this machine back in forty-five.'

'Shit, my grandad died at Auschwitz,' added Zak and there was an involuntary lane change.

'Ping,' said Manny and the audience erupted into rapturous applause.

'The bell development site was meant to be about two hundred miles from Auschwitz,' said Allie.

'Now we're cooking on gas, boys and girls,' said Manny with a single hand clap. 'It ain't nature bubba, it's Auschwitz.'

'It has to be,' said Allie. 'My mom told me about my grandfather. This is what he told my grandmother. I remember the story but now I know what it means. What if they took some of the prisoners to the bell testing facility and experimented on them? That's what these Nazi assholes did all the time. What if they were exposed to something during the experiments.'

'So what if this departure from the normal loop of time was another effect?' added Zak. 'My dad said his folks died there but he never wanted to talk about it. Shit, so my dad did see the changes.'

'Boom. So who's to say they didn't die a couple of hundred miles away at the bell site and not in the camp?' concluded Manny, helpfully drawing into focus for those in the front of the car what he'd figured out a dozen miles back.

'Just murdering Jews from Auschwitz but in a slightly more interesting way,' said Allie.

'Maybe somehow this effect, seeing the changes, started then but it was an effect of their whole timeline not just their bodies.'

'Dude, it's perfect. You guys are the descendants of the people they experimented on.'

'A beautiful irony.' said Allie. 'They killed them but also created us, and we're going to fuck them up.'

'Fuck them up.' toasted Manny with many crunches of tortilla chip.

'So what story did your grandfather tell your grandmother?' said Zak.

Allie stared straight ahead.

'When enough people didn't come back from where they were meant to be, my grandparents knew they weren't coming back. Then it was their turn, filed into their carriages, cattle bound for the slaughter house.'

'Nazi assholes,' said Manny.

'Benjamin and Hertha Aaronheim. Taken in the winter of forty-four. They'd come and take people to the showers and they'd never come back and one day they came and took Benjamin and Hertha knew she'd never see him again. But that night Benjamin did come back and she was allowed to see him for the first time since they got there. They made love and Benjamin told Hertha as much as he could remember of the place they'd taken him to.'

'The Bell site?' said Zak.

'They didn't see anything. They were blindfolded the whole trip. The truck took about four hours to get there and they were taken into this room. Benjamin knew it was big the way it echoed when the Germans spoke and it felt like it was a hard concrete floor. They were told to stand still and a door closed and the talking stopped. Then a low humming noise started. It sounded like it was over the other side of the room. It hummed and vibrated for about ten minutes as they stood there. At least it was warm in there. Then the noise stopped and they all were quickly back on the truck.'

'So he was OK.'

'Every few days he'd go off and every time he'd come back feeling sicker. Until the time he didn't come back again. Hertha would never see Benjamin again. After that, the Germans started filing as many people onto trains as they could. Thousands left the camp but they hadn't taken Hertha yet. It wasn't long after Benjamin's final trip that the Germans left them all behind and the Russians came.'

'And she survived.'

'Hertha was loaded onto another train and soon ended up in a Leipzig in what was now East Germany. Not long after that, she knew she was pregnant. Benjamin would live on in this baby. She also soon realized East Germany was far from free, just different assholes. After my mom was born, Hertha had to make an important decision.'

'Escape to the west,' said Zak.

'She handed over everything she had to this agent. On the night of her escape, little Katherina had already been passed through a carefully cut fence to another agent in the west, car waiting, but then the agent in the west got into his car and drove away. Hertha was now being held at gunpoint by her agent, who told her she's not going anywhere, turn around and go back. Suddenly she was hit by spotlights. The East Germans opened fire and she was killed.'

'Holy shit, were literally everyone assholes back then?' said Manny.

'Siegfried and Anna Muller from Berlin couldn't have kids and paid good money for this little Jewish baby from Leipzig. When Katherina was delivered, there was a letter hidden under a blanket in her basket. It told the story of Benjamin and Hertha Aaronheim and Auschwitz and how their little Katherina came into being. Siegfried and Anna agreed, after they all moved to America, they would change Katherina's name from Muller to Aaronheim, the name of her real parents. One day they would give Katherina this letter. It was a sad story but it was hers.'

The car absorbed several minutes of contemplation and then Zak needed to elevate the mood and return to logistics.

'We need to get you a room at the hotel when we get there, buddy.'

'Don't worry dude guess who got the King Suite.'

'Manny that's four hundred bucks a night.'

'I know right. Care of some shitbag company, thought they'd sit on their cure for Addison's disease. Pretty generous of them to release it onto the internet and donate so much money in the bargain, do you think or don't you think? Answers on a postcard...'

12

rabbu tahumu

Zak's alarm brought him into this fine sunny morning with a sweaty bang. This time, he was falling into the sea from a fair way up and woke just before he hit the water. Allie wasn't in bed and he heard the machinery of a human in a bathroom at the end of the room.

'Why still the water?' he said to himself. All the water stuff was about leading them to that Mayor in Billings then here. Maybe he was just dreaming of yesterday, dream worrying Manny would jump over the edge of the cliff.

He couldn't feel his legs and had to check in case there were mystery amputations in the night. There weren't but, as sensation returned so did the pain.

They'd parked in a public car park about two miles out and got a cab to the hotel, a critical trial run for the disguises. The cabbie seemed fine. They checked in under their ISI names, now joined by Manny, who had become Jesus Blista for some reason.

He looked like a pedophile in his disguise, a major coup for a fifteen year old.

'Got superglue on your chin, Manny?'

'No. What?'

'It just looks like you got pubes stuck to your face when you were sucking yourself off.'

'Asshole.'

They'd enjoyed some clam chowder for dinner. Manny was no stranger to letting people get on with their own thing and he'd gone off to do 'something.' Zak and Allie had taken a walk down the little sandy path to the beach with a bottle of wine. They just lay there getting used to their disguises and pulling bits off them.

Their room was top drawer, big and nautical, ceiling fan, ropes and driftwood, white stones and linen and the whole bundle all for a hundred bucks a night.

Not many yards below the balcony was the beach. This was a room to kick back and enjoy the ocean. This was also a place to get naked quickly and christen the room. At one point, Allie acquired a portion of Zaks beard, looking up at him with a fuzzy-cheeked love he thought he'd never experience, and he laughed himself to an early finish.

In that bathroom at the end of the room, Allie just about got her head in the toilet before she blew. She tried to keep it quiet but when you can't, you can't and Zak was treated to the possibility of there being an angry troll in the bathroom, not a small, pretty human.

Allie had realized by now that whenever she dreamt about a baby, namely Aaron again last night but when he was about ten, she would wake feeling tediously pregnant. How this would go down with the father, there in bed, oblivious and calm and not being fucking sick, who knew but right now this Allie didn't care. What's her cover? Clam chowder. Done.

Zak was staring at her when she finally got rid of what she needed to and she was already more annoyed at him than he deserved, or was she? She knew the standard first two questions in these situations and was ready for them. Don't get wound up.

'Why do you think Aldebaran was shining twenty percent brighter last night?' said Zak.

OK, that wasn't one of them.

'What?'

'Just checking out the usual stuff. Just odd that's all. Anyway who were you killing in there?'

That was one of them.

'Clam Chowder.'

'Can't be, can it? I had the same thing.'

And so was that.

'Not a clue then.'

Uniforms and disguises were retrieved from couch and lamp-stand and they were once again, techie people who knew what the fuck was going on. They made the mistake of looking at each other before they left the room and pissed themselves laughing. This didn't bode well for a nothing-to-see-here entry into Rabbu Tahumu.

Allie came out of it first and steadied Zak.

'Are we past the point of no return?'

'We passed that the day I met you.'

'OK then. No going back.'

'No going back.'

Manny was already there at the table hammering into bacon and eggs.

'Jesus, Manny,' said Zak.

Manny had added Groucho glasses to his disguise. He thought it was appropriate for the sort of guy he was pretending to be. He also had one of those foot long wooden things from the room, in that vase on the table. He looked up at Zak, calmly raised the wood to his mouth and did the eyebrows. Zak lost it right there. Allie took a jug of water and a glass and sat opposite Manny, don't even think about it kid.

'Cock,' said Manny as Zak took a seat.

'Pedo.' Click.

'Post that and die, my friend.'

'Whats up, Allie?' said Zak.

'Seriously, apart from literally everything I've ever eaten getting flushed into the ocean just now?'

'Dude, gross.'

'Look can we just get this breakfast done? Jesus, the smells…'

'Allie, waiting for toast and jam over here,' said Manny.

Wisely, they were quickly through breakfast and into the hotel parking lot to wait for their cab. Manny drifted off across the lot to check something out. It looked aimless but Zak knew when he saw something, he had to dig it out.

Manny looked back and smiled and waved them over. There he was, standing next to a nice shiny little car with ISI's light blue logo on the doors. He'd 'borrowed' the car from the driveway of some people nearby, he discovered they were on holiday for two weeks. He opened the trunk to reveal all their tech gear sitting neatly inside. That was his 'something' last night, or some of it.

'You knew you were coming the minute we told you on the cliffs, didn't you?' said Zak.

'Or did I know before then?' said Manny with a disturbing wink.

Zak caught the keys from Manny and they were off on the few short miles to Rabbu Tahumu. Manny reminded them cameras would be on them from the top of the Rabbu Tahumu driveway so 'act ISI.'

Their little ISI car cruised slowly along Latigo Shore Drive past some massive space aged houses and then turned into a sandy track bordered by palms trees. There was only one building at the end of it and Rabbu Tahumu came into view.

Allie immediately got the building, a square glass palace morphing into a pyramid. The thirty yard driveway opened out into a parking bay for probably thirty cars. They took a bay, extracted tools and parts from the trunk and made their way towards the steps up to the main doors. They were visible from every inch of the building. Allie felt like a single great eye was focused on her and was tracking her inside.

Through the front doors they could already see the terraces out back and the beach not far beyond that. The whole building looked like a giant frame, just edges and glass, people wandering about like they were floating. They approached the large semi-circular reception desk. Behind the desk sat two women who looked more at home in the pages of Cosmo than office reception.

Their badges checked out and they were shown to the lounge area opposite reception to wait for their escort. Stage one complete.

On the marble clad wall behind the receptionists, there was a simple phrase. 'Dream. We are the Designers.' Allie lingered on it for a moment or two. She didn't know why but it felt familiar. The nausea and this 'oh hello, now a headache' felt familiar as well. At any moment, she could be back with her head down that toilet bowl. She needed to have close sight of bathrooms wherever she went in this building.

They were joined by a young blonde woman on one of the couches opposite them, sitting cross legged in a light orange knee length dress and boots, oozing class and no doubt a serious ability of some flavor. She was flicking through a Hello magazine.

Manny was captivated. He'd never seen a woman like this, she was the perfect design in every way. He could see her chest move when she breathed. It was impossible not to stare and then she looked up and offered him a smile that could have won Vietnam by sixty-five. Manny thought he returned it and she returned to her magazine.

Zak noticed the only items on this large glass coffee table were Hello magazines, dozens of them, some in piles, some strewn around. It seemed less than stuffy corporate and Zak wondered if the bods here at Rabbu Tahumu owed that as well.

The blonde woman got up, straightened her dress smooth over her long legs and made her way round the table past Zak and Allie, pausing briefly to drop her magazine on the table open at what looked like a pretty top flight boat party. There were loads of pictures, most of them focusing on some old fellow having a very dignified and sunny time of it.

She looked at Zak, smiled and made her way out of the building towards the car bays. Zak wondered why someone would wait in reception after having already seen someone here. Maybe she just lost patience waiting.

Allie reached across to pick up the woman's discarded copy,

enticed by the sunny pictures or maybe seeing something she recognized, but just as her fingers prepared to tickle the edge and draw it closer, a voice diverted her.

'Miss Kay, Mister Garling and Mister Blista,' said the voice as it approached from beside the reception desk. It was attached to human form and a friendly smile. They all stood and hands were limply fumbled around with.

'You ISI guys are getting younger all the time,' he said, scoping Manny.

'People always say that,' said Zak. 'He looks younger than he is but Jesus here is something of a prodigy. He pretty much designed our new Dimension systems.'

'Dimension systems, sexy. Well it's an honor to have a prodigy in the building,' he said. 'Please follow me.'

Their immaculate pin-striped guide took them to the right of the staircase and through a glass door into a corridor. He was Augustus. He was nice and there were no signs of suspicion. As they walked, he handed out access cards and explained these allowed them access to the various areas of the building requested in their session spec. He ensured they knew where they were going and deposited them outside a room with a less grandiose wooden door. He asked Zak to try the card to check it worked and bid them adieu.

'Augustus,' said Allie. 'Where's the nearest bathroom?'

'That door there, gaudy red sticker on it, the card will get you in,' and Augustus was off.

The three invaders went inside and closed the door, free for now to their nefarious devices.

Manny was up. His first task was install the patch he'd created to simulate the installation of the things they were meant to install.

He diverted keypad alarms to an anonymous pay-as-you-go cell phone. It had an automated coded response simulating the alarm was received and being acted on. Cameras would loop whatever Manny told them until he told them not to. He'd planned one or two subliminal messages of love and peace and a Laurel and Hardy scene, the one when Stan gets stuck in the boat.

The system would recognize if people came into an office and switch to live mode. And to cut the guts out of snake, he disabled all motion sensors in the building. They could wander about free from the prying eyes of technology but perhaps not from humans, who have no trouble seeing through glass.

'OK,' said Manny. 'Still can't find any mention of Peter Hendricks. Time for the floorboards. We're going upstairs, load map.'

The target was the office that spanned the whole top floor. Manny saw there was no-one in it from reception earlier and there still wasn't. The door was delicately shut behind Allie. Manny sat behind the PC on the desk and Zak and Allie pulled out fictitious spec sheets as they scoped for things unusual, a bit of upturned carpet, dust not where it should be.

This office had no pictures on the desks or walls, no nic nacs, no teddy bear little Jenny had given Daddy. Manny's systems were all doing fine but there was no sign of anything helpful in the desk drawers and only a fine scotch whisky in the cupboard.

If Hendricks was ever here, this had to be his office but there was no sign Peter Hendricks or anyone else was ever here.

Then Allie remembered.

'Go up the channels,' she said. 'Look at people lower down the chain. This guy has to have a PA of something. Maybe they call him boss or the old man or something.'

Manny was on it and soon a smile appeared.

'It's not boss or old man, he said. 'It's designer. Jesus, arrogant much? A shit ton of emails from someone called Nancy Figueroa talking about the designer, arranging things for him, everyday conversations.'

'The logo at reception: *dream, we are the designers,*' said Allie.

'And he likes purple. Nice...'

'Where is she?' said Zak.

'She is located...'

Manny raised a pointed finger and followed his scanner round the room until it ended up at the door.

'Just outside here on the inner terrace, ten yards to the left.'

That would have them into open space, visible from everywhere. The terrace looked down on a maze of glass and calmly moving bodies. Manny hooked into Nancy's PC and Zak was quickly down on his knees behind her desk. The drawers were unlocked again and again there was nothing in them. What was this place? Did no-one here have any family or was it some kind of company policy?

Then Manny got a hit.

'Hang on. Nancy will be at the Dover Street Wine Bar at eight tonight... Oh...'

'Oh, what, oh?' said Zak.

'I'm locked out,' he said, which brought Zak off his knees, drawer mission aborted.

There was a slight increase in the speed of movement from various bods on the formerly sedate ground floor, all aiming for that side door Augustus took them through to the server room. Time to leave.

They were down the main stairs, every step potentially bringing big guys to greet them with no smiles. They made it to the ground floor, heads down for the doors. They were interrupted only by one of the receptionists asking didn't they need to sign off the sheet. Zak offered a single lopsided smiling head shake as the doors had them outside, in the car and off at a fair rate back onto Latigo Shore Drive.

'Stop the car,' said Allie.

'Are you crazy, stop the car?'

'Seriously, stop the car.'

Zak obeyed and Allie wondered where the fuck it all came from behind a palm tree. She was back in the car quickly though and they were back on their way.

'Jesus, how much Clam chowder did you have?' said Zak.

Allie mulled a response, something to do with fucking off but thought leaving her head half out the window with the air washing over her was a better idea.

'It's cool, they don't know who we are,' said Manny.

'Need to ditch this car,' said Zak.

A couple of miles down the road they parked the car up close to a taxi station and left the uniforms and ISI stickers in the car. Soon the cab was kicking them out at the hotel. Allie hit the bed and curled up, looking through the light drapes and through the terrace doors to the sea. She felt the breeze, cuddling her up safe and before she knew it, her and Zak were waking up spooning. Allie felt better. She couldn't help a smile as the sun dipped its toes into the ocean.

It was time to get ready. Downtown to the Dover Street Wine Bar, see what information they could prise away from this Nancy Figueroa.

There was a knock on the door. Zak got up and rubbed his eyes. This room had everything apart from peep holes in the door so all he had was 'who's that?' A giant couple of seconds of silence followed and then a voice of authority from the other side.

'Hotel security, sir. There are two detectives in the lobby, They'd like to speak with you.'

'They know we're here,' said Allie, starting to feel a different kind of nausea.

'No they don't. Relax. I'm a cop. I'll handle it.'

'Now please, sir,' prompted the door.

Zak primed himself, drew a decent breath and pulled the door open. There was Manny, having successfully sounded like a two hundred pound security guard, smiling with his arms outstretched like a game show host entering his theatre.

He was dangled head first over the edge of this terrace for about a minute under the bluest verbal attack from Zak. Allie managed to pour a liter of mini bar water over him followed by a nice little jar of potpourri from the coffee table and at least two sachets of instant coffee.

Eventually he was pulled back up.

'Touchy, people, chillax,' he said, shaking the right way up back into his head.

13

dover street

Manny had searched Nancy Figueroa and he had a picture. By the time they walked into Dover Street and took a table near the corner, they knew where she was.

As they waited for their drinks, a small kerfuffle persisted at the table behind them, bringing unwanted attention in their direction. Some old boy was kicking off about the wine. The nose was dipped in soil and the taste more farmyard that vineyard, in short, unacceptable.

The waitress was still and calm as the old boy showed her the offending bottle, which turned out to be extra virgin olive oil, poured to taste but quickly rejected. The waitress did well to conceal the laughter that was already putting pink on her cheeks, seconds away from erupting with colleagues backstage. She agreed to replace a bottle never ordered in the first place and bring another.

The attention from customers to the confused antics of the old boy had included Nancy Figueroa, sat a few tables away. Zak thought her gaze rested on him slightly longer than it should but maybe this was a little paranoid.

Nancy Figueroa was a sophisticated looking lady in her late sixties and she was on her own. It wasn't impossible to drain the color from the scene and imagine her sitting here, lighting a cigarette, waiting for Bacall to join her. She'd arranged to meet someone, Adeline according to her calendar. Soon, Adeline joined her and Nancy got up to greet her with a hug and a smile. In the midst of this smiley hug, a Manny they didn't even notice leave the table walked past and bumped into Nancy, slipping out of sight into the toilets before she could turn to say no problem. Seconds later he emerged and returned to the table.

Manny pulled out a bizarre looking cable with all sorts of adaptors and possibilities. He plugged his own phone into another phone and looked up at Zak and Allie.

'What?'

'Is that her phone?'

'It certainly is and in eight seconds it'll be my phone too.'

After eight seconds, there was a subtle double beep.

'Done.'

He unhooked Nancy's phone, headed back over and popped the phone she'd just dropped on the floor back on her table and with a smile he was away. He was past her before Nancy could thank him. She mouthed what looked like 'what a nice young man. I'm such a ninny' to her friend and Manny again returned to the table. He spared a few seconds to feel pleased with himself, eyeing up Zak and Allie in turn and smiling briefly. Then his head was down into his phone clone.

Zak and Allie watched his every eyebrow and expression, waiting for the smile of a boy who'd found something.

'Fuck it,' he said. 'Nada.' He placed his phone on the table and sat back to take delivery of his fizz.

'Can I...?' said Allie.

'Sure, your password is m.i.l.f., sorry.'

Allie smiled and picked up his phone. She started swiping through photos. Fairly soon she stopped and looked up at Zak with a half smile.

'There is this,' she said laying the phone on the table.

It was a photo of Nancy, arm in arm with some old guy on the deck of a pretty serious yacht, sun blazing down on both of them, a picture of some tranquility and affluence.

'Who's the old guy?' said Manny.

Manny got busy on his phone again and eventually conceded image search, no results.

'We're getting nowhere,' said Zak. 'Maybe this Hendricks isn't our guy. Maybe it would have been easier going out to fucking Kalenjin and finding that asshole.'

'Square one, bottom of the pit, no ladder,' said Manny and couldn't help a chuckle.

'Alternatively,' said Allie. 'And you're too young to be that morbid...'

'Or am I the perfect age?'

'Alternatively... can we please be positive, boys. It's got to be Rabbu Tahumu and it's got to be Peter Hendricks. We followed it up the channels with the Mayor of Billings and we followed it up the channels to find Nancy. We're here for a reason. The richest guy in the world isn't just going to tell everyone where he is.'

Their next immediate move was governed by Zak spotting an agitated Nancy and her friend. They were staring at her phone and then over to this table. Her friend was summoning a couple of large guys over near the bar. This didn't look good.

'Whoops,' said Manny.

'Let's not wait around to see what that's all about,' said Zak and the three of them abandoned their drinks and headed for the door. Just before the door, Zak looked round to see the two big guys had joined Nancy and her friend's stare across at them and had started to walk over. It might well have been Nancy buying Manny a thank you drink for finding her phone but Zak knew how people looked when they were buying people drinks and this wasn't it.

They hit the sidewalk and fortune provided a loitering free taxi cab right outside the door. The driver received the only obvious command from Zak. 'Drive, anywhere, just go.'

Taxi drivers are no strangers to this type of urgency and he reacted quickly, getting them several dozen yards from the front door of Dover Street Wine Bar before the two big guys came through it, all large and confused. The three of them were glued to the back window, just their noses resting on the back seat. The big guys looked left and right and over the street for people walking or running and at no time saw the cab. They were clear of whatever that was.

'Manny. Street cameras.'

'On it.'

'These fuckers probably own all the cameras.'

'OK, cameras disabled from where we are now... what's this, Lasille Street, right, Lasille street all the way back to the hotel. We'll show them some different streets, might let them see what Tango street back home is up to.'

'Nice. You're a legend.'

'Word.'

'But don't get too cocky and fuck it up.'

Manny put on his Groucho glasses and did the eyebrow and Zak lost it. Consequently, Allie lost it. Manny wouldn't mention the finale to his hour long show, Pluto's birthday party on every camera in Malibu.

Zak wondered how convenient was this cab, drawn for exactly that moment in time?

'We can't go back to the hotel for another night,' he said. 'Something was badly up at that bar. The next knock at the door might not be this dick and you're still a dick by the way.'

'Whatever, massive tool.'

'Home.'

'Home.'

I-5 was quiet.

'Maybe we did get close,' said Allie.

And these were the last words this car heard for a hundred miles. The car was full of mulling brains, exhausted by a day of subterfuge and escape.

'Maybe you're right,' said Zak. 'Something pushed back. That's a reason to keep pushing.'

'Do you get the feeling something's guiding us?'

'This weird feeling we can't lose.'

'That's exactly it. There's no reason for it.'

'Yet.'

'Yet there it is.'

'Are we ready to be right?' said Allie.

Zak offered a fist pump and it was quickly returned. No comment was available from Manny who was spark out across the back seat.

Soon they were at the point. Manny was tweaked into action and slung out into the mist gathered over the cliffs. Just before he shut the car door behind him, he poked his head through Allie's window.

'Seriously, don't you dare go off and do stuff without me. Whatever's next, I'm fucking in.'

'Sleep well, now fuck off.'

Manny left a departing finger behind him and was quickly into the mist.

'Izzi's at Sarah's tonight,' said Zak. 'Don't take this the wrong way, I am looking forward to seeing you naked, but can I crash here with you and just go to sleep?'

'You can certainly risk it,' said Allie with a smile Zak had seen before.

'We need to go see Mom. I think maybe we didn't go up enough channels.'

'How do you mean?'

'We started too high up. There is something up with Rabbu Tahumu I know it but let's go back to where it started. Mom knew it started with the Nazis.'

'Same goal, different route to it, are we going to be able to talk to her?'

'Most days I wouldn't get anything back but I've just got a feeling we will this time. It just feels like its the right time.'

Zak spooned her on her bed for no more than a few seconds before sleep came. Allie's final thoughts rested on his hand on her belly.

14

carajillo

Zak opened his eyes. All the light that would normally be falling on them from another bright California morning was taken by Allie's face.

'Zak, seriously wake up,' she said, her hands cupping his head, which he realized was a sweating throbbing head.

'What?' he said, shifting up from horizontal to make use of the big fluffy pillows.

'You were shouting like you'd fallen off a building,' said Allie, releasing her grip on Zak's face. 'I was having this bizarre dream and then you suddenly appeared in it. You looked really scared. You were shouting something at me but I couldn't make it out and then whatever you were shouting in your dream brought me out of mine.'

Zak spun round and put his feet on the ground, waiting for a couple of twinges to fuck off before getting up and heading through the archway to the bathroom. His head was needed in a sink of cold water. When he came back into the room, Allie's eyes were still all over him. He started to remember his dream. Allie had jogged something when she said he was shouting at her.

'You were there,' he said. 'I was trying to get you to see this woman.'

'The blonde woman,' she said.

Zak looked at her and they both knew.

'In the orange dress, Rabbu Tahumu, sat opposite us?'

'Yes, her, Jesus, Zak.'

'So much for a quiet start with coffee and croissants,' said Zak. 'My dream was at the waterfall on the island, the beach we went to, just inland from that. I think it was the day Izzi found that pipe but in the dream this blonde woman just appeared right next to me and something became completely clear to me at that moment… fuck… I just had it.'

Zak shuffled on the end of the bed seeing if a different aspect on the room could jog more of it out of him.

'They don't know we exist, Allie. These assholes don't know we exist.' He turned to Allie and grabbed her face with both hands. 'At the waterfall I'd been wondering how could it be so easy to find this Peter Hendricks name and Rabbu Tahumu and she made it all clear.'

'Of course, how could they know we exist?' said Allie. 'As far as they know the whole world has always seen what they've changed it into. They don't need to hide from us because we don't exist to them, we're impossible.'

'But here we are,' said Zak with a developing lopsided grin.

'Existing.'

'If they knew about us, your mom wouldn't still be here, none of us would. Did the blonde woman say anything to you?'

'We were all in Rabbu Tahumu,' said Allie. 'She was there reading that magazine. Then she started reading it out loud, some weird language, just the same thing over and over.'

Allie closed her eyes and took a deep breath. It was right there, getting closer to the surface and then she had it.

'Amaru, edu, rab siknani, she said. Then she looked over at the wall behind the desk at the writing, *Dream. We are the Designers* and looked at me and smiled. It was so real but I knew it was a dream. Somehow I was aware in my dream. I could look round wherever I wanted. I got the feeling I could go anywhere but I needed to find something first. I was back to yesterday right there in that reception, could even hear the noise of high heels on marble, smell the jasmine. She got up, left her magazine on the table and said Izzi is the future. Protect her at all costs.

'Izzi?'

'Then she left and Augustus appeared. I knew that text on the wall was familiar when we were there yesterday but I didn't know why. Now I know. Jesus, I recognized it from the future, a day later, my dream last night.'

'That's all seven shades of fucked up,' said Zak. 'And I've heard it before too, not what they wrote on the wall but whatever you said in that language. It sounds like something Izzi says when she's stressed. She gets all bent out of shape about something and babbles on in some language, sounds exactly like that. What is that language and what did she mean about Izzi?'

'No idea,' said Allie. 'By the way, ever wonder why there were so many Hello magazines in Rabbu Tahumu?'

'Yeah, I know.'

'And then she left the magazine open in front of us. I didn't have time to look at it before Augustus came along.'

'What was it?'

'It looked like it was an article about some party on a boat. A boat's a boat to me but it did look like the same boat as that photo with Nancy and that old guy. There was a shot of the boat from the side and there was something written on the side of it.'

'What?'

'Couldn't see.'

'We need to get a copy of that magazine. Let's get out of here and get a coffee.'

Allie's place was a skip and a jump from a sedate little coffee shop called Carajillo. Allie went off for the magazine and soon rejoined Zak and their coffees. She flicked through the pages, seeking just the one article. After about twenty pages of advertising and unheard of 'celebrities' dribbling on about nonsense, the first article appeared and soon after that, she found hers.

'This here,' she said, opening the magazine out onto the table.

'That's him from Nancy's phone,' said Zak.

'He's in most of the pictures... but I can't see a name anywhere in the damn article. Doesn't look like there are any names of anyone there.'

The photos were blurred like a long range paparazzi effort but, as they read through the minimal almost ashamed copy, there remained no sign of names or addresses.

There was a forlorn attempt to call Hello magazine and discover more but the guy there was distracted. He couldn't get off the phone quick enough. The photographer and the editor were both on holiday. Bye.

'The boat's called Designer's Dream.' said Allie.

'Same boat in Nancy's phone.'

'Same old guy.'

'Dream, We are the Designers. This guy is the main guy at Rabbu Tahumu.'

'Hendricks.'

'Hendricks.'

'So we've got a name and now we've got a face.'

Zak's phone pleaded for attention. It was Manny. Zak listened carefully then looked into space and hung up.

'What?' asked Allie.

'That was Manny,' he said. 'He got back into his research this morning...'

'And...'

'And he thought there were a couple of angles he could try.'

'And,' said Allie again, this time tightening her grip on Zak's arm.

'And, Rabbu Tahumu's HQ was never in Malibu. It's in Laguna Beach. And there was never anyone there called Nancy Figueroa.'

'Holy shit' said Allie.

'Yeah. Holy shit' said Zak. 'Looks like we rattled some cage after all and Rabbu Tahumu could only cluster bomb the situation, you know what that means?'

'They're guessing. They know something is up but they have no idea it's us.'

'And no idea what we know.'

'And we've got two photos of Peter Hendricks,' said Allie.

'One. Manny also said the photo we got from Nancy's phone of her and Hendricks on the boat is now just Hendricks and someone else.'

'Shit,' said Allie. 'Poor Nancy.'

Allie looked around the cafe and beyond and she made herself feel a little better. There were no street cameras out here and her and Zak were the only people. The sun beat down on their morning heads and the sea breeze made its way over them and their table lifting a sugar wrapper and taking it down the narrow lane. And then she sat up and reasserted her grab on Zak's arm.

'Manny,' she said. 'How does he know?'

'What?'

'Well we know Rabbu Tahumu was in Malibu, we were there. And we know Nancy Figueroa existed, we saw her. Manny lifted her phone. But how does Manny know this if they've always been in Laguna Beach to everyone else?'

'He's the right age and no-one knows who his parents are,' said Zak. 'Shit, Manny's seeing the changes.'

'Has to be,' said Allie. 'How many people see this? What are the chances we'd all be living in San Sebastian?'

'It don't think it's chance, Allie,' said Zak closing in on her. 'Remember that feeling, something's guiding us, the feeling it's meant to be?'

'The woman from Rabbu Tahumu.'

'Why not? We shared a dream last night and it was her. The vibe I got from her was so peaceful but so powerful.'

'Same. I wonder if my mom and Izzi had the same dream,' she said and just as she did, Zak's phone interrupted again. It was Izzi and Zak's thoughts fixed on the warning to keep her safe.

'Hey baby, wassup?'

Zak's face darkened and he leant forward in a posture

demanding action at any moment. Once more Allie stared at him trying to extract something from his face.

'Baby, don't worry we'll be there in ten minutes. Don't move.'

Zak was up, threw a ten on the table and the two of them were in the car heading to his place before Allie heard any real details.

'The answer to your question is yes, Izzi had the same dream.'

Zak hadn't waited for the full story on the phone. He needed to wrap his Izzi up to hear it. She was waiting on the front porch. He ran in for a huge cuddle and took her inside and sat her on the couch.

'She said you had to go away. It was at the waterfall. She just appeared. You're not going away, are you Dad?'

'No baby, relax. Who said that? I'm not going anywhere.'

'This woman. I believed her Dad. It was so real. I was there. She said it's almost time. I shouldn't worry because I can change it all, I control everything. Control what, Dad?'

'I don't know, baby.'

'She put her hand on my shoulder it felt like Mom was there holding me and as soon as she did I woke up and remembered I'd seen her before.'

'Where?'

'The day you, me and Mom went on the boat'

'Tomatoes.'

'Yeah, tomatoes. The minute I realized the cafe was called the bistro and the menu was different and stuff, I saw her on the boat. She was looking at me and smiling then she went inside. It was her I dreamt about when I found my pipe behind the waterfall that day. What's she talking about, Dad? Control what?'

Zak had a million thoughts in his head all fighting for the vote. It was one thing to go that step further than his dad did and tell his little girl what was happening to her but another thing to involve her in it. Keep her safe, the woman said but Zak already knew that.

'It's just a dream, baby' he said, gathering her in for another cuddle. Pretty soon she looked past him at Allie.

'Is this Allie?' she said.

'Yes baby, this is Allie.'

'Off you fuck, silly parent,' said Izzi shoving her Dad away and focusing on Allie. They shared a smile. Izzi didn't need Allie to speak to know she was the woman in the apartment that day.

'I'm Izzi.'

'Nice to meet you, Izzi, your dad's told me all about you.'

'I see what you're saying,' said Izzi. 'But this Tardosaur doesn't know that much. Nice to meet you too.'

'You OK now baby?' said Zak. 'Dreams can be horrible but it was only a dream.'

'Yeah Dad, I'm fine thanks.'

Izzi ran into her silly Dad for another cuddle and then hit the stairs to her room, throwing Allie another smile. If her silly dad was up to something, he was doubly up to something now. She knew he'd try and protect her and not tell her and how sweet and all but fuck that. She was going to get under this skin and she was going to control it, just like that woman said.

15

katherina

Zak was nervous as he and Allie headed into Bayside. He didn't know why. He was never nervous meeting new people. It wouldn't be a top ranked quality of a decent cop but, there again, this wasn't just an average new person. This was someone who might have a lot to say about this shit they're all bogged down in if she was in the here and now. He knew Allie could tell as soon as she walked into her mom's room and that moment was almost upon them.

'She won't bite, you know?' said Allie, taking Zak's hand.

'But you might,' he said. He was right and she did, little finger inserted and gently nibbled.

Allie paused briefly at the door to muster some of her own hope. Zak squeezed her hand and she took a deep breath. The door swung open gradually revealing the room like a new powerpoint slide and the day was reflected in the lake through the windows. There was no movement this side of the windows though and Allie's breath was released, damned to the realization this would be another quiet visit.

She moved over to check the armchair and just as she saw her mom wasn't in it, her mom made herself known.

'Hello darling, wasn't expecting you yet,' said Katherina, who was on all fours poking behind a chest of drawers over by the bathroom door.

'Mom, what are you doing down there?'

'I've dropped an earring behind this blessed thing. Oh, hello, who's this?'

'This is Zak, Mom.'

'Well, get him over here to shift this thing will you?'

Zak obliged and Katherina located her earring. She stood up and smiled at Zak, pausing a few seconds, maternal analysis almost complete.

'Thank you, Zak, very kind.'

'Not a problem.'

'Come on sit down you two. Tell me all.'

Katherina sat in her chair and Zak and Allie on the couch opposite. It took a few seconds before Allie got used to this sparkling lucidity and yielded to the laser stare from her mom. She knew her mom had been waiting for the time she brought a boy to see her and she already knew her mom liked Zak. She also prayed the pregnant comment wasn't just round the corner and braced herself for the oncoming irony. Today couldn't get stuck in stuff about boyfriends though. She knew the thoughts were probably gathering in her mom's mind about weddings and getting pooped on in her dotage but this lucidity would have a shelf life.

'Mom, there's something I need to talk to you about.'

'OK darling.'

'Zak's like us, Mom, he sees the changes.'

Katherina held her gaze on Allie for a few seconds and switched focus to Zak.

'We're going to find out who's doing it and stop it,' continued Allie.

'Zak, I'm so sorry. Darling, I think we need to talk about this quickly. I might not be compos mentis for too long, better make the most of it.'

'Mom, you've never said that before. You know you drift off somewhere sometimes? You always said that was nonsense.'

'I didn't realize till this morning, darling. I must have blocked it out. Maybe if I refused to believe it could happen, it didn't happen. But I just woke up and it was suddenly all so clear. Huge chunks of my life were being spent in some mystery zone. Zak, I've been seeing these infernal changes for fifty years and I haven't felt as good as this for fifty years. It was like half my life was taken out of a drawer and stuck back onto me. Something must have just switched on in my sleep last night. I'm so sorry, darling it must have been awful trying to talk to me.'

'Where do you go, Mom?' said Allie, wondering if a tear or two might appear.

'I don't really know. I just remember getting back to this, like now when I know where I am. I know I've been somewhere but no idea why. I get flashes sometimes. I know I could go off at anytime so I'm going to try and figure out any signs telling me I'm about to so maybe I can stop going.'

Allie had to run into her mom and cuddle her up and one or two tears did pop out into her mom's shoulder.

'I woke up and I just knew something was going to happen today. And then you and Zak turned up and Zak's one of us.'

'Have you told Hopkins?'

'No darling and don't you either please.'

'Why Mom? This is a really good sign.'

'And because I realize that, I don't need Hopkins.'

'What are the flashes you get,' said Zak,' when you're elsewhere, what does it feel like?'

'I think it feels good,' said Katherina. 'Like I go to a good place, but I still can't remember where. Maybe it's like dreaming. Oh, Allie, It feels wonderful. All these years of it and now maybe I don't need to just sit here. Maybe I can do something.'

Zak looked at Allie. She knew today would be different. The more he looked at Katherina, the more he saw bits of her in Allie, the confidence, the driven response to her revelation. He hadn't known Allie or Katherina long enough to fine tune the genetics but he was pretty sure they both put their heads back slightly when they were trying to remember things.

It was a nice room, more an apartment really, two large couches facing each other in the loungey bit and Katherina's armchair between them, little stone topped table in the middle, very Morocco, light yellow and olive green wallpaper, rugs from a bohemian market somewhere and an overburden of ornate low lamps. Two large full length windows with cushioned ledges drew you to them and a hum of peace was here. It was so different to the cold slice of room Zak had seen strolling past when he first met Allie.

'Let's take a walk?' said Katherina.

Overgarments were prepared and wrapped and they were off down the corridor, Zak leading the way.

Allie and her mom had rarely been closer than that arm in arm short walk down the corridor to the front steps. The sunset was already coloring things as the sounds of the day prepared to hand over to the sounds of the night. The crickets were thinking about getting in shape for a song and the air was dropping a fine musty layer on it all.

As they slowly moved round to the other side of the grounds, a swirling flock of white birds vortexed in to take up residence on a little island no more than a few dozen yards into the lake and the three of them took up residence on a bench just over a little path down to the lake's edge.

A few quiet moments passed to absorb this peace. Zak found himself between Allie and Katherina, holding them each by the hand. The ballet of the birds entered a repositioning phase as each flank rose and circled and deposited themselves gracefully on the other flank.

'Goodness, my dream last night,' remembered Katherina. 'I've just remembered this woman. She was sitting on the window ledge in my room where you like to sit.'

'Blonde, orange dress?' said Allie.

'Yes darling, but how…?'

'We all dreamt about her, Mom. She told us different things but it was her. We think she's helping us somehow.'

'I think she is too,' continued Katherina. 'She told me to trust her, don't let the darkness come over me. When I start to feel departed bring myself back. She said I need to help you, darling.'

Suddenly between her dream and what her little girl was about to say, Katherina saw a speck of light, like she was about to find the key to her door and a life away from Bayside. Hopkins would know soon enough about what happened today but not yet, not until she knows what it means.

'Mom, we've found this guy.'

'What guy, darling?'

'We went up the channels, like you said.'

'Up the channels, darling?' said Katherina.

'It's something you said, Mom, and it really helped. Find the small changes and see who benefits then follow it up the channels from them to who's behind it. We did and we found the Mayor of Billings' Montana. This Mayor suddenly appeared so a hydro dam happened so we found who was behind him. It was this company, one of the richest companies in the world.'

'And the guy in control is called Peter Hendricks,' added Zak. 'We know what he looks like but we've got no idea how to find him.'

Then Allie remembered her last trip to Bayside, the first time she met Zak. The visitor's book.

'Mom, have you had any visitors apart from us?'

'I don't think so, darling, apart from Hopkins and people from here, unless I did but wasn't exactly in the same room as them. Why?'

'There was someone called Hendricks in the visitor's book last time I came to see you. It said he came a couple of weeks ago. You don't remember?'

'No darling, sorry.'

Allie's hand tightened on Zak's and Zak's in turn tightened on Katherina's.

'This is Peter Hendricks, Mom.'

Allie pulled out a torn out page from Hello magazine and

showed it to her mom. Katherina showed no emotion, focusing on the picture without movement. She knew who it was the instant she saw him but was absorbed in the transition of then to now, memories of how it was.

'Friedrich,' said Katherina as her eyes absorbed themselves into his picture and lost a little focus. Zak felt her hand start to tremble.

'Allie, my darling, this is Freddie.' A fledgling tear appeared underneath Katherina's left eye and she couldn't help it's release.

Allie couldn't have imagined a more logical group of words to swim into this place. Freddie, the son of the man who orchestrated the Nazi bell project, her mom's sweetheart in her twenties and now most definitely without a shadow, their man. Freddie was Peter Hendricks.

Katherina pulled out her own dog eared, wrinkled photo.

'This picture was in a frame over on a table by the windows,' she said. 'Just this morning I got back to my room after breakfast and the frame was broken on the floor. I thought how dare someone come into my room but it looks like it might be a sign.'

There in front of them was the unmistakable picture of a young man who became the Peter Hendricks of today, Freddie back in the day, and the reason Allie thought she recognized him before. She'd been coming to see her Mom all these years and there he was by the window all this time. Kathleen looked at Allie for the longest time and finally broke into a smile, the first truly peaceful smile Allie had seen from her mom since she came to Bayside.

'This is the guy who came over twenty years after his father was meant to have come?' said Zak.

'Someone with the power but not the bloodline,' said Allie.

'The club the Nazi couldn't get into. The hybrid bloodline. It is an extermination. He will never get in so he removes it and every member it could ever have. It's a holocaust of eye changers.'

'Still not convinced,' said Allie. 'But we do know him or Freddie has the machine. It has to be'

'The Bridge Cafe,' said Katherina.

'At Berkeley?' said Allie, checking this wasn't another black stared departure from her mom.

'It was 1967, a really warm summer evening,' said Katherina. 'That's when I really met Freddie. I'd seen him before though. He was beautiful, blonde hair, crystal blue eyes. He was the most beautiful man I'd ever seen. I saw him on the steps just as my left shoe decided to try and slip off my foot. Typical. I knew he'd seen me and all I could do was look up at him like some shoeless urchin as I scuffed past.'

'Don't forget the head flick, Mom.'

'Oh darling, well, yes, I suppose that was a touch nonchalant.'

'You shameless flirt.' Allie knew this story back to front but loved hearing her mom tell it. It was a jump back to when her mom was happy.

'It was the longest few steps after I passed him. I had to turn round and look at him again and when I did, he was looking right back at me. We just kept looking at each other. We weren't ashamed of it.'

'Brazen,' said Allie.

'Careful darling,' said Katherina. 'I might have to ask you about how you two met,' which had Allie back in her box.

'I didn't stop smiling for three days...' Katherina was right back in that moment and she let the windows keep her there.

'Mom, the note.'

'The note, yes, the note. I got a note in my locker, a small folded note on lined paper. The message was in thick black pencil. Oh, Allie I was a teenager all over again but when I was a teenager, I never got a note in my locker.'

'I know, Mom.'

'I knew it was him. It said *Seven PM, Bridge Cafe, matters non-scientific, F.* It was so deliciously spy movie. Where is he now, jumping from a plane, negotiating peace or scaling a wall? I couldn't think of anything else between then and seven PM that night.'

'So, the cafe,' said Allie.

'The sun had been blazing all day and it was so warm and cosy in the street. Everyone was outside all the way from my apartment to the cafe. There were cocktails and chats, even a little dancing. There at the nearest table to the border with Fond du Poulet was Freddie, natty wide grey forties style pinstripe, wide light blue tie and a gold tie clip. He pulled a chair back for me and a vodka martini arrived not long after my bottom hit the seat.'

'Shaken not stirred. Very James Bond, mom.'

'Oh yes, it felt like it, darling. The way the waitress looked at him when she was bringing my drink. But he didn't take his eyes off me. He said 'Name, immediately. I'm Friedrich.' He was nervous, you see, deflecting it with this adorable arrogance. I told him my name and said I'd call him Freddie. That's what his mother called him, he said. I have to admit, although it was nice to be in tune with him, syncing with the same name as his mom did make me a little jealous.'

'What did you talk about?' said Zak.

'Well there was the clear and written prerequisite of no Berkeley talk so I talked about Utah, tractors, just the one nice dress, hay and bare floorboards and the most peaceful, loving childhood a girl could ask for. I wish you could have met the Mullers, darling.'

'Me too, Mom.'

'Freddie talked about Germany, the fallout after the war, his anthropology studies in Munich, his walks in the Bavarian mountains and coming over to America two years ago to meet his father for the first time.'

'Yes, Allie told me about that.'

'There he was happily twenty years old in Munich figuring out where he wanted to be if not somewhere in line with his degree and one day he was told to sit down, told that his father didn't die in 1945 somewhere in Poland, he was still alive in America. Apparently his father was a war refugee and needed his family with him. I asked him why the twenty year gap and he said his father had been working on something with the Americans all this time and only then did they allow him to reveal himself. Well, I thought that was just horrible of them.'

'But he was a Nazi, Mom.'

'I know darling but the family. Poor Freddie. When him and his mom arrived in America, his mom still had this thought in the back of her mind. Was it all real or some nasty trick so long after the war. Then they saw him at the airport. They expected someone in their mid sixties but there waiting for them was a man in his mid forties, the exact same shape and color as when Freddie's mom last saw him in forty-five. Freddie had seen all the photos of his dad and he saw that very same man right there. The only thing they could imagine was America was really a very healthy place, maybe lots of green stuff and mountain walks.'

'And they didn't suspect anything?' said Zak.

'How could they? The only options would have been some kind of everlasting youth experiment or… well… the thing we're dealing with today. Freddie said his father had been working on this thing for the Americans, this craft they called Die Glocke in the war, the bell. He'd been given the best brains in Germany back in the war to work on this project, an anti-gravity device or something about propulsion.'

Katherina sighed as the birds continued their fevered and constant repositioning and someone dropped what sounded like a metal tray of breakables somewhere down the corridor outside her room. Katherina didn't even notice it.

'I had a few too many martinis and we just talked well into the small hours. It really was one of the happiest days of my life. Over the next couple of weeks we went to the opera, dinners, parties, even a tennis match. Goodness me, I don't think I spent more than a couple of hours not thinking of Freddie. It was wonderful although one or two in the faculty did have words with me and they were right. My studies had taken a bit of a back seat. Then Freddie took me to his parents' mountain retreat. It was an hour or so drive into some of the most beautiful countryside. Freddie's forty-eight

Tucker was an undiluted lump of a car. Horrible thing. The climb up the mountain roads gave me the wobbles. It was like a boat swaying all over the place. The road was so close to the edge too. I was grabbing on with white fingers onto the sides of the seats. I only let go to give Freddie a punch and tell him to slow down.'

'A forty-eight Tucker?' said Zak. 'That crazy one with the three headlights?'

'The exact one. Gosh. You're the first person I know who's even heard of it. The house though, Zak, Allie, my goodness, gothic stone, old oak. It was beautiful. There were huge boulders piled up and strewn around all over the lawns, lining the driveway. Over on the left it looked like stables or garages and whatnot and the main building tapered off on the right into smaller bits and then a big pile of logs.'

'Sounds expensive,' said Zak.

'Very and I hadn't seen inside yet. I had my mouth open from the top of the drive and all that came out was oh my God, Freddie. When we got out of the car, we immediately experienced the sort of wind a mountain can throw at you, almost took my headscarf. I wouldn't have seen that again. The inside was a massive atrium, all lovely old wood. Everything was big, big couches, big fireplace, massive rugs and a chandelier. From the terrace out back there was a gorgeous view over the mountains. Freddie lit various oil lamps and candles and asked had I ever you ever chopped wood? I looked at him as if a Utah farm was on Fifth Avenue. Yes I'd chopped wood till my hands blistered, nincompoop, but today he was warmly invited to do it himself and I'd search around for something to drink.'

'And his dad owned the house,' said Zak.

'He did. I asked Freddie what his father's name was. Maybe I'd recognise it, some movie producer or something. Freddie's name was Paternoster. His father was Hugo and his mother was Klara. I didn't recognise it. I sat in the most enormous comfy couch wrapped in a blanket and Freddie dropped a magazine about turbines on me for some reason and went for logs. My mission wasn't turbines though. It was booze. When Freddie's in the room all you notice is Freddie. Now I was alone in this sublime space, I started to notice some of the other things in it. There was a row of pictures all over the back wall and the sherry I'd found compelled me to investigate. There were a lot of pictures of Freddie growing up in Germany with his mom, Klara, that fringe and his little schoolboy shorts, and a lot of pictures of this Hugo Paternoster. I asked myself who the devil is this Hugo Paternoster. You know I'd always been keen on history, darling.'

'I do, Mom.'

'Especially the Germans in the war for obvious reasons but if Hugo had been so influential, how come I didn't recognise the name? Well, I found myself mesmerized by one picture of Hugo. When he was about the same age Freddie was now, they could have been twins. This could only have been Freddie's father. It was the eyes. But as those eyes of Hugo searched out of the frame and locked onto mine, I felt a sharp stabbing pain in the top of my head, which then reeled a dozen images in front of me and reminded me who the man in this picture was. I'd seen this picture before and he was exactly the same age as he was here on this wall. This was the SS General who controlled the concentration camps. This was Hans Kammler. I'll tell you what, the icy wind accompanying Freddie when he returned with logs gripped me long before he opened the door.'

16

something napolean said

Freddie sat at the corner table in Eve's Diner and watched a man with one leg quite a lot shorter than the other labor across the floor and stick some coins in the Wurlitzer.

Pretty soon Bing got Galway Bay underway and at the same time the front door opened, rattling the blinds and ringing the tinny little bell, moving one or two heads to have a look. Most of the twenty odd people here just carried on as they were.

A black trilby hit the table throwing off a puff of dust and a weary looking old man slumped down on the bench opposite Freddie. The banners had started to go up and probably the shortest waitress in the place had been given the job of finishing off the decorations with a few balloons and the mandatory mistletoe. 'Welcome 1950' was the anticipated mood here in this warm little diner over the next few hours.

The old man was dusty and bothered by something. He'd dispatched two of the most innocent creatures, a preacher and little Garfield Jnr so the smart money would be on there being some poor expired person nearby. Freddie sat opposite him quietly shaking his head.

'I just don't understand why you insist on doing this yourself. Why do either of us bother. Just pay someone.'

'Friedrich, again, because no-one else can be trusted and no-one else needs to know.'

'Is it done?' asked Freddie.

'Of course it's done.' Freddie took a sip of water and knew to back off a bit when his old man was in this sort of mood.

'All the time we've wasted.'

'I know, but we're getting close.'

'Close? My wrinkled balls, close. How long have I been hearing we're getting close?'

'Father, relax, not long now. Were there any problems with this one?'

'No.'

'So where is she?'

'In her chair watching Ed Sullivan.' Freddie could see Hans lighten up a little as a sinister grin appeared. 'Those fucking eyes.'

'No doubt it's her then.'

'None at all. I looked in those fucking eyes as she sat in her chair and they changed right in front of me. Fucking freaks. I wanted to wait until they'd gone all the way to blue. What if I plug her right then? Would they change back?'

'Did they?'

'No, they stayed blue, just lost a little… shine.' Hans enjoyed the word 'shine' and lingered on it.

The two men shared a covert smile and it seemed another job was efficiently done. A waitress appeared and Han's murderous joy relaxed him back to Munich 1945 and 'zwei kaffees.'

'Two coffees please,' corrected Freddy, and threw over a quick glance at his father that said 'for fucks sake.'

'She knew what I meant, the barrel of shit,' said Hans referencing the ample midsection of the waitress.

Hans wasn't impressed with the coffee from its first scent and Freddie could see it coming. He was used to this. His father could call anyone a cunt at any given moment for no reason at all. Here again the word was about to escape from him into open play but Freddie headed it off at the pass with a protracted cough, just about covering Han's venom at the waitress and her vile coffee.

The plan used to be straightforward but most of the time now his father was in a pit of despair trying to figure out how he was never given that seat at the table. Freddie had tried to tell him seriously fuck that seat at the table. It was too long ago. It didn't matter. But it did.

Security and wealth had been secured decades ago. But this new mission, deleting the eye changers, this was driving him. These eye-changers owned that door that wouldn't open to him. They were special alright, so fucking elevated, fucking alien spawn. They had to be wiped from the face of the Earth.

Freddie could see his father start to transform on his bench. He was as still as a corpse looking into his coffee cup, eyes widening.

'I was the one,' said Hans slamming his arms down on the table and drilling his eyes into Freddie.

'I know father but...'

'Fucking Speer and that fucking inbred Goring. I was their fucking superior.'

Freddie noticed one or two glances diverting from breakfast and a few eyes hit their corner of the room, two of them from the waitress.

'Father, for fucks sake, again? Every time?'

Hans maintained his laser stare into Freddie and threw his left arm across the table sending his coffee several yards over to the Wurlitzer in disarray.

'Fucking foul shit. Better a floor cleaner than a fucking beverage.'

More than a few eyes were now on them. Freddie could only sit back and ride it out. Maybe this was the slip that was bound to happen. There was some woman dead in her chair watching Ed Sullivan and some nut job started spraying off about aliens in the local diner. Even local law enforcement might see a link.

It had become too easy for Hans. Just go somewhere, pop someone and they never existed, they were never there. He didn't even care if people heard him talking about it. He'd just kill them as well. He was perfectly happy to tell all these confused people here all this stuff, knowing it was their last meal. There had been so much killing it didn't mean anything to him.

'Do you know what I went through?'

Freddie didn't answer. Yes, he did know what his father had been through but it didn't matter what he said, this rollercoaster had begun. Hans stood up and turned to his audience. The one or two that were not already looking at him were now.

'Do you people know what I went through?' he said again. They didn't. The soundtrack was the gentle sizzle of something on the grill and Galway Bay nearing its end.

'We had it,' he said banging one hand to his chest. 'We had it and we made it work. Do you know what we did?'

They still didn't.

'Aliens crashed in the black forest, did you know that? No you fucking didn't. 1937. And we had it. It was magnificent just hovering there above the ground, humming to itself. It would just vanish and reappear only a second later. We put a clock in it. The next time it vanished we checked the clock. It was six hours fast. It had travelled somewhere, past or future who knows, but for six hours in the space of a second and returned.'

Freddie had had enough. This was seriously fucked up. 'Father for fucks sake, we have to go. We're so close. Don't fuck it up.'

Hans waved him away with a growl and Freddie sat back on his bench, watching for any signs of unrest in the audience. He had a quick look outside but there was no-one else around. Freddie really didn't want it to come to this on these people's New Years Party night. He'd tried but needs must. The risk to the timeline from twenty people deleted here in 1950?

'We can travel in fucking time ladies and gentlemen,' said Hans with a half flourish and bow. These twenty people would scratch an itch. Freddie loaded both guns under the table and did the same for his father.

He scanned around the diner. There were about five or six in the back by the toilets. He would head to the toilets and take care of them and then he and Hans could pick off the rest from two sides without too much fuss. Hans heard the guns load and his show picked up pace. His adrenalin started to flow with what was about to happen.

'And what did we get for creating fucking time travel my friends?'

Nothing from the crowd.

'We got murdered ladies and fucking gentlemen. Our own people were killing us because we built it. But I didn't get murdered. You know what I did? I got in that machine and ended up here in the U S of fucking A, just like that,' clicking his fingers. 'Instantly. What do you think of that?'

Maybe it was a little early but he was getting nothing from this crowd. Useless. Dead robot faces, some chewing, one drooling. They didn't think anything of that but Hans did. The next thing he knew he was still inside the machine and he was hearing English. Americans. His arrival in a ball of flames across the cold sky had been witnessed by most of the town of Kecksburg, Pennsylvania in 1965. It would have been a frightening sight, not so much fear of aliens, more a Soviet first strike.

He was alive, although in enemy hands. He knew something of Americans. They'd been on him like vacuum cleaner salesmen to flip, trying to woo him over to them towards the end of the war. Americans tended not to piss on their own boots. They would have to keep him alive, the person who brought them this fine machine.

They scanned and prodded it and finally extracted him from it, like a giant Nazi shit emerging from a giant Nazi elephant, quickly on the ground and encased in Americans. They loaded it up and took it back to where Americans did sneaky stuff, somewhere in Nevada.

'It was either that or a Luger to the back of the head on the way to lunch,' laughed Hans. 'Do you know what it is to do that? Do you know what it is to jump over the edge without knowing what's down there? Of course you fucking don't.'

'I had to leave my wife and newborn son behind,' he said turning to Freddie. 'They didn't see me for twenty years. Ha!

twenty years and… let's see… twenty of you. How poetic, I'll make a fucking note.'

Hans had reclaimed one or two of the audience.

'Here's one for your underfed little brains. I'll bet you don't know the fundamental rule of time travel.'

One member of the audience thought she had a shot but was also smart enough not to bother.

'Anyone? Anyone? Come on… OK fine, I'll tell you. You can't travel back in time before the time machine was invented.' He looked at them all like there should be applause. 'But…' he continued with a wagging finger. 'Our machine wasn't created in 1945 or 1937 or nineteen fucking anything. No, no, no. It was not. It was just recommissioned. This time machine, ladies and gentlemen. This time machine was invented by whoever those fucking aliens were that crashed in the Black Forest. It was built thousands of years ago, maybe millions. Way before 1945 or 1937. Do you know what that means? Still nothing? It means we can go back to anytime in human history, maybe before that.'

A sneeze came from the audience and a young girl started to cry as a result. But Hans just smiled at her.

'Any time in human history. We've been back to Jericho just as Elijah was being abducted. We've seen Neanderthals in northern Spain. Did you know Napoleon wore a wig and had both sets of genitals?'

They didn't and although Hans had spent an educational night in Napoleon's camp just before the battle of Waterloo, it was unlikely Napoleon did wear a wig or have both sets of genitals. It was just Hans stirring any pot he could think of.

Han's and Freddy were very wary of too much risky killing too far back in time. The further back you go, the further into the shadows you should really sink. The resulting changes can grow. With the usual business of getting fabulously rich and controlling things they only ever needed to go back a couple of generations but for these eye-changers that whole idea went out the window.

There had to be a final solution to erase all of them, the ultimate holocaust. This was the overriding driving force behind them right now, to track the eye-changers back to the original hybrids way way back to ancient Sumeria and delete them, taking care of all the rest that would follow at the same time and humanity would return to humans not fucking alien mongrels. Everything else was business but this was deeply personal to Hans. He would erase all those that kept him out in one single glorious killing. The greatest murder ever done. The trick was finding them.

Hans always said it was an inspired choice of Freddie to choose anthropology as his major. Hans wanted him to be a physicist but Freddie didn't. He wanted to trace civilisations, dig up evidence of what it was like millennia ago. Now it was their essential tool to track down who these people were thousands of years ago.

Freddie's skills were being put to the test now as he tried to find the first instances of this alien breeding programme. Odds were if they found just one from long enough ago it would delete most of them today but there was no disguising the preference to delete the very first ones. It had been a long time coming but Freddie was on the brink of something that would give them a time and place and maybe an end to this mission.

Freddie saw the natural break in his father's monologue. He placed two guns on the table for Hans and got up to head to the toilets in the back. Hans waited till he was there and a single glance at each other unleashed a swift and precise massacre of all twenty people in this diner. If it wasn't so horrific for the twenty people you might see the poetic perfection of their ending. No more than twenty five rounds were used. Freddie moved through to the back and located a couple of cowering kitchen hands and they were dispatched while Hans put second taps into all those in the main diner, humming an old Marlene Dietrich tune as he went.

They returned to their seats and Freddie looked out of the window. The town must have been at home, getting dolled up for the New Year's shenanigans here at Eve's later. There was no-one else coming and if they did they'd join this lot but now it was definitely time to leave.

Hans knew it too but there was still time to have a chat with his boy on another matter.

'Have you see the Jew lately?' he said.

'Don't call her that.'

'What do you want me to call her? She is a Jew.'

'Her name is Katherina and don't start on me, you cantankerous old cunt.'

Ever since his forced removal from Katherina's orbit in 1967, Freddie had never forgotten her and he'd never stopped loving her although he knew she would never love him back again if she knew what he'd become. He'd humored his father's obsession with the eye-changers and had to accept 'the Jew is getting too close' back in sixty-seven but he'd come to really fucking hate him for Katherina. He'd even been to see her from time to time but she was never able to respond to him. It made him very sad.

'Answer the question, Friedrich.'

'Fuck off.'

Hans was still popping from this wonderful carnage but the two of them left slowly and quietly leaving the tinny bell to signal their departure, the Wurlitzer confused and silent and only the sizzle of something on the grill.

17

venomous little cakes

Back at Bayside, the birds had finally stopped messing around and settled on their island, happy to preen and poke around and prepare for night.

'That Nazi bastard,' she continued. 'Suddenly here I was in his house in the mountains with his son. I was crazy about Freddie but he'd lied to me about who he was.'

'The first lie and trust starts to melt,' said Allie.

Zak shuffled to change position.

'Did you ever get your car back off that idiot?' said Katherina.

'Nope.'

'He was such a horses ass. I was still thinking about Freddie all the time but now it was just sad. It changed from what we would do together to what we would never do together again. Those glances would be briefer, less crystal, those conversations less passionate. I could feel the love seeping out of the edges and it flooded out of my eyes. Freddie would be back any minute with logs. I couldn't let him see me like this. By the time he got back with the logs, I'd changed from a girl in love to a pretty angry spy.'

'Spy?' said Zak.

'I was a spy. I was a completely different person, inhabiting the person lying on this couch. I was impersonating myself. My world would become subterfuge and planning until the job was done. When the door opened and Freddie heaved the logs over to the fire-place, I already knew what I had to do. You see, Zak, Kammler coordinated the construction of the concentration camps but he was also in charge of advanced nazi military projects and used concentration camp slave labor in those projects.'

'That's where my grandfather was taken with Benjamin,' said Zak.

'I told him, Mom.'

'Why fate conspires to drop technology like that on the Nazis of all people is anyone's guess. Perhaps fate likes stirring the pot as well. I'd drunk my sherry and pretended to be asleep on the couch. Even then he was so lovely, it just made it worse. I left a foot hanging out of the blanket and he came over and tucked it back under. I was still trying to keep the tears back. Luckily, when he came in for a hug, he was freezing cold from outside and I could push him away.'

'What was it you decided to do?' said Zak.

'I pretended to go back to sleep and heard Freddie moving around the room. Then there was the crackle of a roaring fire and I realized my pretend sleep head wasn't pretend and I woke up. Now I remember. I dreamt of that same woman as last night. Allie. I've only just remembered.'

'What did she say?'

'Nothing. I just noticed her walking past a shop I was in. I noticed her because of how striking she was, tall, blonde, just had this presence. I could feel her even from through the window, like the air warmed as she walked through it and sent it out in ripples.'

'And there she is again, the blonde woman. Hang on, you dream about being in shops?'

'Funny, darling, but the sacred spy mission of this new person on the couch was kill Freddie's father. All I wanted to do was leave and go home but I had to keep up the pretense. I know it sounds cold but I would use Freddie to get to him. We spent a really nice evening. Freddie was wonderful all night but I had to say I was too tired to play.'

'Didn't Freddie sense a little distance?' said Zak.

'He must have done, Zak, I'm sure of it but he didn't show it. Once or twice I even wondered if I should be thinking about doing this but every time I did, I thought of Kammler glancing over at another truckload entering his new facility for disposing of them, eradicating them from history. I thought of him subjecting my father to this infernal machine. Over the next few weeks, I told Freddie we had to cool it off a bit. My studies were suffering but I couldn't think about anything else apart from killing Kammler.'

'What was the plan?' said Zak.

'Freddie called me up one morning and said his parents had invited us back to the house in the mountains that weekend to stay.'

'That was your chance.'

'That was my chance. I remember waking up early, really early, the morning we were going. I couldn't sleep. I was so nervous. Freddie was picking me up at ten and we'd head up to the mountains in time for lunch. I'd only had a few days to get my plan together and this spy had to get used to a new nature, murder. It was the hardest few days of my life even if it was a Nazi I was murdering.'

'Stay the course, Mom.'

'Oh I did stay the course, darling. All I had to do in the end was think about all the people who had to do this sort of thing in the war, the people who made the difference. And this was a rekindled war after all. I would poison him.'

'How did you do it?' said Zak.

'Macaroons.'

'Macaroons?'

'I had to have a little smile when I thought of it. I'd never poisoned anything before, no idea how to, so I looked into it. All I knew was the Nazi's used this horrible stuff, Zyklon B. The active ingredient in Zyklon B is hydrogen cyanide. A very small dose would have Kammler dead pretty quickly. It smelt like almonds. Macaroons are made of almonds. So I could bake some macaroons for the lunch party and watch him squirm with my after-lunch treat while I enjoyed a nice cup of tea.'

'You really took to this spy thing, didn't you?' said Zak with a smile. 'Cold. You sound like a pro.'

'Deliciously cold,' said Allie.

'Where did you get cyanide?'

'I had a friend working in the Berkeley chem labs, Bernie Brinkelow. Bernie was such a sweetie. He was a persistent chemistry PhD, one of the nicest guys you could ever hope to meet, always smiling, affable, couldn't do enough to help those around him, had a slight stutter especially when he knew the answer to something, he couldn't wait to enlighten you. Not an attractive man but he had just about every human quality besides.'

'And he had a big fat crush on you, Mom.'

'But he was a complete gentleman, darling. I think he read women very well. When he knew his amore wasn't going to be returned, he made sure they never knew how he felt. It would be poor taste to make them guilty not to love him. Bernie would be happy just being in their company.'

'So Bernie got you the cyanide?'

'I felt so guilty. I was about to use my dear friend to have it away with a dose or two of cyanide and, worse than that, commit felony and murder because of it.'

'I guess the world would see you as the cold-blooded killer of poor innocent Hugo Paternoster,' said Zak.

'They would. I would have duped his son into a meeting and carried out my devil's work.'

'But you'd be dispatching one of the sons of bitches though,' said Allie.

'Oh yes I would. Everything was worth it to see that murdering Nazi gasp for his last breath.'

'So did you get Bernie to play ball?' said Zak.

'She wooed poor old Bernie into a late evening tour of his chem world,' said Allie.

'I slipped a few doses of some pretty nasty laxative in his coffee at the lab.'

'Nasty,' said Zak.

'Bernie was showing me some black liquid frothing over the top of a jar in a glass cabinet. He said 'don't worry, it can't get out' but as soon as he said that he lost focus and stared into space. I knew he'd started gurgling. I could hear it. He looked at me and almost managed a smile before finding the sort of speed I didn't know he had and slamming through the doors. He'd already shown me the poisons so I decanted a fair bit of the cyanide into this little bottle I'd brought.'

'Was he OK?' said Zak.

'He was but he was so embarrassed. He blamed it on these prawns he had for lunch. I was going to buy him dinner for the tour anyway but I thought it had better be a pretty fancy dinner after what I'd just put him through. I took him to Fond du Poulet but I could see he wasn't feeling it, bless him. He struggled through it like a gent but really he only pushed a bit of fruit round his plate for an hour or so and then had to go home. It's OK, he was fine the next day. I called him.'

'One murder was probably enough,' said Zak, bringing a subtle smile and a hand squeeze from Katherina.

'When I was making them, I still wobbled about doing it but wobbling before a murder is acceptable, don't you think?'

'Definitely,' said Zak.

'Zak's a cop, Mom.'

'Oh gosh, you're not going to arrest me are you?'

'Maybe.'

'I'd like to see you try,' said Allie.

'I thought maybe I won't bother with the poison, just take them along without the essence of murder and just be happy to imagine him in agony?'

'But the spy was always there, Mom.'

'She was. I made myself promise to do it. I had to make sure there was enough cyanide and, most importantly, to identify the one with the poison.'

'The venomous little cake,' said Allie.

'The offensive little pie,' said Zak.

So, Mom, how did you identify the fraudulent little pastry?'

'OK stop it, you two, this was serious.'

'Sorry, Mom.'

'Sorry.'

'Anything out of the ordinary or generally wonky would spell danger to any self-respecting pathologically paranoid Nazi. The one with the poison had to be marked, something only I would know. There were thirty of them and they were all topped off with a whole roasted almond. They were laid out in the box in five rows of six. My favorite number was seven so the first macaroon on the second row was the one. If they separated it would be the one with the almond upside down, pointy bit down. I had to serve them individually, not some wild west free-for-all in the middle of a table. The upside down almond one contained enough cyanide to fell an elephant.'

'Probably make a brontosaurus poop for a week.'

'Yes, probably, darling, have you two been drinking?'

'No, sorry, Mom, just happy to see you back.'

'Happy to be back, darling, thank you. Anyway, the day we were due at the house, Freddie was at my apartment bang on ten AM and we were in his silly car heading for the mountains. He asked 'what's that lovely smell?' and looked at my box of macaroons on the back seat. He insisted on having one. I said no, they're for lunch but when he asked how many there were, he wouldn't give up. I yielded on the third attempt and Freddy was handed a safe macaroon.'

'Definitely not the one with the upside down almond.'

'Definitely not or this car would be over the edge before we got to the top of the mountain. It was in his face in one go. His cheeks were puffed up full of it like a ten-year-old.'

'Infants.'

'Indeed, and when a man's mouth is full to the nozzle of cake, it's apparently vital to have something important to say and Freddie did. I was pretty sure he said how lovely it was but shared much of it with the dashboard. His request for a second was refused.'

'So the good news was they tasted nice,' said Zak.

'They tasted divine. Before long, we were heading down the driveway and I felt the same twinge I felt when I left here last time. I was so nervous, like I was heading into a black cave and I knew there was a demon in it. It was the last chance to back out, drop them all in the driveway and call it a day.'

'But you didn't,' said Zak.

'No, and as soon as I went inside that opportunity was gone for good. When I saw Kammler, it was obvious he was far too young for Klara.'

'What did it feel like to see him?' said Zak.

'The front door swung open and the family Alsatians, Wolfgang and Pete, ran out towards Freddie and then over to me. They were gorgeous and so excited, their tails thrashing everything in their path. I had to give them a good fluffing first. Then I saw Kammler, standing there. He didn't really smile. It looked like this whole idea was a chore to him. I shook his hand and tried to put it to the back of my mind that I'd just touched the Nazi scum who killed my father.'

'Tough intro,' said Allie.

'I couldn't let it show. My mission was in full swing. I even smiled at him, partly to maintain my cover but also because I knew he only had a few short hours to live. Klara had made roasted boar with potato dumplings. I wasn't the kind of Jew not to get stuck into boar and it was wonderful. I couldn't help feeling the swine test was rather obvious but that just drove me on. Soon it was my moment. I'd prepare the macaroons for the spotlight.'

'Did you get that shaking thing?'

'That was it darling, no I didn't. Zak, when I was nervous my hands used to shake, had done way back since I was a kid. But today, they were still, just when they needed to be because I was terrified. This was the moment I was going to murder someone. My heart was racing so fast. I hopped up the steps to the kitchen but I was stopped dead in my tracks. Wolfgang and Pete had pulled the box of macaroons off the worktop and were more than halfway through them on the floor. 'Oh my, the dogs,' I said. Kammler rushed in and Wolfgang and Pete were shown the terrace door with malice.'

'No. Not the dogs,' said Zak.

'He said he was so sorry and I started to pick them up and bin them. Two of them had lost the almonds on top.'

'So which one was the nasty one?' said Allie.

'Suddenly there wasn't the coded layout of the box and no tell tale upside down almond. Only if Kammler ate all of the others and Wolfgang and Pete had avoided the nasty one would my mission stand a chance. Just as I thought all was over, Kammler took one without the almond and ate it, citing the ten second rule with a smile. There was nothing I could do about the dogs. They were long gone, banished into the woods for their impertinence. If probability was on my side, maybe pretty soon Kammler would start to feel the three teaspoon's worth of cyanide, the headache and nausea, then his breathing would become labored and he'd lose consciousness, signing off in seizures.'

'Did he?' said Zak.

'No. He was fine, not a sausage, the lucky swine. The rest of the day just carried on with no-one knowing what it was meant to look like after lunch. Freddie and I took a stroll round the grounds and we drank wine.'

'Did you feel just a little relieved though?' said Zak.

'No. I'd committed everything to it and all for good reason. There was no going back once the macaroons came inside the house with me. Eventually, the day was ready to be left behind and we all went to bed.'

'And that was that?' said Allie.

'Mission aborted but not quite it yet, darling. Wolfgang and Pete, remember?'

'Oh yeah, Wolfgang and Pete.'

'When I woke up there was no Freddie next to me. I went downstairs and he was moving things around out on the terrace ready for breakfast. Then I heard a hearty woof from the terrace. The dogs, thank God, I thought, but actually it was only Wolfgang, begging at Freddie laying out the sausage and more than keen to get involved. He was considering a repeat of the trick last night but maybe hung back a little having seen Pete this morning.'

'No Pete?'

'No Pete. It was a beautiful sunny morning although still one for a blanket or two for eating outside. I was about to head onto the terrace to see Freddie when there was a mighty operatic female scream from upstairs. Things would have rattled and moved up there. My fear of killing Pete moved onto my delayed delight of killing Kammler.'

'No, it couldn't be. After so long?' said Zak.

'Freddie was up the stairs like a shot but I stayed right where I was. It was Pete or Kammler and the clock was ticking. I had to steady myself, make sure my look of shock and horror was believable. Pretty quickly, Freddie came rattling back down the stairs and smiled at me, not the sign of a man whose father had just been discovered contorted and dead. Pete was unfortunately back to being the favorite. Klara had seen what she felt was a decent enough sized spider, which had woken Kammler with a start, and Freddie had scooped it out of the window.'

'A spider,' said Zak.

'Eventually, everyone emerged out onto the terrace, said good morning and started talking about coffee. I looked at Wolfgang, who was perfectly fine getting Pete's share of sausage. It looked like last night had been the end for Pete but, seconds later, another woof signaled the late arrival of Pete to the party. Pete didn't know why I gave him such a big rubby cuddle and got instantly involved with the idea of sausage.'

'Yay, Pete,' said Allie and she and Zak shared a smile.

'Then, I just got the feeling there was something over there in the trees. I stopped fluffing Pete and looked up past Freddie to the far side of the terrace. Pete buried his nose into my hands to remind me he certainly wasn't done yet. It was the strangest thing. I could have sworn I saw something move, maybe just a change of light, but there was nothing there. It felt like whatever it was stopped moving as soon as I looked over.'

'What was it?' said Allie. Katherina looked into her eyes and smiled.

'I have no idea,' she said. 'But there was definitely something there. I went back to giving the most welcome pooch a solid fluffing about the face and another piece of sausage and spared a thought for probability. Of the thirty macaroons I'd baked, Freddie had one in the car, which I knew was fine. The other twenty nine were mixed up like a box of smarties on a rollercoaster. Kammler had one off the floor and only five or six were binned. This left about twenty three to the dogs.'

'Two very lucky pooches,' said Allie.

'Here they were, alive and well and consuming sausage. Maybe something somewhere was speaking through probability to skew the odds against murder.'

'Maybe, Mom. What happened after that?'

'Well, that's just it. Nothing happened. I spent the next two weeks expecting Freddie to call or drop round. I hadn't seen him in college since the mountains. Apart from my foiled murder plot, had I done something wrong? Had his father ordered him to ditch me, realized I was onto him somehow and left his life behind, pulling his whole family along with him? Or had Kammler actually had the poison cake in the end and the effects were much slower than I'd figured? There was nothing in the papers about a murder in the mountains'

'So where did Freddie go?' said Zak.

'I went to see the girls in the admissions office and asked about Friedrich Paternoster. After a deliberately long and sniffy search by one of them, I got an answer. 'Friedrich Paternoster, here we are,' she said. 'He dis-enrolled last Thursday.'

'So he just dropped out and vanished,' said Zak.

'I never saw him again. I returned to my life pre-Freddie and continued my studies and my career against the backdrop of the ever present changes, but I never stopped thinking of him.'

Here on this bench the birds were just about done with their preening on the little island and the leader announced with wing and flap that it was time for them to head off to their next stop. In waves the rest followed his path into the air and were away over behind the trees.

Katherina turned to Allie and Zak and offered them both a smile as they pulled themselves from her remarkable story. If Kammler had the power of time at his disposal he would be as wealthy as he needed to be to remain invisible. He could have hundreds of houses all over the world, keeping them all safe from the government and continuing to manipulate time for his own ends. He could move the machine, or whatever it had become by now, at will.

'Mom, we will find them and we will end this,' said Allie.

Katherina had done what she'd been told to do in her dream. She hugged them both and started to walk back inside. Seeing Freddie after all these years had knocked her sideways. Then she stopped and walked back towards them.

'Finish what I failed to do, darling, and say your grandad's name when you drive the knife into him.'

Katherina ambled gently up the steps and headed off to her room to bring out the emotion she couldn't show to Zak and Allie. This will be many years in the making. Allie desperately wanted to follow her in but knew she needed to be alone with this.

Zak and Allie had an address at last.

18

raid on the mountains

Allie got ready for what the night had for her. They had a pretty decent idea of the layout of the mountain house from Katherina. This wasn't a ring the doorbell type thing, this was covert subterfuge, reanimating her Mom's 1967 spy. A win would be find Kammler and his machine and blow the shit out of everything. A fail and maybe pretty soon, none of them would ever have existed.

What would they do if they found Freddie here and what if they found his father, the real target? Could they really call themselves cold blooded murderers? Her Mom had been faced with the same moral question and she'd arrived at a simple logic. Murdering a Nazi isn't the same as murdering someone who isn't himself a murdering asshole.

It couldn't have been clearer to Allie. If Hans Kammler was still alive, the only thing she had to rehearse was her small monologue as she inserted a nice long knife into him and watched him squirm. 'Benjamin Aaronheim' would be the last thing the Nazi prick ever heard.

All the things you could do with such a machine, she thought, and Kammler had chosen to destroy generations to obtain as much money and power as this world allows and make nothing better.

Zak pulled up outside Allie's building just after a very black midnight. It was like the stars couldn't bear to look, hiding themselves away till it all passed. Last night had been one of the hardest things he'd ever had to do. It was no more than a few days since Izzi had shared their dream and pleaded with him not to do what the woman in her dream told her he'd do and leave her yet here he was, doing just that. He had to keep telling himself it was better an Izzi without a dad than no Izzi at all. He would carry that lump in his throat and the tearing at his stomach to the end.

Zak and Allie had perhaps reached their point of no return up in Malibu and poor Nancy Figueroa was no more because of it. Their incursion in the mountains might bring them face to face with the truest evil and tonight was the night. Izzi needed to be safe and sound at Sarah's.

He'd picked Izzi up at Frio and, after a quick smoothie, he'd got her home for a rare and usually hilarious dad-cooked meal. Izzi let him know at regular intervals she was sure of the culinary disaster to follow and by the time they got in the house, Zak had decided that an attack was in order.

As soon as the door closed behind them she was off her feet and upside down, defenseless on her way to the couch and there he gave his cheeky little daughter the tickling of her young life. To anyone passing outside, perhaps taking a fuzzy mutt for a walk in the twilight, the pleas, jettisoned lamps and breathless laughter inside might make them stop briefly to consider emergency services.

Izzi recovered from her dad's first-strike tickle attack and would plan revenge during the evening. She returned to the kitchen and caught him in the act of wine. Izzi always came up really close to Zak and looked up at him with cartoon blinking and a cuteness that made his knees liquify. Normally, this dad's way of saying 'seriously, no' was a little flick on the nose but tonight he smiled and poured her a glass.

She welcomed the glass with a smile and a little kiss for her old dad but her Izzi sense was on fire. She smelled a dry white rat. She'd been looking forward to eating very little of Dad's inedible muck and had questions for him about Allie, but now she sensed something else.

'Baby, you need to stay at Sarah's tonight?' said Zak and there it was. The message in her dream was becoming louder and clearer.

He was definitely up to something. She knew exactly how to deal with it but, for now, just let it go.

'Sure, Dad,' she said.

'Me and Allie have just got to go see someone and we might have to stay overnight.'

'Sure, whatever, Dad.'

This matter of fact presentation, delivered complete with a nonchalant shrug and sip of wine, might have breezed over any other human but not this Izzi. It didn't breeze over her one little bit. It stuck to her like tar, ready for the feathers.

'You want any more spaghetti, Iz?'

'Hell no. Thanks all the same. Is the spaghetti meant to be all joined together in one long lump?'

'I thought it was nice.'

'No, Dad. Not really. Might also help if the meat wasn't still frozen in the middle.'

'Come on. Sarah's.'

The car was quiet for a while. Zak put his hand on Izzi's knee and gave it a squeeze. The barefaced cheek of it. She felt like dismissing his silly hand with a huff but stayed quiet. They rounded the corner onto Sarah's street and pulled up. Zak's stomach was twisting. He wanted to take her right back home and cuddle her up. He was dreading this.

Izzi was out of the car and heading up the steps to a waiting Sarah on the front porch. Sarah was such a sweet little thing, she doted on Izzi and Izzi liked her too. Sarah presented herself as really quite boring, all pink and fluff and let's listen to pink fluffy music but really she was the only one at school who had the required degree of insanity to be interesting and she had a knack for deliciously underhand adventures.

Izzi gave Sarah the sign and Sarah went inside. Izzi knew her dad would call her back for a goodnight hug.

'Oy, squirt, cuddle for your old dad, please.'

Izzi stopped on the step and slowly turned. She was still pissed off at him but saw him there, her dad, she had to run into him and she held on tight. Zak pulled her in and held on even tighter. He tucked his head into her shoulder and her hair washed over his face. He picked her up and quietly released the most secret tear into her.

Izzi had now run out of breath, squeezed flat by her silly dad. She grounded herself and pushed him away with 'silly parent' and turned back round up the steps towards Sarah, who was now joined by Sarah's mom, Jenny. Jenny waved and Zak knew he had to go say hello to her. He hopped up the steps and the girls went inside.

'Really appreciate this, Jenny, thanks again.'

'No problem, Zak, anytime. You OK?'

'Sure, yeah. Just got stuff to do out of town tonight.'

'Police stuff?'

'Something like that.' Zak saw Sarah wandering about inside and spied a chance for another hug from his little Izzi.

'Is Izzi still there,' he said.

'Sarah, where's Izzi?'

'Gone upstairs, Mom, just taking some ice cream up.'

'It's OK, don't worry, see you tomorrow and thanks again, Jenny.'

Zak pulled away and the tear on Izzi's shoulder was joined by a few more here. The day had been a long one. He had everything he thought he'd need for this. The police had given him tactical and weapons skills and access to things that were not officially available to him. He knew this would have him in trouble if it wasn't returned asap but if all went well, he wouldn't be returning it.

He had more C4 in the trunk of this car than he should ever need to take out the machine, the house and possibly some of the mountain and enough ammo to handle Pancho Villa and all his brothers. Anyone who stood in his way would feel some San Sebastian PD.

From the moment he woke this morning he felt different. His first glance out of the kitchen window spotted a black car with tinted windows parked across the street and everywhere he went he felt someone was watching him, summing him up. He was sure there were at least two guys he'd seen on more than one occasion. As they say, just because you're paranoid, it doesn't mean they're not after you.

Zak peeked through Allie's window but it was all dark and quiet inside. Where they hell was she? He rang the bell again and let another minute pass. After a *WTF?* text, he retreated from the door and his paranoia spread. Had they got her? He could see her paintings on the wall so if they had got her, they hadn't erased her yet. Maybe she'd just had enough of what would seem to anyone else pure insanity but he doubted that, not Allie.

As he got the bottom of the steps and headed down a narrow path through the garden, he sensed something in the bushes to his left. He didn't look over, just adjusted his field of vision to his left eye and turned just enough to notice anything emerging. He slowed his pace and moved his right hand to unpop his holster. Again he saw another movement in the shadows among the bushes. It seemed to be tracking him. His first thought was that there might be a dead Allie in her apartment and whoever this was fleeing that scene was only here in this garden to create a very dead Zak as well.

The time for pretending not to see it was past and he pulled his weapon and ordered whoever it was out of the bushes and get on the ground, hands behind your back. There was no response and no further movement. Playing dead wasn't going to work, he was heading for the bush. His pistol was cocked and ready, his heart was pumping and all faculties on full alert.

About fifteen yards from the bush he was stopped in his tracks by 'Don't fucking move, cop' from behind him and the touch of steel to his right cheek. His heart carried on skipping but decided his mouth was the place to do this. He lifted his pistol to a less offensive position and said 'Take it easy now,' and the steel pressed a little more urgently into his cheek. If this person wanted him dead, he'd be dead. He would already have heard the last thing he'd ever hear. The sound of his head exploding and him dropping to the ground like a roofer's mistake wouldn't be his problem any more.

An uncomfortable silence followed and he could pick up the slightly heavy breathing of his attacker, who was still not issuing any demands. Zak was seconds from taking the bull by the balls and turning to fire and take his chances when his attacker finally spoke. 'Lucky I'm coming, Zak,' followed by a short nervous chuckle.

Zak turned and saw a small ninja type creature complete with an all-black skin-tight outfit. The steel he was feeling in his cheek was now being held to his face in front of a smile. It was a large nail and that smile belonged to Allie.

'You fucker,' he said, picking her up and turning her upside down, holding her by her knees. He should have been aware the next logical move for someone upside down was to grab his balls and start a meaningful squeeze. A truce was declared and he helped her up.

'Jesus, I was just about to shoot you, Allie,' he said realizing here was a woman with a skillset far beyond delicious paintings and a wicked sense of humor.

Unknown to either of them, the person who was really responsible for the movement in the bushes had now reached Zak's car. He applied an interesting gadget to the trunk lock and the trunk popped open and his eyes widened.

'Who the fuck are you?' said Izzi, who was curled up in the trunk, squinting from a streetlight.

'Who the fuck are you?' said Manny.

'Er, this is my dad's car, mega-tard, I refer you to my previous question.'

'I'm Manny.'

'You're the guy who lives up on the point.'

'Tis I, who be you? Hang on, you're Izzi.'

'And what? Speak' but before Izzi could beat an answer out of him, they heard the approaching voices of a father and his accomplice. Izzi grabbed Manny round the middle with her legs and hauled him inside the trunk and clicked it shut.

The mountain roads started to narrow and twist and reveal the night time vista in a mesmerizing distraction from the edge.

Zak pulled over in a siding and they would take the rest on foot through the woods. Just as Zak was about to open his door he heard a banging noise from the back of the car.

'What, again? Jesus,' said Zak and moved round to the trunk. He popped the trunk and couldn't believe what he saw, pretty much exactly what he tried to make sure he never saw, two faces peering up at him.

'Dad, seriously, let me out. If I have to spend one more second with this dweeb-o-tard, I'm gonna barf. This guy is insane. It's about time you organized a better class of stowaway in your trunk, please, silly parent.'

'Skank,' said Manny.

'Anusaurus, off you fuck.'

'Both of you, out,' said Zak. 'Jesus, do I really have to check you two kids aren't in my trunk every trip I take?'

'Yes, I rather think you should, don't you?' said Izzi.

'Come on, out.'

'Right, so, where are you two going?' said Izzi. 'Please don't tell me you've driven all this way just to make out in the woods, not again.'

'What do you mean not again, and hang on right there daughter, I'm doing the interrogating here.'

'You certainly are not. I heard you two in her apartment the other day. Thanks for that by the way, Dad. I thought I'd hit some porn channel. That's a memory that's never going away.'

Zak pulled back from his failing interrogation of his daughter and closed his eyes. Allie put her head in her hands but under those hands there lurked a smile.

'What are you two doing here?' he said.

'More to the point, what are you doing here?' said Izzi.

'Izzi, please, come on.'

'Thanks for including me as well by the way. I thought we were in it together,' said Manny.

'Shut up,' said Izzi and Zak.

'I knew you were up to something, Dad. I know it involves me so, guess what? I'm involved and what does this moron mean, in it together? How come he's involved and not me?'

'You're not involved, baby, and you're not going to be involved. You're thirteen. We're turning round and we're heading right back home.'

'OK, sure, Dad. You just take me back. Let's see if that guy's still around shall we?'

'What guy?'

'The guy I told you about, the old guy? Remember? He was in Frio?'

'You've seen him again?'

'Yep.'

'When.'

'This very morning. I might have honored our agreement to tell you if you'd honored our agreement not to lie to me.'

'Was he at Frio again?'

'Yes, he was and you know what else?'

'What?'

'When he smiled he had the same lopsided silly grin you've got. I'll ask you just one simple question, Dad.'

'What?'

'Am I safer on my own at Sarah's or here with you?'

The same chill crept into Zak as when he first heard of this mystery stalker on the flag day. That car earlier today. Was their faceless enemy closing in on them? Here he was this stalker guy again. Was he part of their conspiracy? Zak realized she was right, the little squirt. She needed to be near him. He can't protect her if she's not.

'Fuck,' he said.

'So what's the plan? Where is this?' she said.

'OK. Remember Peter Hendricks?'

'Yes.'

'We got an address.'

'I knew it. What is he, some hobo, lives in the woods?'

Zak pointed through the woods to a clearing.

'No. There's a house through there. Izzi, you need to stay in the car and lock the doors. Stay put, don't move.'

'What and this dweeb gets to come? I think not.'

'Skank,' said Manny.

'Got anything else, tard boy or is that it?'

'How long have you got?'

'OK stop it you two,' said Zak. 'Izzi please, baby, get in the car.'

'OK sure, Dad. I'll get in the car and as soon as you're gone, I'll unlock the thing and follow you.'

'Iz, please you're not making this easy.'

'It's my job, Dad, you just getting that? I refer you to me previous statement about being left alone.'

'Why don't you tie her up and leave her in the trunk?' said Manny, attracting a pre-ninja look from Izzi.

A few moments passed as Zak weighed up the suggestions of a thirteen-year-old and a fifteen-year-old.

'OK just stay right behind me all the time and do exactly what I say.'

'Unlikely, Dad, but lead on. Oh and by the way, what's C-four?'

'I told you what C-four is you blue-tipped mong,' said Manny.

'Seriously one more...'

'And what?'

'I think it really is time to do this or not, people,' said Allie. 'Hanging around here won't help.'

She was right and they were soon into the woods. The moon was bright enough not to need flashlights and they gradually dropped through the trees and there was the house, exactly as Katherina described, definitely Kammler's.

There were no lights on inside or outside and their first impression was this was an empty house. Approaching from the front wasn't the way to go. All it had was a doorbell and a thick oak door and that wasn't in their plan. They skimmed the boulders until the house obscured them from the right side, flirted with the open ground for just a few yards before heading over to the left side and the barn attached to the main house. Katherina said these were garages and stables. Maybe there would be an entry point.

Zak listened for any signs of horses chewing and shuffling about but it was as quiet as the house.

'Dad, here,' said Izzi. She'd spotted the slimmest gap between the wooden strips that made the wall. One of the strips was loose.

Zak carefully took hold of the panel and it moved for him. He looked behind it to see its likely hinge point and successfully slid it aside until it wedged onto its neighbor.

He tested the strength of other panels. They might be moveable but not without a fair bit of noise. Before Zak had finished repositioning the panel, Izzi had one leg inside the gap and she vanished into the darkness inside.

'Izzi, Jesus.'

Zak couldn't get his head through the gap to see where she'd gone. It was still all quiet inside.

She'd been gone for about thirty seconds and there was a noise about ten yards down. A door started to open. Zak pulled Allie and Manny behind one of the big boulders. He had his Glock all dressed up and ready to dance. Still the door creaked slowly open.

A figure slowly emerged from the door. He couldn't be sure it was Izzi. A few slow seconds sifted through the increasing wind off the mountain and then the figure turned away and vanished back through the door and closed it. Izzi would have made herself known if it was her, Zak thought. This was someone else. They had her inside. Jesus. Zak gestured to Manny and Allie to stay put. He started to move slowly towards the door but then a small head popped back though the open panel.

'Dad,' came the voice of a daughter and a ton of angst lifted off Zak.

'Iz. Was that you opening the door?'

'What door?' and that angst circled and landed back on Zak.

'Kidding. Yes, it was me. Jesus, I found the door and came out but you lot had fucked off.'

'OK, sorry baby we were hiding. Open the door.'

'Might do. Here for a reason am I suddenly?'

'Iz.'

'OK, OK' and that little head vanished back into the darkness and the door opened again.

Zak suddenly realized Izzi did need to be here, she was right, with him at all time. The existence of all of them was wrapped up and inseparable. He knew deep down she was ready and it tore him up but she deserved to have a say and play her part. She was his little Izzi but, for the first time, he saw a young woman in front of him and a surprise wrap up hug took her by surprise.

Inside this barn there were signs that several cars had been sitting here but not for a fair while. It was a big enough barn to get five or so cars in and at the house end there were two doors, the side door Izzi just appeared from and this one at the end.

Allie tried the new door carefully and she looked round at Zak. It was open. She carefully started to pull the door towards her. There was no light the other side of the door and it opened without creak or fuss. Inside was a stone walled corridor that bent round the curve of the mountain. It led to a door at its end and another to the right.

Katherina hadn't mentioned anything about a door further round the corridor. She had seen everything there was to see inside. She said there was the corridor from the lounge door to the barn but no corridor going the other way. This was new.

They approached the new door and stopped. There seemed to be light visible under the door. There was no noise, just the faintest light. It couldn't have been the moon coming through a window, the glare of the moon was behind them as they came through the woods, it was the other side. They stood behind the door and listened.

There was no noise. They looked at each other and the door was eased open carefully. They headed down a ramp to the space below. Only the moonlight bouncing off the opposite mountain entered the space through a large panoramic window. Apart from that there were only boxes. Zak kicked them. They were all empty. There was another small room off to the left but that was empty too.

This space had clearly been dug out of the mountain to house something since 1967 but whatever it was wasn't here now. They abandoned this space and split into pairs to check the rest of the house. The bedrooms were where this time of night might find people but again, they were all checked and vacant.

This beautiful house, so full of life and lunches in the sixties, was now deserted, home to only dust and rodents. They had been so sure it might at least point them in another direction but there was nothing, no clues, no Nazis and no machine.

Their only course of action was to slink away and retreat back down the mountain, think again. This enemy of theirs remained truly invisible. The drive back down the mountain was quiet. It felt like they were being teased, played with. They kept discovering things and making headway but as soon as they followed up, they hit brick walls. This brick wall tonight seemed finite. They'd exhausted their final source in Katherina. Their best chance of finding the elusive Freddie Kammler was gone. Their bubble at finding this place had popped.

'Fuck it, let's get back to mine, rethink with a drink,' said Allie.

'Solid idea,' said Zak.

Izzi and Manny nodded in approval and soon they were back at Allie's apartment. Allie rustled up lemonade and Rum and coke for Zak. Manny took no time to dig out the tortilla chips.

'Where's yours?' said Zak.

'I might have one later but this lemonade is lovely. My Mom said Anna Muller told her how to make it.'

The room was quiet apart from Manny's crunching.

'Can you eat those things any louder?' said Izzi, which provoked only a double intake and fierce open-mouthed crunching from Manny. Then he stopped mid-crunch.

'You know when I called you the other day?' said Manny.

'What, about Nancy and Rabbu Tahumu?' said Allie.

'Yeah. I forgot to mention my dream.'

'Dream?'

'Yeah. I had a dream about that woman.'

'What woman?' said Zak.

'That blonde woman we saw in Rabbu Tahumu, orange dress.'

'Right. Did she say anything?'

'I was in bed and I woke up with her sitting on top of me. I thought this wasn't the worst way to wake up. I kinda went with it.'

'Slut,' said Izzi.

'Chill, Cookie Monster, it was a dream.' Izzi couldn't help a small smile but he definitely wouldn't see it.

'She was just looking me right in the face and talking complete shit to me, like a different language or something. Then this feeling hit me, like I had to listen to her. It was so important but I didn't understand it. I remembered exactly what she said when I really woke up but I still had no idea what it meant.'

Allie came over and sat next to Manny and took his hand.

'We all dreamed of her that night,' she said. 'Do you remember what she said?'

Manny put his head back on the back of he couch and closed his eyes.

'I just can't,' he said. 'I can remember what it sounded like but not the words.'

'Amaru, edu, rab siknani?' said Allie.

Manny opened his eyes and looked at Allie.

'Jesus, that was it, but there was so much more.'

'So how long was she riding you, then?' said Izzi.

'Oh long enough. Why? You jealous?'

'In your dreams, slut-o-tard.'

'Stop it, you two,' said Zak. 'Izzi, you know it sounds like the things you say sometimes.'

'I never hear it, Dad, remember?'

'I know baby.'

'In your dreams,' repeated Allie. 'We've all seen this woman in our dreams. When I dreamed of her she was pointing me to the words behind the desk in Rabbu Tahumu.'

'What's Rabbu Tahumu,' said Izzi.

'It's a place we went,' said Zak. 'It's Peter Hendricks's company.'

'Dream: We are the designers,' continued Allie. 'Is that language a translation of what she said to us?' and then she sat upright on the couch and looked at Zak.

'The machine,' she said. 'The bell.'

'What about it?' said Zak.

'The machine has symbols on it. They reckon it's like ancient Sumerian. Jesus how did it take me this long?'

'What?'

'She's talking Sumerian. What are the odds it's on the machine?'

'So maybe the rest of the stuff on the machine can give us some clues,' added Zak.

Manny had seen Allie's computer in the corner. The three of them crowned round it as Manny unearthed image after image of the Nazi bell and saved them off.

'Larry,' said Zak.

'Who's Larry,' said Allie.

'It was one of those parties no-one really wanted to go to, some political award thing. It was probably worth a drink and a bit of food but other than that, standard fare boredom. Megan was reporting on it and I was at the bar waiting for the barman to stop chatting up some girl. We got talking. We had nothing in common at all apart from being pissed off at the barman. Segler. That's right, Larry Segler. Professor of Anthropology, University of San Diego. He gave me his card. He said give him a call sometime if PD ever needed any help. I said I couldn't imagine we would need that kind of help and he just smiled, said 'no-one ever does till they do,' and went back to his table. I think that random meeting happened just for this.'

'Like something knew back then,' said Manny.

'Exactly. If anyone can decode this, it's this guy Larry. Larry is in my phone for a reason. This reason.'

Zak flicked through his phone.

'Dad, I know we can get pretty much anything 24/7 in California but I don't think waking a university professor up at four AM is really included.'

19

utukagaba

Zak grabbed his phone the second he woke up. First of all, there was a quick text to Sarah's Mom, Jenny to mention he'd come and got Izzi really early and then Larry.

'Jees, who is that? Zak? What's up?' said Larry.

'Hey Larry. Sorry to call. You know you said I won't know till I do?'

Larry was quiet. Zak left it a few seconds.

'Larry.'

'Yeah?'

'At that party we met at.'

'Yeah, sure man. Sorry I was just getting in sync with it.'

'I need your help.'

A few more seconds passed and Zak was surprised to hear his next words.

'Julio's Bar, Jolian street, eleven AM,' and the phone clicked dead.

This time the I-5 took them in the opposite direction, south and by the time they got to Julio's Bar in a bohemian little area north of San Diego, Larry was already there, waiting at one of the outside tables.

Zak made eye contact with Larry, who lingered a little, not expecting four of them. Zak was glad to see they were the only ones outside. Introductions were made and they sat down.

'Larry, I'm really sorry. I can't tell you what this is all about yet but thanks for helping.'

'In what form is that help required?' said Larry.

Larry was an Indiana Jones nut. He couldn't help love the whole idea of this intrigue and secrecy. Maybe this was a chance to be Indy just for the day. As soon as he hung up the phone he was quickly scoping his bedroom for socks and couldn't countdown quick enough to eleven AM at Julio's.

'We've got some symbols.'

'Symbols?'

'We think they kind of relate to Sumerian script and we need them translated as much as you can.'

Larry studied the photos on Manny's phone and laid the phone on the table as the waitress brought them coffee.

'It's not exactly Sumerian,' said Larry. 'But it's close.' He got the sort of little eyeglass out of his pocket jewelers use to study diamonds and started to mutter not quite under his breath. Various words came out of him, none of which Zak could follow. Larry was frowning like a man in tortured ecstasy, moving his focus between his phone and laptop.

'I can make out some words and others can be assumed from the ones I know but it's going to be pretty rough.'

'Fine. Anything you can get.'

'I'm going to require alcohol.' said Larry and he quickly acquired the look of a man absorbed in a puzzle. Zak signaled the waitress.

'Scotch whisky. Single malt, 10 years or older.' Larry smiled.

Larry loved puzzles of all shapes and sizes. Zak was lucky to catch him stateside. Zak did look him up after they met. He was one of the leading lights in his field, pulled off to every corner of the globe to tell archaeologists and various other folk what they were looking at.

They needed to sit back and wait for the gems to emerge from Larry. Larry flitted from phone to laptop to his old school notepad and pencil.

Half the whisky had gone down without a sound and Larry began.

'LU SHARUR, a man, a hunter. He has a weapon, a tool, no, an instrument, RESUSSUN.'

Larry was quiet for a moment.

'This one's a bit of a mystery. Maybe wildernesses or forest. SU KASADU KHARSAANU. He'd arrived through a thick forest and found this instrument. SAQUUTU UTAKAGABA, near water, but hang on, not just water, still water like a pond or lagoon. OK a hunter had this instrument that he'd found near a lagoon. This looks like it could be some folklore of whoever these people are.'

Zak's mind immediately strayed to their lagoon on the island. He started picturing this hunter in his and Izzi's island domain.

'USH ABNU ITTI SAGKAL. This place had three large stones and one larger stone, dominant, in front of the other two. PANA UTAKAGABA, facing the water.'

Zak stopped mid sip of coffee. Jesus, was this actually describing their lagoon on the island? How the fuck? At his and Izzi's lagoon, there were three large rocks facing the lagoon. The largest one at the front almost dipped its toes in the water's edge. Zak looked at Izzi, who was already looking right back at him.

Larry put his head back down to it and continued 'DANU, that's try or use, no, he plays it, he plays this instrument. UL NEGELTU MA BALTU. Now he's not awake but living.' Larry scratched his head with his pencil 'right that's it, dreaming, AMARU. He played this instrument to fall asleep and dream. In his dream, he finds himself QEREBU KHARSAANU, at the edge of the treeline by the lagoon where he originally found the instrument. He has to find the instrument again in his dream, EMUQ AMARU, to have the power over his dream. It's an instrument that dream dwellers need to control their dream, WARKI AMARU and he finds it...'

Izzi jumped in. 'Behind the waterfall.'

'Yes,' said Larry. 'After the moving water, yes, after the waterfall but more logically, behind the waterfall. How did you know that?' Zak knew the place described here and so did his Izzi. He couldn't imagine how it was possible. It just was. He gestured for another single malt from the waitress, who was now officially abandoning her 'quiet night, get home early' ideas.

'This next phrase is tricky,' said Larry. 'It could mean so many things. WASABU, he sits down. QABA NARUM AUM, he speaks a song, that's it he chants AUM, Om. Om that's it, like the Buddhists do, Om. The Buddhists define it as a cosmic sound, evoking your deepest soul to merge with the cosmos, with the divine spirit. He sits and chants Om. He meditates, that's better, yes, he meditates.'

'He then plays the instrument in his dream. When he plays the instrument in his dream, KHARSAANU SAQUUTU SHI, the forest breathes life, the forest comes alive and, SANU SU ASAR NEKELMU, takes him to where he needs to be, where he projected himself, to look for food, he's a hunter so I imagine where there are pigs and fruit and the like. AMARU MA KASADU, dream and you will arrive. NURU SU MINA JER. Finds him in his desired place. OK he finds himself where he wants to be. He's projected himself there.'

'And he just appears in the place?' asked Zak.

'Yes this is a dream pipe legend. The Mesopotamians had a similar story. If you find this dream pipe in your dream, you can gain control of what you do and what happens to you in your dream, control your subconscious, access all of your brain, actually all of your dimensions literally, commune with the world, function on a higher level.'

'That's what this is, Zak, it's a dream pipe legend. This hunter plays it to access his dreams. He falls asleep. In his dream he finds the pipe where he first found it and plays it again this time to enable him to control his dream. It takes him where he needs to go in his dream, he wakes and he's actually there. It's a lovely idea, really, where is this from? I've not seen the legend from this culture. I'm not even sure who this culture is.'

This text, this message could only have been talking to him and Izzi. Geniuses of all colors would have translated it as well as Larry but it would have meant nothing to them. Instantly it meant everything to Zak and Izzi. This was their sign. They shared a smile. They now knew something was guiding them.

That day with Megan at the waterfall. Izzi had brought it home. Jesus, it was in the house.

Larry continued and brought Zak out of his trance 'this next text talks about someone called... Mass, Massy, Mary, no, more like Maria. SARAT IRKALI, she was a goddess of their world, she was called Queen of the Netherworld. She was apparently the most beautiful woman ever made. Her eyes were green and blue at different times. Her voice resonated and held you captive and she was desired by all their kind.' Larry broke off and took a sip of whisky. He pulled back from focus in stages. He was unsure of the next bit, not necessarily what it said but what it meant.

'She was the purest hybrid of two races, it says, a perfect specimen of mind and body and better than the sum of those two races. She was both human and...' Larry broke off, unable to translate the next symbol. 'This must be the name of something,' he said. He looked at Zak and this time insisted. 'Where the fuck is this from man?'

Larry knew of the sci-fi folklore about the Sumerians and their alien hybrid origin myths and he loved it. Here before him was a story of one of their kind, this Maria. This Maria had to be the famous Maria Orsic.

The text went on to highlight Maria's journeys around the universe, including Earth, and her communion with the natives.

'Zak, have you ever heard of this Maria before?'

'No, I haven't' said Zak, but he didn't need her name to know who she was and she was an eye changer. There was always a soundtrack when he dreamt of her, sounded like static at first then maybe wind but now he know, it was a waterfall. His and Izzi's waterfall. She was guiding them.

'Maria Orsic was a member of the Vril society,' continued Larry. 'A secret society in Germany in the war. Vril means godlike. They believed in the coming of a new age and communion with races from other worlds. Naturally at the time, it got absorbed into Nazi bullshit pretending it meant Nazis were that new world order.

Maria was supposed to be a medium capable of receiving signals from these other worlds. They said she received her messages in Sumerian, Zak.'

Zak imagined this before Larry said it. It was all slotting into place although he didn't believe Maria was just communing with other worlds. She was from another world and she'd led them here. He also recognized the Sumerian as it emerged from Larry's mouth from Izzi's stressed moments. Izzi was speaking Sumerian. She didn't know why but maybe Zak now did. Izzi was connected to all of this in a much deeper way than just seeing the changes.

'What about RABBU TAHUMU? What does that mean?' said Allie.

'RABBU is fourth. TAHAMU, that's domain or realm, the fourth realm.'

'The fourth reich,' said Allie, nodding her head at Larry. She wasn't surprised, given the Nazi fuckbag nature of their target. This fourth reich had established dominance on this planet now how far would they go? Was Zak right, another Holocaust, this time of people whose eyes change color?

'Zak, what's going on, please,' said Larry, so close to where they were but just unable to know why they were there.

'Larry, I can't tell you buddy. I will one day I promise but not now.'

'One more thing,' said Manny. 'I know what the answer is but what does this mean?' Manny showed him his phone and AMARU, EDU, RAB SIKNANI. Larry put his head back down and a simple line came back, *dream, we are the designers.*

The four of them were done there. Zak got up and offered his hand to a Larry resigned to this day of secrets. He would hit Zak up for that 'one day' very soon. Zak grabbed hold of Larry's shoulders and looked him right in the eye and just said. 'I won't forget this, bud, but please, please,' tightening his grip on Larry's shoulders. 'Please do not tell anyone. It's too dangerous. Literally life and death,' and they were off to the car, leaving Larry with the most delicious Indy moment.

Zak hadn't been in Izzi's room for months. It had changed, different bands, more purple and orange, an odd new smell and a general essence of Megan, bohemian hippy cool. Izzi would allow this mass incursion for only this reason and dweeb boy was already pushing his luck scoping around her photos but then she saw him stroke his finger over the face of a new photo of her and suddenly the sunlight hit his stupid face in a slightly different way.

Izzi headed straight for the closet and lifted one or two sweaters. There was a light brown box with orange trim around the edges. The contents of this box were Izzi's secret prizes, things she'd keep her whole life, things that would take her back there to the smells and sounds and she's right there. She looked up at them all, considering how fucking awesome it was for her to be showing them this box.

There underneath the photos, concert ticket stubs, curious pieces of colored string and handwritten notes was this little stone dream pipe.

20

pipe dreams

Zak knocked up some coffee. Manny was laid out on the couch with the big flower next to it. That's Izzi's spot. She stood in front of him plotting her strike points and expecting a sooner look up than happened.

'Move.'

'Why?'

'Don't get smart, not-smart boy.'

Seconds passed. Izzi had no option but sit on his face till he moved.

'Jesus, rapey skank, wash much?'

'As my dear old aunt used to say after a few glasses, off you fuck.'

Eighteen seconds after coffee arrived they realized they were exhausted. They were close enough to natural sleep anyway but their next sleep would not be natural. It would be simulated and forced. It would send them into a world unknown to them.

'I've just remembered an episode of *The Next Place*,' said Zak.

'The what what?' said Manny.

'What if the technology for the machine came from somewhere else? This guy said you can't travel back in time to before the time machine was invented but then said 'unless…'

'Unless what?' said Allie.

'Unless it was invented somewhere else.'

'Like this one.'

'Like this one, maybe millions of years ago on another planet. This one wasn't invented in 1945. It was acquired.'

'No limit how far back it goes.'

'Could be millions of years and, if they can do that,' said Zak. 'These fuckers can wipe out hundreds of generations in one go.'

'If they know about it, they're trying to do it,' said Manny.

'If this really works,' said Allie. 'We go back to 1945, ninth of May 1945 and destroy the machine and that Nazi asshole Kammler right there before he goes anywhere.'

'Agreed,' said Zak.

They all looked at each other but Manny wasn't sure.

'Woah, hold on,' he said. 'Kammler went to the US in 1965 from 1945 Germany, right?'

'Yes,' echoed Zak and Allie.

'Well we can't go back to forty-five.'

'Why,' echoed Zak and Allie.

'Because he has to end up in the US in sixty-five so he can go back and kill that Russian dude.'

'Beria,' said Allie. 'Of course. He has to go back to fifty-three and kill Beria or World War Three would have happened over Cuba.'

'So we go back to fifty-three,' said Zak. 'We kill Beria then we go back to forty-five and kill Kammler and the machine?'

'Uh uuuuh,' came the Family Feud fail buzzer from Manny. 'No, dude, same thing. If we go back to forty-five and kill Kammler at any time, before or after anything else we do, he still won't go to the US or ever go back to fifty-three and kill the Russian dude. Allie, you got any more tortilla chips?'

'Cupboard over the hob.' Manny set in motion more coffee and there was soon crunching coming from the kitchen. Then the crunching stopped and Manny returned.

'Kammler goes back to fifty-three and kills Beria,' he said. 'So we know he's there and the bell is there.'

'So we go to fifty-three, we kill Beria in his cell and then destroy Kammler and the bell when they arrive,' completed Allie.

Plan. They had it. It was flawless. World War Three in 1962

wouldn't happen as soon as Beria was dead. Kammler and the bell would be ended soon after that.

'So we blow the pipe,' said Manny.

'Fall asleep and dream,' said Allie.

'Wake up behind the waterfall,' said Izzi.

'Find the pipe again, play the pipe again. Go where we go,' said Zak.

'Nice. Can I suggest something?' said Manny.

'Not really a question is it?'

'The future, anywhere, don't care, me wanna see.'

'Me too,' said Izzi.

'Guys, can we start dicking around on joy rides later, get this done first?' said Allie.

'Fine.'

'Cool.'

'We know Beria's date of death, December 23rd,' said Zak. 'We don't know his time of death, get there at midnight and follow the plan.'

'And we're done, get the flock out of Dodgeski.' said Manny, flipping a playing card in the air and catching it with the other.

A few seconds passed and they ignored the soundcheck of the sun, coming round the bend, ready to crank up the amps of the new day.

'One small thing,' said Izzi. 'Which cell is it?'

'I think that's what the dream pipe legend said,' said Allie. 'You don't try and find a location. You try and feel what it would be like to be there, the smells, the light. Specific things that can only mean that person in that spot at that time.'

'The hunter didn't know where the food would be,' said Zak. 'He had to be able to picture food, pigs running around, trees with fruit and stuff, then he got taken there.'

Jesus, this playing card, up and down and up and down. A carefully planned swat sent what better be his final card out of orbit.

'What are you twelve?' she said.

'No, what are you, like, eight?'

'I'm thirteen, cock-tard.'

'So just think of the waterfall. We've all seen it,' said Zak.

'I haven't seen it,' said Manny.

'Falcon Island.'

'Have seen it.'

'When did you go there, oddboy?'

'Loads of times.'

'Off you fuck from that island. That's my island.'

'My island, yay. Welcome to my island, island stealing muppet.'

'Do-you-get-any-weirder-o-tard?'

'Fuck yeah. Listen to what your dad's gonna say next.'

'Once we're there and we find the pipe again,' said Zak. 'We do the chant and we get in the zone for a 1953 Soviet jail cell.'

'Picture yourself there in that cell with the rest of us,' said Allie. 'Immerse yourself in it, the smells, sounds, colors, everything that's around you.'

'Like tuning a radio,' said Zak.

'What does a Soviet jail cell look like?' said Izzi.

'Grey, boring, paint chipping off the walls, graffiti in Russian,' said Zak. 'If there's a window it will be a tiny window high up, no glass just bars.'

'It'll be cold,' said Allie. 'Moscow in December cold. There'll be a man in a bed, round glasses on a plain wooden table next to the bed. It would smell of feet and shit, it would smell of fear. This guy knows he'll be executed when he wakes up.'

'Harsh,' said Manny.

'Now picture a small mirror over a tiny dirty sink. You're looking into it and you see the four of us looking back at you. Smell the feet and shit, pull your coat over you to keep warm, feel the fear of death in the room.'

'And if he's having trouble sleeping we need to be ready to jump on him,' said Zak.

'Check,' said Manny.

'Check? What are you, Starsky and Hutch?' said Izzi. 'Don't see any ninja in you, soft boy. So Dad, we just blow it again to get back here.'

'Yeah, make sure you can picture back here as well,' said Allie. 'Us on these couches right now.'

Zak looked at Izzi and then he noticed something. Next to Izzi, Manny's eyes very gradually started to change from his usual green to a very bright blue and stayed there in the middle of a face completely unaware of its transition.

'Manny, blow the pipe.'

'Why me?'

'No way, Dad, my pipe, tard boy's getting nowhere near it. No-one else can blow it, remember?'

'Iz. Trust me.'

Izzi lobbed the pipe to Manny and they all lay back ready for whatever happened next. Manny put the pipe to his lips and then a sound washed over them, wrapped around them, filled the room with a vibration that matched every molecule in their bodies. It felt like a precisely orchestrated powering down, slipping away. Nano-seconds before feeling the spray and sounds of falling water, Zak thought was this the end? Had they just fucked around with dark joojoo and done themselves in? Or had the enemy located them and this was what it felt like to never have existed. Would anyone come and take his hand for the final journey or would he be alone?

He opened his eyes. His face was wet and his vision was hazy like a bank robber with a stocking over his head. His head felt woozy, like a few drinks had gone down and then he turned to see the others looking back at him.

'Reckon that worked then, Bud' said Manny. 'Wait. Bud... Bud... Bud... Bud, awesome echo.'

'Holy shit,' said Zak.

'If it looks like a waterfall, it probably is,' said Allie.

'When I said I was going to bring you here one day, I didn't imagine this,' said Zak.

Izzi didn't need to sift through rocks and stones. She knew where this pipe was.

'Exactly the same as that day, Dad, but with different people.'

'I know baby.'

'Hands off, pipe stealing tard. Wrap up, people,' said Izzi. 'We're going down the rabbit hole.'

They joined hands. The Om chants started to vibrate in them. Images flooded in from that cold dark prison cell and Izzi blew the pipe. The waterfall and its cooling powder spray on their faces started to diminish and the smell of almonds hit them.

'Shit, really sorry,' said Allie as they realized they weren't in a prison cell, well not a Soviet prison cell in 1953, more an executive San Sebastian prison cell in 2017. 'I just pictured my Mom telling me the story of Beria.'

They were in Katherina's room, time slot unknown. Was this the future with no Katherina living in this space? No. It was still all her stuff. Just having breakfast.

'That smells nice,' said Manny and scoped around the room for the source. A little tin on this dresser was still warm and he opened the lid.

'Allie is this your mom's room?'

'Yeah and, come on, hands off stuff please.'

'Can I just snaffle one, please, just one, I fucking love macaroons?'

'Wouldn't bother, seriously,' said Zak.

Too late. This boy must have been hungry. In fact they were all hungry. The shame of demolishing a whole tin of Katherina's macaroons was overshadowed by the joy of it.

A decent gulp of air came in through Katherina's open window. Drapes danced and ornaments shuffled and Manny moved over to the window to see what this place was really like. He'd heard about it. Everyone had. He half expected scenes of chaos and madness to be playing out, people screaming and chasing each other with sticks, restrained in straitjackets, throwing their shit at passing cats, perhaps even a naked man standing upside down.

Then Manny somehow managed to catch the edge of a table full of pictures and assorted ornaments. One of the pictures wobbled like a drunk at closing time and finally gave up its fight for stability, topping over the edge of the table and smashing on the wooden floor.

'Nice move, tard boy.'

'Woah, shit, sorry,' said Manny, compounding his felony by spitting bits of macaroon on the table. 'Woah, shit, sorry again.'

'This is the photo Mom showed us the other day.'

'Jesus we broke it. So we're only a couple of days back in time,' said Zak. 'Why, because you thought of your mom?'

'Must be, did anyone else think of anything else?'

'No,' was the consensus.

Allie bent down to start picking up the glass but suddenly they heard the door handle squeak very slowly downwards. Someone was coming. Zak and Allie dived behind a couch in a heap and Izzi and Manny took a drape each. Whoever it was would enter a room populated by the keystone cops.

They'd travelled in space and time. If they were to be caught doing it, better to be Katherina than Soviet soldiers in 1953.

The door gently opened and Katherina entered her room. She lingered by the door for just a moment and came inside, shutting the door behind her. She seemed preoccupied. She moved right over to the offending table, missing Manny's shoes peeping out of the bottom of the drape. She glanced downwards and noticed her picture, smashed on the floor. She carefully picked it up and took the photo from the redundant frame. A small smile came over her face as she brushed tiny glass dust off the photo with her fingers and then looked into it. She took the photo with her over to her chair and held it as she stared out of the window to the lake and the birds enjoying their morning routine, much the same as their evening routine.

Katherina then turned to look right over at their end of the room.

'Is anyone there?' she said. 'Allie, is that you, my darling?' she continued, unable to see them but just as sure able to sense something. Nobody moved.

'Yes, Mom, don't worry,' Allie thought to herself.

'Oh good,' said Katherina and turned her gaze back to the window and the birds and enjoyed a genuine smile.

But there was now the small but meaningful problem of their next move, chanting their way to Moscow in 1953, and creating a noise that would definitely bring Katherina out of her peace. But, as if by magic, there was a knock at the door and in came a nurse, who asked if everything was OK, she'd heard breakage.

Katherina said a picture had been broken and was there anyone in here earlier? The nurse said no. Katherina huffed secretly but said don't worry she'll go with her and get a dustpan and brush and clear it up.

Katherina and the nurse left the room but not before Katherina looked back with a smile. Hands were joined and they once again focused on Beria in his cell back in '53. Their chants accompanied their focus and the room started to fold in around them, the corners of it becoming distant points of light drawing them in and soon they were in a new space.

But this still wasn't a Moscow winter scene. It was a bright and sunny and the day was pouring through two large windows onto the wooden floorboards and bouncing off them to create sash window patterns on the wall and its door. There were no drapes and no furniture.

As the fog started to lift, Zak heard someone walking about the other side of the door. He knew exactly who it would be.

'My bad,' said Zak. 'I thought of Manny's eyes changing and then Izzi's eyes changing.'

'We really need to work on not doing this,' said Manny. 'And what do you mean eyes changing?'

'Don't worry, it's really cool. They change from green to blue sometimes.'

'Fuckin what now?'

What was clear from their new space was that there was nowhere to hide. The door opened and a woman, mid-twenties, shoulder length blonde hair and a summer dress strolled in, shut the door behind her and looked over at them, growing a smile as she did. Zak froze. Izzi froze.

'Hey Dad,' said the woman, as calm as a hidden pond, like they'd just dropped round to pick something up. 'Bit James Bond,' said the woman. 'But I've been expecting you.'

Zak was looking at the unmistakable form of his little Izzi, but his little Izzi from the future. He looked at his Izzi and this future Izzi. Outside the windows he heard the laughter and gurglings of an adult male and children. This was her house.

Future Izzi knew what was next before her Dad did. Zak ran over and wrapped her up and squeezed her tight, kissing her on the top of the head and flicking her tiny nose, eventually being pushed away with 'silly parent.'

'You knew we'd be here, Iz,' said Zak, quickly summoning a tear or two from his left eye.

Future Izzi spared a glance and a smile for Allie, who smiled right back and took her hands and then she spared a more lingering glance and a smile at Manny.

'Hey.'

'Hey.'

Her gaze remained on Manny for a few seconds longer than he anticipated. Time travelling Izzi came out of her freeze to tweak the back of his arm.

'Slut.'

Zak didn't want to stop looking at his little girl all grown up but he had to go to the window and see who was there. There was this guy and two little boys bumbling around, maybe four and two. The younger one was upside down having just rolled off a big bouncy ball. He looked just like Izzi did when she was that age. The other was escaping daddy into the trees, loving every second of it, both pursued by a fuzzy little puppy of uncertain design. Zak couldn't see who the guy was. He was chasing the boy away from him. Through the trees at the bottom of the garden the vista opened up and he could see the sea. Maybe this was still somewhere near San Sebastian.

'Those two are your grandsons, Dad, Zak and Billy,' she said and the tears now cascaded from both of Zak's eyes.

'Yes, Dad, I knew you'd be here today. I have stuff to tell you.'

'What, baby?'

'That blonde woman. I saw her in a dream, remember?' Zak nodded. 'Her name is Maria. You saw her too. You all did. She's always there in my dreams. She's been teaching me.'

'Teaching what, baby?'

'How it all is. How I fit into it all.'

Manny sat on one of the window ledges, transfixed by the antics in the garden. Future Izzi and time traveling Izzi tracked him every step of his way there. He turned from the window into Future Izzi's eyes and smiled. Future Izzi was expecting it and smiled back.

'You're all destined to do this. It's been set in stone ever since your grandparents were at Auschwitz. You know the aches you get in the morning? You're feeling the same aches your grandparents felt in the cold of Auschwitz. The paranoia? That's what they felt each new day as they wondered if it was their turn to take the trip to the showers.'

'That's exactly what it feels like,' said Allie. 'How did you know that?'

'I started feeling it myself and Maria told me all about it and so much more. Maria said us silly humans actually turn out to be quite important to the universe. We have a really important part to play. I don't know why yet but we have to believe we do.'

'Why? What can we do?' said Zak. 'We're not important to anyone but us.'

'You have to believe you are, Dad. Have faith what you're doing is right. Have faith you'll win. You have to win or I won't be standing here. None of us will. Trust Maria. She's watching over all of us.'

'I knew it. I knew she was guiding us.'

'She is, Dad. Larry was right. They consider her the most perfect universal being.'

'They?'

'Her kind, the ones who came and created hybrids. I'm one of them, Dad. There are things I can do. She said I had a vital part to play in our future on Earth and that will all become clear to me one day.'

'Jesus, baby. Why's she doing this?'

'It was their mistake. It was their spaceship that landed in the Black Forest in 1937. They handed this technology to the Nazis.'

'Jesus, like giving a gun to a really pissed off monkey,' said Allie.

'They had to correct their mistake and this was the only way. They can't get involved themselves. They can't interfere. We humans have to do it.'

'So they made us see the changes?' said Allie. 'So they could have stopped all this shit before the Nazis even happened.'

'Yes, but they can't get involved.'

'Crashing that spaceship sounds like getting pretty involved.'

'I know, Allie. Their mistake cost lives, a consequence of a war no-one knows is happening. It will cost even more lives if Dad and me and you and Manny don't finish it. The moment you started seeing the changes, you were destined to be in this place at this time.'

'So this is some kind of rule? Don't interfere even if you caused a while load of shit in the first place. Stupid rule. The universe is full of shit.'

'So what they did in the war,' said Zak. 'The Nazis, the extermi-nations, they're doing it all again but this time it won't just be the

Jews or Muslims or gay people. It'll be anyone with the pure blood of Maria's people, like you, baby.'

'Fraid so, Dad. They need us gone. We're a threat.'

Allie wasn't sure who to hate more, the Nazis or the fucking stupid clown footed aliens and their stupid rules. Maybe she'd start with the Nazis and move onto having some serious words with this Maria after that.

'But this is what Maria wanted me to tell you. You've got to clear your heads before you travel. You're close but you don't know how to do this so here it is. You've got to give up sight and sound, smell, everything. Blank it out. Enter a kind of humming void. You have to feel where you're going. You're blind, feel along the wall for direction. You can tell when you touch silk or fir, wood or metal, feel for what you need.'

Izzi smiled again and came in for a big hug from her Dad.

'One more thing,' she said. 'You can never make physical contact with yourself from another time. It's like antimatter touching matter.'

'Woah, very bad joojoo,' said Manny.

'Fine, hug everyone else, what do I care?' said time travelling Izzi.

Allie joined the hug. Manny came closer but he wasn't sure where to slot in. Future Izzi looked up and tugged him in after another long stare into him, almost believing it could become a kiss. Time traveling Izzi felt like kicking future Izzi in the shins.

'Time to do this,' said Manny.

They parted like skydivers ready for parachutes, this time with a 'silly family' from future Izzi.

'By the way, Dad,' continued Izzi as the reached the door, stroking a handle she wasn't yet ready to use. 'You and Allie are coming round for dinner tonight. What do you want to eat? Lamb or Salmon?' She had that head-down-looking-up-at-him look, that cheeky, guilty look she always did. 'Tell you what, I'll surprise you.'

Zak's future Izzi tugged the handle and she was gone. She was here in the future with two kids. He wiped the residue of tears from his face, held out his hands and the three of them joined. Their chant began and at a time of Izzi's choosing, she blew into the pipe.

The next thing that appeared to Zak was his and three other little faces staring back at him from a mirror, a very small mirror on a very dirty grey wall. He quickly scanned around him and it didn't take long. They were in a tiny cell about twelve feet by ten. Over against the wall opposite this mirror and sink arrangement was a bed. In that bed was the unmistakable lump of a human topped off with it's head on the pillow, completely unaware of their materialisation in his private quarters.

Fuck it's cold, Zak thought. Then Beria stirred and rolled over on his left side, facing the wall. They froze. The thing that should have occurred to him first had to be done now. He knew it was a coward's murder, should he at least wake him up first?

Too late. Allie had already moved up alongside Beria and slid a long knife along his throat, her heart racing with the horror. She stepped back leaving a gurgling, dying man. There was no time to offer an apology.

'Now we wait for Kammler,' she said.

The final moments of Lavrentiy Beria spurted out of him and dripped down the wall onto the floor and the gurgling stopped.

'Is he still alive?' she asked, the shock starting to tremble her.

'Not after that,' said Zak.

Zak approached the bed and confirmed this was indeed Lavrentiy Beria, only few months ago President of the Soviet Union, and he was very dead.

Allie washed her knife off in the sink, dried it on his face towel and reabsorbed it into her sheath, a series of icy cool movements not unnoticed by the others. And then it hit Manny.

'Fuck,' he said. 'Kammler's not gonna come.'

'Why?' said Zak, starting to prep the C4.

'I can't believe we missed it.'

'Missed what?' echoed the others.

'Anyone… anyone?'

'Manny.'

'OK. Look. As soon as we killed him, chilling assassination by the way, Allie, he was dead.'

'Of course he was dead.' said Zak.

'Yeah, but the timeline changed as soon as we killed him. There's no World War Three as of one minute ago. No-one ever needed to come back and kill him.'

'Jesus, it was us who stopped World War Three,' said Zak. 'Kammler probably never even thought of Beria.'

A few moments passed as another opportunity started circling to go down the plughole.

'What now?' said Izzi.

'Well the plus side is World War Three won't happen,' said Zak. 'At least we couldn't fuck that up. But we still have no idea where Kammler or the machine is.'

'How about if we come back to just before we did just now but not kill him?' said Allie.

'We'd just see ourselves arrive and kill him anyway,' said Manny.

'Couldn't we stop ourselves?' said Zak.

'We've already decided not to,' said Manny.

'Why?'

'When we got here just now, were there the four of us waiting for us?'

'We can't come into contact with ourselves,' said Izzi. 'Eight of us in this tiny cell and all.'

'Fuck,' said Zak.

'One thing I do know,' said Allie. 'If we hang around any more, this cell will be full of Soviet soldiers and World War Three will be back on the agenda nine years earlier than planned.'

'Home?' said Zak.

'Home,' said Izzi.

Thoughts transferred to Zak and Izzi's place, the coffee and tortilla chips and that flower by the couch, flicking soft boy's fucking card into space. The four of them joined hands and started to chant. But instead of feeling the pipe take them home, Manny broke the circle.

'Woah, hang on,' he said. 'We can't got back to '45 or '65 so where can we go where we know exactly where the fucker is at a specific point in time?'

The room didn't. And then Allie did.

'1967, the mountains,' she said. 'Mom's lunch with Freddie, the macaroons.'

'Ping,' said Manny.

'Of course, June 15th 1967.'

'Manny you're a genius,' said Zak.

'What, still?' said Manny.

'Arrogant much?' said Izzi.

'We know Kammler's there but we don't know the bell's there,' said Allie.

'It's there,' said Zak, staring straight ahead. 'Katherina didn't mention any door to that basement in '67.'

'That's right,' said Allie.

'But there was a door a few days ago. The space has always been there, so why was it hidden in '67 but accessible in 2017?'

'It had something to hide,' said Manny.

'It has to be there,' said Zak.

'So it's back to Mom's plan in '67,' said Allie.

They turned to look at Beria one last time and joined hands. Their new formula for their navigational chant set them fair for the morning after Katherina's lunch with the Kammler family.

'Where are we aiming?' said Zak.

'The treeline beyond the morning terrace,' said Allie. 'Mom said she saw something that morning in the trees. It was us.'

'Wait for Katherina and Freddie to leave and see if Kammler goes down to the basement.'

'Check,' said Manny.

Suddenly, there was a noise in what they assumed was the hallway outside Beria's cell. At least two men and keys jangling right outside the door. When they entered the cell, there was just the mess of a murdered President.

Nobody in that Soviet jail, least of all the very deceased former president Lavrentiy Beria, heard the chants and the sweet tune of the dream pipe as once more they were projected across time and space to the mountains in Southern California on the morning of June 16th 1967.

21

what's that song called?

A strong smell of sausage and a gentle rustle of early morning leaves brought them into their new space. They appeared as planned, behind the treeline on the far side of the terrace behind Freddie as he served up a fine fare of sausage to all and sundry not least the two happy alsatians.

Allie smiled as she saw the relief her mom felt when Pete showed up. From 1953 to 1967 everything seemed as it was meant to be, as it always was. There'd been no changes to the continuum, nothing untoward trickling down the timeline and they were where they wanted to be.

Katherina pulled away from her luxurious fluffing of Pete and stared right through the trees and straight into Allie's eyes. She scoped around the rest of this far side of the terrace and then returned to the mutt and his pathological desire for sausage.

There was Kammler. It was like seeing a movie star in a restaurant, more like seeing Charles Manson in a restaurant. There he sat, ready for sausage and the day, large as life and at ease with himself.

Everything Katherina said was true. Here was a man born in 1901, a man who should have been sixty-six years old as he sat on this sunny terrace yet here sat a man who looked the twenty years younger he was. Twenty-two years ago to everyone else and two years ago to Hans, this Nazi had been suffering under the very real threat of being murdered for his knowledge of the machine.

This was another irony the Nazis loved to fulfill on each other. They would invite a select group of highly expendable people to a celebration, a party to commemorate their great work for the glorious Reich. Food and wine and cake would be all around them.

Gradually and slowly those of a certain office would ooze out of the room until only their targets remained and then the doors were locked and those who remained started to wonder where everyone else went. When they saw the guns drawn and ready, they could only close their eyes, all their hard work, all their loyalty served only their own destruction, for the future of the glorious reich of course. They'd be martyrs, guarantees that it all stayed in house and the idiot Americans or stinking Russians never got hold of it. They would pay this price of spoof immortality with their lives.

Allie wondered how lovely it would be for Kammler to somehow feel the paranoia that today would be his last day alive. They were joining Katherina's mission no sooner than she'd failed in it and how lovely as well if she knew they would be finishing it for her. Allie couldn't help feeling that perhaps she did.

In another segment of time, unknown to the Hans having break-fast here, the Hans and Freddie of 2017 had something to celebrate.

'Remember, they won't look like the people around them,' said Freddie. 'They'll be gods to these people. The blonde woman will definitely be hard to miss.'

'Maria fucking Orsic,' chipped in Hans very much looking forward to this moment of epiphany. Hans had known this Maria Orsic in Nazi Germany. She was one of the Vril fuckers behind that eternally closed door.

'Seven thousand years, that spawning breed. Seven thousand fucking years will be gone starting with her and the other fucking gods. This first spawning breed will be no more and every slip-eyed freak that followed will be no more. You've been discovered and you've been marked.'

Freddie had finally made sense of it, this time in ancient Sume-ria, extracted everything he could from scrolls, caves and carvings. There were more and more signs pointing to this woman 'not of their kind' and those she came with, Gods, come to improve us, teach us. And then there was this stone tablet, dug up in Iraq three weeks ago and the first mention of a beautiful queen's eyes changing color, a queen with powers beyond the imagination of anyone else. She'd appeared to the people of the age soon after the great chariots from the sky had shown themselves and come among them.

Hans and Freddie were headed for Babylon 5445BC.

They would blend in from a distance, find their way to this woman and her kind long before she became Maria Orsic. They weren't far off making what they hoped was their final journey. Hans couldn't help wonder if he'd feel the vanishing of her kind, a release, the opening of a door. After all, if a door never opens, what do you do? You burn it down. Would he enjoy the truth they never existed. Would he hear screams? Probably not. Pity. Would he see the terror of oblivion on their faces and feel his victory as he drove his knife into them? Definitely.

Breakfast on this 1967 terrace was a quiet affair but seemed to take an age to finish. Katherina held her own after the chaos that had invaded her and this house in the mountains last night. She even managed a smile or two at Hans. Allie was rooted to this scene and her Mom's playing of it.

Soon, Freddie announced it was that sort of time and he and Katherina went inside to pack Hans and Klara had a brief chat about spiders. Klara knew when to let it go and sat back and smiled. It would be a matter of a car kicking up gravel in the driveway before she brought out bottle number one of the day and good luck to her.

Katherina and Freddie left and by this time, Manny's attention to sausages was primordial.

They didn't understand the German that confirmed to a surprised Klara it was also time for them to go and do whatever they needed to do. The terrace became quickly empty and the plates of sausages put down for Wolfgang and Pete. Manny left it almost a minute before he broke cover, slipping the attempted restraint of Zak and Allie and introduced himself to Wolfgang and Pete.

Wolfgang and Pete's attention moved from sausage for the sake of sausage to this new friend. Manny gave them both a solid fluffing and returned to the trees with every morsel of food left on the terrace. As breakfast was being shared in the woods, Klara returned and congratulated Wolfgang and Pete with another fluffing for their obvious appetite. Klara was dressed smartly. It looked like she and Hans might be off somewhere themselves.

Before the last of their breakfast had been chewed, the front door closed behind the last residents of this house, who got into their car and headed off down the drive.

They were alone and free to do their mischief. It mattered not that Hans had left. They knew it was temporary, there was stuff to clean up and doors to lock, which luckily they hadn't bothered to do. The trust alive and well in this remote fiefdom was welcome. They probably didn't have much time but now was their chance to sniff about and discover the secret door that must exist to the basement.

The three of them spread out to various areas, tapping walls, looking under rugs and finally Zak found it. There was a bookcase built into the dead space under the stairs. Zak had noticed a copy of The Black Obelisk by Erich Maria Remarque, not due to his familiarity with the author, but because it wasn't flush with the rest of the books in the row. He reached to pull the book out only to find it wasn't to be pulled out, existing only as a catch release. The whole bookcase shifted slightly towards him, revealing a staircase to a lower realm.

Zak went first and drew his pistol. They weren't to know if there was a team of scientists or security personnel lurking down there. But there were no sounds coming from below as they rounded the oak spiral and soon they were in the basement area they'd accessed from the corridor a few days ago.

This wasn't the dark, dusty basement they found the other night back in 2017. There were still some boxes stacked up over by the wall on the left side but here and now, this was a large clean space dominated by a vast panoramic window out onto the mountains. It was bigger than the entire floor above, maybe there was a Tardis-like force at work.

The beautiful stone walls persisted down here and the only things interrupting the complete openness of the space were the boxes, a small oak desk and two armchairs facing the window. It looked like a place of modest activity soaking up its view.

Zak noticed in the far corner of the room to the left of the panorama, there was a door, the only sign that this space had company. Zak signaled Izzi and Allie to stay back and he and Manny headed over to the door. Their nerves were tingling like pins and needles. The door was locked. Zak ran his fingers over the top part of the frame but there was no key. He turned to ask Manny to look in the desk drawers but found the lad already there, carrying a big smile and holding up a key. The key was the key they needed. The door creaked open slowly and soon it became clear this small circular room, about the size of a squash court, was what they'd been searching for all this time.

All around the wall of this room was a concrete structure that looked like a small version of Stonehenge and in the middle sat the machine, quiet and aloof, hovering about two feet above the ground with no visible means of doing it. They approached it slowly like approaching the cage of a lion at the zoo. This unmistakable bell shaped machine was levitating effortlessly absolutely still in front of them. It was bigger than Zak had imagined and he could easily see at least three of them fitting into it although a way in wasn't obvious.

'Can you feel that?' said Izzi. 'like a really quiet buzzing noise.'

'I can,' said Manny. 'Makes me want to itch my ear.'

'You guys stand a bit further back from it,' said Zak.

Zak applied a very light pressure to the machine's surface, which was warm, brass type material, pushing it slightly, mindful of it toppling off any invisible moorings but it didn't move. He gave it a heavier nudge but still nothing. Finally, he ran a shoulder into it.

It was like it was cemented to something but it was totally free, suspended in the air.

Allie crouched down on the floor and ran her arm underneath it and there was still no physical device to explain how it was levitating.

'Its hollow inside,' she said. 'As far as my arms can reach.'

'Good. we can place the charges in and out,' said Zak.

She ran her fingers over the markings engraved into the metal, the symbols Larry had revealed to them in San Diego, symbols created countless millennia ago on another world that only made sense to Zak and Izzi.

They stood back in awe of where they were. Zak had to think to himself, as time machines go, this bell was clinical, industrial even. You really want a beautiful brass and steel, mechanical and leather-bound comfort time machine like HG Wells, a big observation window to see what time looks like being travelled, like a first class cabin on the Orient Express. Levers need to push and pull and you need to hear the ratchet noises as you speed up and slow down. There were no clues to how to use the machine. Maybe its designers weren't that bothered about how they got somewhere, just get there. Now where's the fun in that?

Zak couldn't help feeling a twinge of shame as their plan of destruction returned to him. He had plenty enough C4 to split this bell into a peeled banana, possibly a million pieces with just a few symbols remaining to baffle anyone approaching the aftermath, maybe take Kammler's whole private fourth reich with it down into the valley.

Zak suggested the others leave the room while he lays the charges and they agreed ten minutes was enough on the timers for them to get well clear.

As he placed the charges in their ideal positions for maximum damage, he pulled back. The machine started to vibrate. Then it started to hum. Maybe this is what Izzi and Manny heard. It wasn't consciously audible, just enough to shake his atoms, not enough for him to feel it but just enough for him to know it.

Perhaps this machine was aware of their attack on it, perhaps it possessed the same fear animate beings possess when they know the time of their ending is inevitable. Perhaps this was its machine sense.

Then a noise was heard back where they came down the stairs. It was the unmistakable noise of the false bookshelf door creaking open quickly followed by the sound of two men talking in German and footsteps descending a staircase. Allie ran in to warn Zak.

'Zak, someone's coming,' she said, whispering but urgent. She turned to exit the room but noticed Zak wasn't moving. 'Zak,' she said again, now giving it more volume, but still he was just standing there with his hands on the machine. He'd laid the charges but looked like he was bidding the thing farewell. She ran over to him and punched him high on the arm, releasing him from his trance.

'Boxes,' he said. They ran over behind the boxes, their only available cover down here, but Zak noticed a desk drawer left open following Manny's discovery of the key. Despite Allie and Izzi's attempt at restraint, Zak ran over to the desk to close the very obvious drawer but had just turned to head back for cover when one of the men appeared at the foot of the stairwell. He and Zak froze.

The others remained undetected behind the boxes but the lack of footsteps back over here to the boxes, told them Zak had been seriously detected. The man holding Zak where he stood was Hans Kammler. He drew a pistol and pointed it at Zak to ensure there was no attempt by this intruder to unfreeze. The man who followed him down the stairs was an equally surprised Freddie.

'Move,' said Hans. 'Over in front of the window.'

Zak half raised his arms and did as he was told. He thought to himself how close they'd been. They would have had to wait for

Hans to return to kill him anyway but he'd hoped to have the element of surprise. This was whole different kettle of fish.

Allie did well not to lend audio to the cold shiver that crawled up her spine. They were barely breathing behind these boxes and could only rely on sound to make out the goings on in the room. She knew there were two men who came down the stairs and she could tell the distance of the one taking but the other one might be inches from them, about to peer round and that was them done.

'Take out your pistol very slowly,' continued Hans. Zak did. 'Now throw it on the floor.' Zak complied again, making sure it was thrown away from the boxes. Freddie moved to pick it up and held it at Zak.

'What are you doing here? What do you want?' said Hans flicking his pistol upwards to imply Zak's arms were becoming lower than he was comfortable with. Zak adjusted his arms to mirror the gesture.

Zak had many possible answers running around his head, none of which seemed to make sense. Was he lost? Was he a common thief? If so what was he after? Nothing had the impact he felt he had to make here apart from the truth.

'Fuck you, Nazi.'

Hans tilted his head to the left and was clearly surprised at this. It had been a very long time since anyone had known he was or had been a Nazi and no-one had ever said 'fuck you, Nazi' to him.

'American,' he said, getting the smallest inkling that the Americans from whom he had defected with the bell had somehow tracked him down. 'I will ask again, who are you and why are you here?'

Zak knew this Nazi was slightly off guard so continued in his current vein of truth. Perhaps his brazen revelation of a truth Hans could not possibly know would further unsettle him. As he was pretty sure Hans would shoot him anyway, he may as well go out with a flourish, making him feel watched, uncovered and unsafe.

'It was so easy to find you, Kammler,' said Zak.

'Who?' replied Hans, unable to hide a slight croak in his voice, raising a smile on Zak's face and a modest frown on his own.

'Hans fucking Kammler. I know who you are, you murdering Nazi asshole. I know you've been changing time and I'm here to stop you.'

This brought out of both Kammlers a broad and deep laugh given the nature of Zak's captivity.

'Changing time? Are you mad? What are you talking about?' said Hans, now moving over to take a seat.

'Oh and maybe I should mention I'm also here to kill you.' continued Zak, starting to enjoy his possible swan song and enjoying the nervous nature of the responses coming back at him. An important lesson for any police detective is to detect signs of the right kind of nerves, nerves that suggest lying, a change in vocal pitch, hand movement, head and eye movements and a general demeanor tends to tell them a pretty complete story. Beyond that, the good detectives have good hunches but this detective didn't need a hunch. They didn't know what he knew and up till this moment they didn't know he existed. Zak also knew these Nazis were about to start matching his truth with their own. He could just see them desperate to tell him how amazing they were, even that he was right but how redundant his life had become as a result. Bingo.

'Alright,' said Hans. 'Let's assume your madness has some truth. How would we be doing this?'

'The machine,' said Zak and spotted Freddie's instant but fleeting glance over to the door in the corner. 'You use the machine to change things in the past and I can see when you make those changes.'

Hans was now more visibly shaken. He leaned forward in his chair, his pistol still very much aimed at Zak but now starting to tremble very slightly. Zak knew he had him hooked.

'How can you possibly know this? And what are you going to do about it anyway?' said Hans, offering another throaty laugh but one filled with less confidence. 'I assume you plan to destroy this machine and your changes would just stop?'

'Something like that,' said Zak. 'And of course turn you two assholes inside out in the process.'

Hans sat back in his chair and it was clear he appreciated it was time he did what Zak hoped he would do and effectively spill his beans. He very carefully entered into a slow but brief hand clap, preferring to cut it short to maximize control over his pistol.

'Bravo,' he said. 'So it was my error that we didn't know people could see what we were doing. Yes, we've been changing the past and soon the Fourth Reich will rise and take back what it was so rudely denied twenty years ago. If only you were in a position to carry out your futile plan, but alas here we are.'

'Here we are,' echoed Zak with a decent smile. 'Master race and all that.' A deep exhale from Kammler suggested he was tiring of this. It brought on his essence, the essence of a Nazi believing himself to be invincible.

'Oh the things I've seen. The places I've been,' began Kammler, now Coriolanus centre stage. 'I've tilted history and just as easily delighted in a whim to leave it be. I have the power to overcome any enemy and create any future and you stand before me, before the dawning of the glorious new reich, daring to challenge me? I can take your DNA and your family would never have existed. Can you even comprehend the power?'

'Wow,' said Zak. 'Yes you are so very powerful it makes me hard. Bet you planned to say all that shit one day in the fucking temple you rule the world from. CBS or HBO? No, all of them, right? Jesus, you fucking Nazis.'

This had done it. Kammler was off his chair, red faced and now furious at the way this subordinate, this nobody had just shat all over his proudest words. Zak was ordered to kneel down and tighten his hands round the back of his head. Kammler was now a mere few yards from him.

'It is now time for me to kill you, insignificant fucking insect that you are.'

Zak began what could well have been his final speech of the campaign. Instead of closing his eyes and waiting for the crack of his oblivion bullet, he looked up at Kammler with a smile and started to laugh.

'OK, don't shoot him,' said Izzi emerging from the boxes with her hands up.

Zak closed his eyes. What was she doing? Baby, for fucks sake.

Freddie got Izzi by the arm

'Off you fuck, Nazi-tard.' Izzi broke free and turned to deliver some ninja on Freddie, who reeled back a little bit it wasn't enough to bring down a big guy like Freddie. Izzi was wrapped up in his coat and made secure.

'So I guess after I'm dead,' continued Zak. 'You'll just carry on doing what you're doing will you?'

'Of course,' said Kammler, cocking his pistol.

'And to do that,' continued Zak. 'You will need to make at least one more trip I guess.'

Hans and Freddie didn't know what to make of this idiot American laughing to welcome his final bullet.

'What are you saying, idiot?' said Kammler, now pressing his pistol against Zak's temple.

'So how are you going to do that without a machine?' said Zak, pointing his head in the direction of the door housing the machine. Both Kammlers followed his head's path to the same door and then Zak went into slow mo.

Freddie took Izzi over to the door. Fuck, he was meant to leave her there. It was unlocked and he opened it. He turned to his father in a gesture of 'WTF?' and Izzi started to wriggle.

'Keep still or I will squeeze tighter,' but it was too late for Freddie. Izzi had got some traction and shredded her heels down Freddie's shins. She was released and followed up with a double high kick and dived behind the boxes. Freddie cleared his head and turned to the bell for the briefest of seconds, enough time only to see the C4 countdown at 2... 1.

'Woops,' chuckled Zak.

Freddie was torn apart in an explosion that shook the foundations and sent a few rocks down the mountain. It obliterated Freddie, the machine and that entire room, shattering the windows into a waterfall of glass and leaving behind it a chaos of smoke and debris.

'Friedrich!' yelled Kammler, in a very different tone to his Coriolanus arrogance of moments ago and this was Zak's chance.

Zak grabbed hold of Kammler's right gun hand with his left and tried to snap the gun out of it but Kammler's grip was strong. His face had changed from the isolated desperation of losing a son to the blind red fury at this killer in front of him, his teeth were bared and his every muscle joined forces to regain control of the gun.

The battle for the gun told Zak this Nazi was a strong Nazi. Zak knew very quickly Kammler would be able to turn the gun back round on him so, risking a loss of focus on his restraining hand, he threw a fat right cross into Kammler's left cheek and Kammler's head rocked back under its weight but recovered and still he held firm on the gun.

Kammler now returned fire with a left cross and Zak saw stars as a fist-sized stone dulled the right side of his face but still the gun remained in limbo.

Kammler also knew he could win the battle of brute strength with this American but perhaps not the battle of agility so his goal was to keep Zak close and squeeze the fight out of him. Once more the gun was coming round to Kammler's command as these two men stood chest to chest, red faced and growling under sheer muscle pressure.

Zak was able to release enough small bursts of energy to continue diverting the gun away but each eventually yielded control back to Kammler. This stalemate had to be broken and as it stood, Kammler would win the ascendancy for the gun if something else didn't happen. If Kammler threw any more of those left crosses, Zak wasn't sure he'd stay in the game and this dance would end. Once more Zak risked focus on the battle for the gun to divert power to other muscles.

Zak brought his right knee right up into Kammler's balls. Kammler closed his eyes from this new pain and lost his ascendancy over his gun hand. Zak brought his right hand round and chopped Kammler's wrist, releasing the gun to the floor and also releasing his left to pile in a solid left cross. He wrapped his right leg behind Kammler's right and applied a new center of gravity forwards, bringing both men to the ground in thudding unison but Kammler refused to let go of him.

What had been a static but exhausting perpendicular struggle centered on control of the gun now turned into a static but exhausting horizontal struggle, one that didn't involve a gun.

The two men rolled on the ground trying to fend off blow after blow from each other but still Kammler was proving the more able at close quarters. Who was this guy? Did persistent time travel give him superhuman strength or had he always been a monster?

Kammler rolled himself on top of Zak and now had his hands round Zak's throat, elbows out to parry any hits coming in at him. Then he was rocked sideways by a charging Manny low into his left side. 'Fucker, that hurt.' Kammler released Zak and grabbed Manny by the scruff. One right cross put Manny away and he flopped back on the floor, head spinning.

Zak spared a tiny second to notice they were both now seriously close to the edge of the room, which was now the edge of the mountain, a straight drop hundreds of yards thanks to the shattering of this huge window.

The tighter Kammler's grip became around his throat, the more Zak tried to pull away and the closer the men moved towards the edge. Zak was starting to lose oxygen and with it muscle strength. Kammler sensed this and, with what he hoped was one last prolonged teeth baring squeeze, lowered his head to drive more force behind his killer grip. Zak's head was now hanging over the edge and fell back with the removal of hard floor beneath, allowing Kammler even more neck to grab onto and even less resistance.

Just as Zak was considering the merits of death by strangulation versus death by means of a plunge over the mountain side, there was temporary relief for him in the form of Izzi.

'Fucker!' yelled Izzi as she came in with a waist high kick but Kammler didn't move. Again he released his grip on Zak to grab her and throw her over by the desk. Izzi landed hard and knocked her head on the desk. It all went blurry. Unknown to Izzi, the dream pipe in her pocket dropped out onto the floor and started to roll towards the edge.

Zak managed to throw a left then a right cross with all the reduced energy he had at his disposal in a desperate attempt to make up the few yards and stop the roll of the pipe but he didn't have the reach and Kammler reclaimed his grip on Zak's throat quickly, unmoved by the actions of this random stone.

Izzi was still seeing stars and Zak could only watch. Time slowed to a trickle and finally showed their dream pipe, their only means to escape this time and space, disappear over the edge of the mountain down into the valley below.

Zak now had his whole upper body hanging over the edge under Kammler's relentless death grip. He knew this was it and his deflation at the loss of the pipe didn't help. He saw Kammlers face recognise it as well as he exploded one final gurgling growl to finish him off.

Zak closed his eyes and surrendered his remaining struggle to the inevitable. He was now out of oxygen and his head was becoming a fuzz, like waking up after a blow of the pipe. Thoughts of Izzi came to him thick and fast, Izzi as a baby, Izzi by the desk in this room, Izzi with her kids in the future. He would never see his baby again.

Then his memories regressed further back in time to the police, high school, his childhood, that day Dad backed the car into a fire hydrant and just started laughing as Mom sat there confused, his first Flat Eric's Burger, his second kiss, so much better than the first, and then, out of the corner of his eye, he saw it, a pinpoint of light slowly growing into full vision. He was mesmerized. It was pulling him in, he couldn't control it but soon realized he didn't want to. He suddenly saw his destination, this was the only thing he wanted. This was the purest light carrying with it the purest feeling, safety and harmony. He was at one with it, no longer in this world, entering the next. As he started getting closer and closer to the source of light, reaching out for it, he heard a loud bang and he was pulled back away from the light and opened his eyes.

Kammler's grip loosened. His face showed only the purest pain. It was twisted and his eyes were closed, teeth still bared but now with pain not effort. Zak rolled him off him and, as he looked up from the edge, there in front of him was Allie holding the gun. The Russian ninja spy had parachuted in at the last moment and Kammler lay barely breathing beside him, unable to move.

Zak was exhausted, he was no more animated than the near-dead Nazi next to him and only managed to slide back from the edge with Manny's help, lying there regaining air with his head in his hands. Izzi was moving. Thank fuck. Then thoughts of the lost dream pipe and maybe a memory of that next place he almost entered in his mind.

Allie was focused on her one final mission. Her eyes bored into Kammler as his breaths became fewer. He stared right back at her and sensed this woman had a plan for him. She approached him slowly and knelt beside him, studying every inch of his face so she could see the difference between his living and dying. She once more pulled out her long knife and held it in front of his face, happy to see his eyes widen a little and breathing increase.

A bead of sweat developed on the bridge of his nose and threatened to descend it. He knew what was coming and it certainly wasn't what he was expecting when he woke up this morning. Neither speech nor movement was available to him. Allie brought her face in close and moved her mouth to his right ear.

'I just wanted you to know I am going to kill you now,' she said in a whisper that only he could hear, summoning a groan from his blood filled mouth and a futile shuffling which served only to dislodge the bead of sweat and send it south down his nose.

Allie wanted to enjoy this on behalf of the millions wiped from the face of the earth in this man's death camps and on behalf of her grandfather who perished but not before leaving this gift for her mom. She pulled away from his ear and made sure he was locked in her murderous stare.

She'd figured out how this would work as soon as she thought they'd meet. It's what Katherina had wanted to do and what Allie wanted to do. Her technique was courtesy of a pretty grizzly youtube video, some redneck survivalist, the right way to access the heart from underneath.

Allie launched into a smile capturing three generations and got closer still to Kammler so a mere breath was enough for him to feel her. She started to apply modest pressure to the knife. Kammler twisted and tried to back away from it but he was done moving.

'Benjamin Aaronheim,' she said. 'My grandfather.'

He could only close his tortured eyes in muffled agony as she drove the knife into him and up behind his ribs and finally into his heart.

As it stuck fast right there, she saw his eyes start to lose their shine and his body lose any structure. He closed his eyes and deep in there he will have been seeing all the things that brought him to this moment, things that now demanded of him an eternity in the other place, perhaps where Jewish tyrants kept Nazis simply to feast on their balls, sautéed with some onions.

He lost air and bodily glue and he was gone.

Zak had witnessed this most welcome of murders although she chilled him to the very machinery doing it. Allie saved him and had the fortune to see Kammler from this world with far a more poignant monologue than he'd offered earlier, the Nazi prick.

Allie left the knife there as a solid photo memory of what Katherina tried to achieve with poison and subterfuge. She sat back on the floor next to Izzi by the desk. Izzi's fuzzy head cleared and she smiled. Manny's head was still throbbing and he moved over to sit in the middle of the floor and crossed his legs.

Back in Bayside in 2017, the receptionist countersigned 'Hendricks' and closed the visitor's book. Katherina didn't hear him enter the room until he said 'Today, I think you are with me, Katherina.' She didn't turn to see him. She knew he'd be coming today. Freddie moved over to the couch to face Katherina. He'd stared into her eyes many times over the years, but this was the first time his Katherina was really staring back.

'Katherina. I've think I've come to say goodbye.'

'I know, Freddie.'

Freddie sat back on his couch and turned his head to the window. The peace of the lake and the woman in this room started to show him the way.

'No more madness,' said Freddie. 'For some reason today was the day I just couldn't anymore. I don't know what he'll do. I think from this moment he might just destroy everything. I wanted to come here. If you'd seen the horrors I've done, Katherina. No God will ever forgive me.'

'Freddie.'

'But it's not their forgiveness I need. I have no right to ask but will you give me your forgiveness now?'

'Yes, Freddie. I will' and Freddie felt the touch of his Katherina's hands for the first time in fifty years.

'It feels strange, something's happening, Katherina.'

'I know, Freddie.'

'Will I ever have known you? Will I ever exist to you?'

'I will remember you. I remember it all. You will always exist to me.'

'And you to me, my Katherina.' Freddie's tears were the final guide to his next place and they had him by the hand.

'If I never existed does it even qualify for heaven?' and with that, Freddie was gone.

The sand was kicking up in this little back street in Babylon. Little swirls were taking pieces of straw and dumping them some-where else. It will only last a minute or two but it was fine red sand, gets right in the fucking eyes, gets in fucking everywhere. Hans wrapped his head up against it. But something had come with the wind. Something was happening inside him.

Fuck, he was so close, what is this? Just at the top of this climb, the high square, was where the Gods resided. He'd plotted out every second of it. First the woman. In a few minutes she'd appear on the terrace of the palace. He will appear and vanish in seconds to terminate each of the slip-eyed fuckers in turn, precise, perfect, a temporal orchestra.

But that something that came with the wind showed itself and he knew something was wrong. The climb became steeper and longer. It didn't make sense. He was trying but he was going nowhere, only further away until his path finally terminated in a nearby star and he stopped. He was starting to lose the feeling in his legs.

A shopkeeper brought a basket of something outside and saw and old man shout something into the street and take a heavy seat on a bench.

Hans couldn't feel anything, just images of the door to their fucking club stuck in his mind. No flashbacks to sunnier times, there were never any sunnier times. There was just this torture. Then the fog started to enter his mind.

The shopkeeper will tell a friend one day about an angry man who sat on a bench and vanished.

There was a four way hug just about to break up with 'silly people' but the only thoughts from all four was the pipe. They all saw it go over the edge.

'OK. 1967 mode,' said Manny. 'Mission partly successful, yay.'

'Tard boy.'

'So, what, in 1967 you'd be minus thirty-seven years old and I'd be minus thirty-five.'

'And what, pointless boy. Dad. How the fuck do we get back?'

Zak knew they didn't get back. He looked at Allie then Manny. They knew as well.

He walked over to check the remains of the machine's room. There was nothing left of machine or room apart from a breezy open vista over the mountain and a small shard of Sumerian symbol. Zak took it and had to smile. He'd have it delivered to Larry Segler in 2017. It would arrive the day after Zak met him in San Diego along with an account of everything that just happened.

When he got back out into the main room, Izzi was no longer standing next to Allie by the desk.

22

family album

Katherina woke in her chair with a start. There was an instant breeze wrapping round her, cooling her. She felt different, like she was coming out of an intense dream or someone had just stuck her with a knitting needle after some shenanigans at bingo.

And then she smiled. The clarity she started to feel a few days ago was complete. She closed her eyes against the sun's reflection off the green vase by the window and raised her arms in the air, stretching out the dust of the last years. She was free. She looked around the room. Her eyesight was better, her hearing was better and her recall absolute. She bounced out of her chair like her arthritis never existed and stood for a moment.

Yes, this is exactly were she'd be if none of that shit ever happened. And now it hadn't. She approved, a little wooden house in a nice quiet street. Kids playing in the street. She'd like it here. She'd need a fair time to figure out who she'd known for fifty odd years and who she hadn't, get the lay of the land, but she would. But first, she thought looking over at her old two man lift TV set, today was the day she would drive into town and have a beer or two, a nice German lager maybe and buy a brand new flat screen TV.

Izzi opened her eyes on her own bedroom in her own house and Fozzie was looking right back at her. That was seriously the most intense fucking dream ever. 'Fuck,' she said and sat bolt up in bed. What the fuck is this now? The back of her head was throbbing and there was a lump. The briefest thought it could have been a dream was gone. She was still in the same clothes and her phone said Tuesday. Yesterday they'd blown up a mountain.

'Dad!'

'Dad!'

She rifled through the house in quick smart time yelling 'Dad' in every room, every so often an 'Allie' and one 'soft boy.' There was no-one here. It was evening, her silly dad wouldn't still be at work so where was he? How did they all get back? Her dad's car was still in the driveway. Izzi got on her bike and did a personal best to the Harbor Bistro. Nothing, no dad, no Allie, no soft boy, in fact no humankind at all. Where the fuck was everyone?

'Frio,' she said and her wheels were turning again. If they're not here, they're at Allie's, and oh yeah, fuck off without me much?'

Frio was a silent and distant cave in the evening breeze. And there he was, just the one guy sitting outside, stalker guy, just going right ahead and smiling at her again like he always did. She pulled up and looked back at him. She still didn't feel intimidated. There was something about his big friendly lopsided grin, just like her dad's, she had to smile back at him.

This still and unassuming space and time hummed quietly and made no demands on either of them for conversation. And then she recognized him, finally, fuck. She was sure she did the first time she saw him, just couldn't place him and now she could. Photographs.

Ages ago when she was about nine, she'd been camped out in her mom and dad's room while her mom got dressed to go out. She had time to wander about and fiddle with things and her mom was too busy to bother.

Her mom had a big walk-in closet with tons of stuff either side of it, dresses and shoes in cupboards and on racks and shelves, and a big mirror at the end. It was the only place a nine year old ever needed to be, sitting on the carpet under the long dresses, feeling the material, smelling the space.

There was a blue box up on a shelf she could just about manage with props. The edge of the lid was just a little raised, taunting her to open it up and see what secrets were inside.

She'd succumbed with no opposition, scaled the small height

using a conveniently placed chair to procure the box by a simple tiptoe on the chair and sat on the rug behind mommy and her mirror in front of the big window.

Small, square polaroids, with the thin white edges, and larger more bendy rectangular ones with no edges were all spread over this rug and under scrutiny from little Izzi. They were all pictures of Mom and Dad in silly clothes and different cars. It was the story of her mom and dad's life. She'll be in there somewhere. This was a treat and her mom smiled as she tucked into it for the first time.

Izzi was sure she'd seen stalker guy in amongst those photos and, somehow she knew she'd find an answer in them but 'answer to fucking what?' she shouted into this street.

'Where your Dad is, Izzi,' said stalker guy and he and Izzi locked eyes. No other atom moved for fifty yards. She could feel a breeze but couldn't hear it rustling things about. A delivery truck pulled up outside Frio and broke her gaze with him. The guy dumped off a couple of boxes of Manuel Zamora's super bueno tortilla chips and left, leaving no stalker guy. That's all Izzi needed.

Her Dad's room was pretty much exactly like it was when Mom was alive apart from the smell and the interruption of the light from the big window when she was getting ready. Izzi could always tell from the light making its way through the open door if her mom was there, even before she went into the room.

Izzi needed to do this from time to time, feel her mom again, gauge her progress.

Today was another day with no such light and no such Mom in the room. Izzi always stopped just inside looking at the mirror capturing her in the doorway. It was like looking at Mom turning round to say hello when she came in.

The blue box was exactly where it was and now no chair and no tippie-toes were needed. Izzi sat on the very same rug, looked past the mirror out of the window and her eyes slowly morphed from green to blue.

A warm smile came over this little Izzi as the first picture she grabbed was one she remembered from that last time with her mom. The look on her dad's face, it was a perfect shot. Uncle Ferdy took it. Her Dad just finished spending ages washing his car, that old Mustang and a few folks were over for a few beers.

A pretty massive bird must have seen the car was nearly finished and was circling with a grin, just waiting. As soon as it was finished, the bird saw it's perfect moment. It deposited pretty much everything it had with a grunt and flourish all over the shiny red roof. It made a decent 'thunk' noise and spread out like a slo mo meteor strike.

The sound turned her dad around, wondering if he could get his gun quick enough. This blurry edged snap showed he'd just seen the roof carnage but hadn't yet computed it, a beautiful study in finding the crossover of a polar emotion. The rough guide to the entertainment behind him was provided nanoseconds after the shot by everyone losing it in the driveway.

Perhaps you might even have just about seen the tips of the bird's cheeky dangling feet, like socks on a washing line, as it banked and climbed after its heroic drop like a dam buster waiting for the noise of cracking concrete. This was one to tell its grandkids about and if a seagull could smile, here would be that smile, broad and long. It might even have looked back at the top of her dad's head and its fine work and remember it forever more until it curled up its little toes for the last time.

The next picture was selected for no particular reason apart from something familiar in the top right corner, a memory unre-membered, yet there it was in her hand. She was just a baby, about three years old. It was Mom and Dad and her dad was holding her. They were facing the sun and all three of them squinted to prove it. She had no idea who was taking the photo. It was a park some-where. She was pretty sure she'd been there since then.

Behind them about fifteen yards down the slope towards the river was an old lady and a guy probably in his forties. There he is. Stalker guy. That's where she'd seen him but he looked a bit younger. The two of them were nothing to do with the photo but successfully photo bombed it, looking straight at the camera and sharing the squint of the protagonists as if the whole world was asked to stop and say cheese at that moment.

So who was this old lady and what did stalker guy have to do with this? If he was something to do with the family somehow why not just say hi or be in the main shot?

Here was another one, Mom and Dad and Izzi even smaller, this time she wasn't too happy and in mid bawl. Her dad was in the process of passing her over to her mom but still in the midst of this well practiced scene they managed a smile at the camera. Her dad looked so young, about mid-twenties.

It was in San Sebastian near where the Harbor Bistro was now. Back then it was a real local government style building barely serving booze and looking like somewhere you go to get your methadone.

Behind the family shot was the calm sunny harbor and the boats were there looking pretty. On one of these boats was the same old lady and stalker guy but now there was an old man with them as well, all smiling like they belonged right there in shot.

Maybe they were Dad's grandparents or something but Izzi knew his grandad died in the war and why were they always relegated to the nether regions of the photo? Didn't they deserve a hint of centre stage due to seniority at least? Or was all this a parade of the finest coincidences ever recorded?

Izzi knew the area of rug that housed the pics she needed. It was a reverse chronological powerpoint of her at three then barely nothing then absolutely pre-nothing, before she was even a thought. How could she be looking at something where she wasn't even conceived as a concept. It didn't seem right.

In each photo all of the players naturally looked younger and wore sillier clothes. And in each photo, there was stalker guy and the two oldies gradually getting younger throughout the show.

They weren't coincidence, they had to be organized photo-bombs. Izzi had never known these people and never heard of them yet here they were in regular captured moments of her folks' history.

This was the same park as the first photo and almost exactly the same place apart from a half tree, bark stripped and long past caring, had washed up on the opposite bank, just sitting there as a lesson to all the trees here. 'Never forget' it said. 'You could have been planted anywhere.'

Grandma and Grandpa when they were young in some street somewhere. That baby had to be her dad. Her grandpa was leaning on a car with his arm round grandma who was holding her dad.

She never really knew Grandma and Grandpa, they died when she was very small but she remembered Grandpa having the exact same nose as her dad. She'd sat between the two of them on the couch probably only a few weeks before Grandpa died. Her mom said squeeze both noses and see what happens and she did and what happened was both noses felt the same and she got tickled to the point of having a little wee right there.

Here were Grandma and Grandpa when they were the same age as her Dad was now. There were these people again, walking towards them from behind from about ten yards back, a couple about the same age as stalker guy is now with a young boy about Izzi's age. The boy's parents looked like the same people in the later photos but was this lad a young stalker guy? What the fuck?

The usual suspects kept on appearing in the photo backgrounds, still totally unknown to the protagonists, and they were all getting younger as the photos became more dog eared and jaded.

Pretty soon the pictures didn't even contain her Dad as he entered the realm of the unborn. It was just Grandma and Grandpa getting younger, now in some restaurant.

At a point where Izzi could not have imagined how bad the clothes and hairstyles got, here was a black and white photo, all wrinkled and crinkled at the edges with a cheeky partial coffee cup ring in one corner. This looked like it was way before dad was around, maybe the sixties some time, and Grandma and Grandpa looked really young and really happy, before the sleepless nights. She wished she'd known him when he was her age. He'd told her he was a wicked little boy and she reckoned he was.

She was sure she recognized the random old couple a few photos back but just couldn't place them. She knew the format by now, the people in the main shot then these others appearing behind them somewhere, two dimensions happening at once, unaware of each other, photobombing of temporal excellence thru the ages. So she started to scan around the other people at various tables. They had to be here as well and they'd be much younger.

And then she found them sitting two tables back and her blood seized, her mouth wide open with disbelief, unable to function. She felt cold and her throat dried. She tried to gulp but it wouldn't work. They were small in this photo but it was unmistakable. It was her Dad and Allie exactly as they were now, like she saw them yesterday, but having lunch in this 1960s restaurant. They were the oldies gradually shedding years as her powerpoint rolled on, and here Allie was holding a little baby. That had to be stalker guy.

Jesus, they never got back. Then Izzi remembered one of the photos, just stalker guy an old Allie, no dad, and the tears came fast an easy.

'Fuck! No!' she yelled wet and snotty into the room. 'Fuck. Fuck.' She lost the pipe. It was her fault. Fuck, they'd spent their whole lives in another time and her dad was dead.

Izzi put her head in her hands and let it all out with noise and curse and then she started to feel her head swim. She thought she was going to be sick. She got up quickly and hit the bathroom and put her head down the toilet but nothing would come. She ran the cold tap over the back of her neck and let it run over her neck and shoulders and then immersed her head in it.

Her vision blurred and she was sure she'd pass out. She hoped movement would get her blood moving again and stumbled out of the bathroom and back into her dad's room but the dizziness persisted and forced her to sit on the edge of the bed.

Was it a really unfunny photoshop session they had? Like those ones playing guitar next to Elvis or some soldier standing behind Hitler at a rally giving him the bunny ears. And then reality dug in again.

Izzi thought her head had cleared enough to think about getting back on her bike, get back to Frio, ask him, get over to Allie's, but her head wasn't ready for it. As she headed for the door, it got smaller and smaller and she got further and further away from it, like it was running away from her. Her head started to fizz again and all other sounds ran down the plug hole. She tried to find the edge of the bed but it was too late, she lost her balance and didn't even notice she'd hit the carpet, her fall blowing photos away from her as she landed.

Izzi's fevered mind delivered her an immediate dream to the only place she could truly be at peace, alone on the boat about five minutes off the island. This dream was different though. She knew she was dreaming, it was like when she travelled yesterday. She knew her real body was in her Dad's room

'Yesterday,' she said and she knew. How come they stayed there and she came back? How did she come back? If she could come back without the pipe, could she return without the pipe?

'The pipe.' The pipe would still be there behind the waterfall in 1967. She needed to tell her Dad back then but how? She knew where her dad was now, in the photo of the restaurant. She imagined him in that time, the senses that would be all around him, the noises and the smells, the sadness. He'd be feeling as a sad as she was when she thought she'd never see him again.

Izzi's dream brought her to a new place. She saw a street. The cars lumbering up it and parked alongside it were old sixties beasts, massive great things with fins at the back like rocket ships. The shop signs were different too, prices were silly cheap and it was all a bit more gentle than today.

There he was, her Dad and Allie walking towards her. Allie had a baby. There they were, arm in arm, at one with their new space and time, strolling down this street.

She told her dream to let her walk over to him and it obliged but, as she stepped towards him, a man suddenly emerged out of the front of her walking away from her like some fucked up alien birthing. This guy had just walked through her. Jesus that felt nasty, cold and clammy. It felt like he'd taken some of her with him. She felt abused. She looked around and she caught nobody's eye. She waved her arms right in front of this kid. Not a blink. She was invisible in this world. How can she tell her dad?

Then, Manny passed Zak and Allie at a far lick on his bike avoiding a clip round the ear on his way through.

'Stop being a dick, watch out for Aaron,' said Zak.

Manny was heading straight for her, another merging of bodies but not in good way. But then Manny looked up right into her eyes and screeched the bike to a stop, vexing an elderly lady leaving a cake shop. He smiled at Izzi and then looked at the shop window he'd pulled up outside. In that window there was poster advertising a trip to the Cedar Creek Falls, dinner and room included for eighteen bucks. He smiled again and waited for Zak and Allie to catch up.

'Hey, how about a trip to a waterfall?' he said.

Zak and Allie examined the poster and Zak's eyes widened.

'Allie,' he said, grabbing her shoulders.

'Manny, you're a genius.' He gave Manny a big kiss on the top of his head, which Manny fended off with 'gross and I know.'

'The waterfall,' continued Zak.

'What about it?' said Allie. 'Cedar Creek? So what?'

'Not Cedar Creek, our waterfall on the island,' said Zak.

Allie took a moment and then she was there too.

'The dream pipe. It's still there,' she said.

'Ping,' said Manny.

'It's still there' said Zak. 'Izzi hasn't found it yet. It's still there.'

Here on the rug in her Dad's room, the photos strewn about the place were starting to change. The photobombed invasions of her Dad and Allie and stalker guy over the ages were disappearing from them, leaving behind only the original images of the day.

Izzi came to on the rug and immediately hunted for a picture, firing through irrelevant shots, spraying decoy pictures around the room, until she found one she recognized. It was her Grandma and Grandpa in that sixties restaurant but now the table where her dad and Allie and the baby had sat was occupied by a different couple and two young daughters.

The other photos had changed as well. The temporal additions were no more. Izzi was jogged out of another brief thought of it being another dream by the sound of a closing door downstairs.

Quietly she descended the stairs. There were people standing in the kitchen. It was her dad, Allie and Manny. Allie was holding that same baby, same little football logo on his little top. Izzi was into them in a flash, smelling them, tugging at them, making sure it was all real. She took a moment to coochy coo the little baby. 'Stalker guy,' she said. Then she grabbed hold of Manny, pulling him for a big wet smoochy smacker right on the mouth.

As they broke off one by one to give her back the air squeezed out of her, she pulled her dad back in for an extra special dad hug and then pushed him away.

'Silly parent.'

about the author

Dominic Schunker was born in London and currently lives up a mountain in Javea, Spain. His very small German Shepherd puppy called Poppy isn't so small any more.

Dominic's fiction encompasses ghosts, time travel, aliens, demons, nasty fat corporations, conspiracies and God, but most importantly, human emotion. It's based on the right of every human being to become randomly haunted and taken to the limit of their sanity.

Machine Sense is his second novel, following the release of An Unfortunate Dimension in December 2018.

 twitter.com/DFusu

subscribe

Don't miss out.

You can sign up to receive emails whenever Dominic Schunker publishes a new book.

Visit www.offworldpublishing.com to subscribe.

There's no charge and no obligation.

Offworld Publishing does not distribute subscriber contact details to any third party.

thank you !

Thanks for helping me take Zak and Izzi where they needed to go. I hope you love that little Izzi and it's so nice to know there are so many out there who do. Are you ready to see what's in store for her next? (see next page).

Friends, book reviews can do wonderful things for an author. It feels like a very cheeky tingle invades me every time I get a nice review.

Feel free to leave an honest review on Amazon or wherever you found Machine Sense.

If you enjoyed Machine Sense, tell your friends, maybe get together and draw wild conclusions about what drives such a thing to happen, maybe wonder what they all get up to next.

coming soon

Coming Soon from the same Author:

Letters from Angels (Release, Summer 2019)

Letters from Angels is the third novel by author, Dominic Schunker, and is due for release in Summer 2019.

10 years after Machine Sense, Izzi's thrown right back down the rabbit hole.

When the end of the world comes, would you care if it was aliens or the antichrist?

Oscar's Square (Release, Winter 2019)

When you're mission is to save every starving child in the world, do you leave it to the people who haven't bothered so far, or do do it yourself? And how far will you go to do it?

And why not go back in time and catch up with the Author's first novel:

An Unfortunate Dimension (Released, December 2018)

The average human mind can perform incredible feats to ensure self preservation. A great human mind can perform incredible feats for the preservation of others. Explore human emotion and its drive to perform miracles when faced with the end in this psychological sci-fi thriller. Explore how VR tech can interface with that temporal, supernatural human emotion and form something beautiful, an answer.

www.offworldpublishing.com

story

Zak sees things change that no-one else does. His best buddy suddenly becomes someone he'd never met, President Garfield is now President Valdez. Something is screwing up the timeline. To everybody else though, it's always been as it is. He's been alone with this since he was a teenager but then he meets Allie, someone else who sees the same changes. Her mum does as well and it seems his daughter, Izzi is showing signs of seeing the changes too.

There follows a tale of Nazis, reverse engineered alien spacecraft, Auschwitz experiments and alien-human hybrids with eyes that change from green to blue for no apparent reason.

They discover this is not a random universal glitch, someone is changing the timeline to benefit themselves and what's worse, they're targeting people whose eyes change like Izzi. Things just got very real for Zak.

"An extremely exciting romp across time."

"Schunker's spiky, effervescent style helps propel the novel along at a great pace and brings much humour to what could otherwise be heavy subject matter."

"This is begging to become a movie - it's perfect."

One Night in Breaux Bridge and other odd things are available via the publisher, Offworld Publishing, in a variety of media, formats and sizes from a six foot lenticular lens to a poster. Just visit *https://www.offworldpublishing.com/offworld-pictures*. Use Access Code **37**

offworld
publishing